C000171155

❧ *the* ❧
LIBRARY *of* SHADOWS

RACHEL MOORE

the

LIBRARY

✤ *of* ✤

SHADOWS

HARPER TEEN
An Imprint of HarperCollins*Publishers*

For Christopher, who never leaves me in the shadows

ONE

❧

Este's new roommate was a ghost and not a particularly good one.

Standing on the other side of the cedar door to Vespertine Hall 503, a teenage girl under a paisley bedsheet said, "Oh, my god, Este, hi! You're here."

On Este's first day at Radcliffe Prep, what she really wanted was a chance to soak it all in. The way the light streaked through the white pines outside the windows. How the original hardwood floors from 1901 felt beneath her feet. The fact that she was finally here, really *here*.

Instead, she walked straight into auditions for *Casper the Friendly Ghost*.

According to her orientation paperwork, the person underneath had to be Este's roommate, Posy Thatch: fellow incoming junior, night owl, and amateur journalist. On paper (or, technically, the roommate assignment quiz new students had been forced to take), they were a perfect match.

But in reality? Two holes had been cut out of the still-wrinkled sheet for a pair of wide green eyes, and they blinked at Este, expectant.

Este nudged the door closed behind her. "And you're haunting our dorm room?"

"Unpacking." Posy stripped off her makeshift costume, revealing a Radcliffe Prep hoodie with the tag still on, a spray of staticky orange hair, and a wide grin. "My little brothers made this as a going-away present in case there's a Halloween party. Mom was not happy. I'm sure you know how it is."

"Not exactly." Este readjusted the straps of her backpack just to do something with her hands.

She and her mom had spent the last three years living on pinstripe highways and borrowed time, never staying in one place long enough to settle down. Even now, her mom must have been zipping back down the Vermont mountainsides on her way to anywhere but here. Hadn't even bothered to walk her to orientation. She'd dropped Este off at the boarding school's towering iron gates, her grief too heavy to carry inside the Radcliffe grounds. Was that the kind of thing you told your brand-new roommate on day one?

She settled on saying, "I'm an only child."

Posy seemed undeterred by her deer-in-the-headlights expression. "Oh, okay. Cool! Let me show you around."

Este didn't bother informing Posy that their suite was small enough that she could practically see it all from the front door. A tiny kitchenette—mini fridge, microwave, a hot plate, and a sink—opened to the shared living space. There, a green claw-foot couch took up most of the square footage, and the rest was occupied by a bookshelf and a coffee table splayed with gizmos and gadgets that definitely hadn't been on the suggested-packing list. Doors on either side of the living room were their bedrooms, 503A and 503B.

All in all, it was a huge improvement from the Motel 6 she had just left.

"I took this room," Posy said, heading left to 503B. "Hope that's okay. The energy just pulled me here. I haven't scanned the frequencies yet, but it totally feels haunted. Don't you think?"

"Um," Este said, shifting her weight between her heels, "can you define haunted?"

Mostly, the room felt incredibly pink. Posy had done some serious redecorating because there was no way this much pastel was school-sanctioned. Christmas lights wrapped around four posters of the bedframe, and a polka dot duvet had been tucked around the mattress. Next to a behemoth of a printer that belonged to the last decade, there was a pencil cup stuffed to the brim with gel pens and a teetering stack of scented candles. And that was just the beginning.

On the wall, Posy had plastered a mosaic of memories. Photos from Posy's past patterned her room—her arms slung over her friends' shoulders at football games, planting a kiss on someone's suntanned cheek, and dressed up in homecoming garb with flowers dangling off her wrist and a boy off her arm. There were family photos with her squished between her siblings, each of them wearing broad smiles and a face full of freckles. This must have been Posy's first time away from her family, her first time standing on her own legs, her first time alone.

Este's chest tightened. She knew alone a little too well. Alone carved out a canyon in her chest, deep grooves of a river run dry. She didn't know how to fill it back up. She wasn't sure she even wanted to, just for it to empty again.

Posy waved her arms around the room as if Este should be able to see the obvious paranormal activity happening right in front of her. "You know, ghosts, specters, spirits that can't move on. Radcliffe Prep is the nation's third most haunted high school, so, I'm not surprised. I swear, I've seen the lights flicker so many times already."

"Is that what all that stuff in the living room's for? Ghost hunting?"

It was easy to see Posy settle into her element—the weight shifted off her shoulders, a light flared behind her eyes. Like she'd been waiting for Este to ask. "Yep. I spent, like, all my summer job money on it so that I would be prepared."

Este forced a smile. She didn't have the heart to tell her she didn't believe in ghosts. At least, not anymore. She wasn't sure she could survive an entire school year if her roommate hated her for being a skeptic. As far as friends went, Este usually kept a grand total of zero.

Unlike the shrine to T.J. Maxx Posy had created in 503B, when they got to Este's room, it looked just like the brochures. Designed for substance, not style. Bed, closet, and a small desk situated in the corner. Gauzy sunlight pooled through windows that probably hadn't been dusted since before the turn of the millennium.

Radcliffe Preparatory Academy was an exclusive college preparatory school with a curriculum reserved for eleventh and twelfth graders on an Ivy League track. And, now, Este.

Excitement flared behind her ribs as she dropped onto the bed. The closest thing to home sweet home she'd had in a long time. She dumped the contents of her backpack onto the mattress, and Posy disappeared into the living room only to return with one of the devices from the coffee table. This one looked like a Nintendo Switch but was evidently supposed to be super serious ghost-hunting equipment.

"What are you doing?" she asked. Were roommates supposed to be this . . . involved?

Posy's gadget chirped in response.

"It's an EMF reader. I'm checking for electromagnetic frequencies," Posy said, shoving the scanner halfway under Este's bed. "They're the telltale sign of a supernatural presence."

"Is it working?" Este grabbed a stack of sweaters she'd used as packing protection and unwrapped them from around three framed photos. It wasn't enough to make an entire art installation like Posy, but they were hers. In each, her dad stared up at her.

There was a picture from her eighth birthday, where she clung to her dad's side, holding up her first library card. Her: pigtails. Him: mustache. It wasn't a great era for either of them.

Next, he was shaking hands with the marble statue in the center of the fountain in the courtyard. Este had passed it on her walk to the dormitory and recognized it in the space between heartbeats. In this photo, it was easy enough to see the way she resembled him. She'd inherited his brown hair, his hazel eyes, and his Cupid's-bowed lips. And somewhere, stuffed in her backpack, she still had the vintage Radcliffe crewneck he wore, except now the sleeves were frayed from overuse.

In the last photo, he was her age, sixteen and spindly, standing in front of the door to Vespertine Hall 503A. The photo was grainy and faded, crinkled at the edges, and he'd written *First day at Radcliffe, September 1997* in the corner, the ink smudged with the heel of his left hand. She'd scanned the photo and sent it to the dean of students to ask—okay, beg—to be put in the room he had. At the time, the school's response had been lukewarm. *Your request has been received and will be considered.*

But here she was. Standing in the same place he stood, filling the same space he did.

Posy hummed, standing back up. "Oh, yeah. There's something seriously spooky going on here."

Suppressing the urge to laugh, Este set the frames on the desk and then dug through her pile of belongings for a book. The green binding was a familiar texture between her fingers. A book of stories, a present from her dad. She must have had every word on the deckle-edged pages memorized, but there was a comfort in her old favorite tales that Este couldn't resist.

She knew every line, every stamp of ink, every dog-eared corner. She used to run her fingers over the blank pages bound at the end—a place for her to pen her own story someday. Blue writing stained the flyleaf with her dad's scribbled penmanship. *From the library of Este Logano,* he'd written and underlined. Beneath it, he wrote, *There is life, there is death, and there is love—the greatest of these is love.*

When he died a few years after writing those words, Este knew he'd gotten it all wrong. They laid him to rest in the dusty cemetery down the road from their little blue Paso Robles home, and no matter how much love her broken heart spilled, he stayed buried.

For a while, Este had been desperate to believe in ghosts, to see her dad's face or hear his voice one more time. Searching for shapes in the dark was like ripping scabs off soft wounds, refusing to let them heal. At some point, she had to give up. Ghosts couldn't be real because if they were, she would have seen his by now.

But at least she had the chance to explore his old stomping grounds, and maybe that was enough.

Posy's gear released a string of beeps that sounded not unlike a stray cat finding a field mouse. "Houston, we have a ghost!"

As Posy swung the scanner around, searching for the source, Este muttered, "All that's dead in here are the batteries in that thing."

"If you can hear me, send us a sign." Posy climbed onto Este's bed, stretching the scanner toward the ceiling the way she'd sometimes seen her mom do to find cell phone service in the desert. "Is the temperature dropping? It feels colder."

A door slammed shut somewhere down the hall. Posy's eyebrows shot up, but Este shook her head. She had to give it to her. Posy was nothing if not persistent.

"It's move-in day," Este said, thumbing over the coarse pages of her book. "Not *The Haunting of Hill House*."

Posy jumped down with a *thud*, sweeping the Magic Ghost Detector over the closet door, the single-paned window, and the desk. Este ducked under her roommate's wayward arm to set her book next to the photos.

"Are you sure?" Posy asked, tilting her head to listen for more signs of afterlife. "Because it sounded like—"

A knock pounded against their front door, and Posy skittered backward with a yelp, ramming her back against the desk. One of Este's picture frames teetered. There were only milliseconds between Este's shocked gasp and glass shards scattering across the floor.

No, no, no. Este collapsed to the damages. Her hand hovered over the chipped frame. Posy had hundreds, thousands, of photos with her family, her friends. Este had only three left of her dad.

Posy's voice sounded faraway, even as she crouched next to her. "Este, I'm so sorry. I really didn't mean to."

Impatient, the visitor knocked again.

"Go," Este said between her teeth.

"Maybe I can help put it back together."

Prickly tears welled in Este's eyes, but she wouldn't let Posy see her cry. They weren't close like that. She forced her voice light as she replied, "Please, just. Get the door."

This time, Posy nodded. When she peeled open the door, a vaguely familiar voice filtered into Este's room. Probably the dorm's faculty advisor Dr. Kirk, who doubled as a history teacher, spouting off reminders about curfews and visiting hours. Este barely heard it as she blew out a shaking breath and assessed the wreckage.

Sparkling glass had scattered across the floorboards as the frame shattered, snapping in half. The frame had slammed against the baseboard, cracking, and its black backing had ricocheted under the desk. Este pressed a finger to the edge of the frame where the corner had snapped off with impact, leaving exposed a patch of unpainted wood. Thankfully, the photo inside was left unscathed. Este and her dad still smiled, frozen in time at the Paso Robles City Library. Safe and unknowing.

Este nudged the sharp pieces into a pile by the wall. That would have to do for now. She slid the photo and the remnants of the frame onto the desk and then crouched to swipe the backing from underneath.

No sooner than Este had it in her hands, she dropped it again. The backing slipped from her fingertips, heavier than anticipated. On the inside, a solid brass key wrapped in a leather cord had been taped down.

Her heart leaped toward her throat. First of all, what was that? And secondly, how did it get inside her picture frame—or, more importantly, why was it there at all?

"You okay?" Posy asked, back again too soon.

Este tried to stand too quickly and knocked her head against the bottom of the desk, wincing. Brightly, she said, "Dandy."

She scooted the backing onto the desk as quickly as possible, trying to look casual. There was no way she looked casual. Finding a key hidden inside her picture frame? That was the definition of *not casual*.

"Here. I hope this helps." Posy hesitated at the doorframe with a broom, a dustpan, and a sorry look on her freckled face, like a TV vampire who had to ask for entry. Which meant that in the fifteen minutes they'd known each other, Este had already pushed her away like she did everyone else. For a moment, Posy's jaw hung open as if she had more to say—another apology, another errant, phantom trivia fact?—but she shrugged, shaking it away. Instead, she said, "Dr. Kirk's campus tour starts in ten minutes. We're meeting in the lobby."

Este thanked her with her best fake smile, and it was enough to convince Posy to disappear around the corner. She lobbed a goodbye Este's way before closing the front door behind her. The moment her roommate was gone, Este yanked the key off the backing.

She cradled it loosely in her fingers, then gently unwound its leather string to stare at the key. It looked like the kind that probably opened doors that had no business being unlocked. The key's bow had been intricately wrought with a flower of interlacing metal, and the cord looped through one of the petals like the chain of a necklace.

The photo from that day at the Paso Robles library watched as she examined it. Her dad had always said this was his favorite photo of them. Twin smiles in a place they loved most. Now, she knew why. Este slipped the cord around her neck, and her dad's brass key fitted itself over her heart. Like it belonged. Like she did.

Whatever it led to, she would find it.

The halls around her quieted as students gathered in the lobby for the tour, and she needed to join them. She literally couldn't afford to make a bad impression. Her enrollment hinged on a generous legacy scholarship, offered so that she could pick up where her father left off since he'd unceremoniously transferred schools halfway through autumn. She'd always thought legacy scholarships were given to people who had *actually graduated*, but hey, who was she to turn down free tuition and the opportunity to wear as many turtlenecks as her heart desired?

Este raced through Vespertine Hall's carpeted floors, down the cedar staircases, until she hit the lobby, but the group was already outside. Campus was composed of sunbaked brick, strewn with creeping juniper and honeysuckle blooms. Students carried stacks of books against their chests, clasped steaming cups of coffee, and whispered to each other on garden benches. A cloud had crawled over the sun, blotting out the afternoon warmth and replacing it with an evergreen breeze. Este could spend an eternity drifting between the trunks of black birches and hemlocks.

Ahead, Posy's burnt sienna ponytail bobbed at the back of Dr. Kirk's tour. Forty or so students filed into the doors of the Lilith Radcliffe Memorial Library, Radcliffe Prep's crown jewel.

Este gasped at the sight of the ribbed vaults and gargoyled eaves. Windows dotted the exterior, and her gaze snagged on a boy perched in a windowed alcove behind the shade of a leafy maple. He'd rolled up the sleeves of his wrinkled white button-down, and black hair curled over his forehead like spills of ink.

He must have been a senior since he wasn't trailing behind Dr. Kirk for a first look at the school. The boy glanced up from the notebook he was writing in, the pages cradled against his knees. Este couldn't look away, and he looked right back.

"Este!" Posy called from up ahead. "I brought an EMF reader for you!"

Her roommate broke off from the rest of the group and fast-walked toward her, one of the coffee-table gizmos clutched in her hand. She now wore a fisherman's vest, splattered with iron-on patches and enamel pins. The scanner chimed with every step.

Of course. A peace offering by way of paranormal investigating.

Este forced a smile. "I wouldn't know how to use it. You should hold on to it."

"Suit yourself," Posy said, wagging the EMF reader toward the Lilith's exterior. It let out a high-pitched ring, and Posy squealed in response. "I told you this place was totally haunted."

Searching the alcoves, Este found the boy again. He'd closed his notebook and instead fixated on the spectacle Posy was creating with a smirk curling the edge of his mouth.

And then, he winked. At her.

Heat flared across her cheeks, and it had nothing to do with the way the late afternoon sun crept out from behind the clouds. Was it possible to die of embarrassment?

When Este finally dared to peek back at the window seat, shielding her eyes from the sun with her hand like a visor, the boy had vanished. Off to read Proust or contemplate Nietzsche or whatever it was private-school boys like him did with their spare time.

Her heart thrummed against her rib cage, but she dug her nails into the denim threads on her thighs. *Good,* she thought. *Stay focused.* She wasn't here to drool over upperclassmen with alarmingly sharp jawlines. Este came to Radcliffe to follow in her father's footsteps, and each one led straight to the library.

TWO

Posy's pockets would not stop beeping, which was not ideal for
a library in general, and definitely not ideal while Dr. Kirk
waxed poetic about the Lilith Library's hundred-year history.

Este had joined Posy at the back of the group right as Dr.
Kirk launched into her spiel. She was a short Black woman,
easily nearing seventy with her salt-and-pepper curls braided
tightly around her head, but the way she walked backward
made Este think she could probably lead this tour in her sleep.

"What's that?" Posy had asked, eyeing the key around her
neck.

"Nothing." Este tucked the key underneath her sweater a
little too quickly and motioned for Posy to pay attention.

Now, Dr. Kirk led them around the perimeter of the first
floor, doing a decent enough job of ignoring the endless stream
of interruptions coming from Posy's fisherman's vest. "The
Lilith has been Radcliffe Prep's academic cornerstone since the

school was founded in 1901. Materials in these collections date hundreds, even thousands, of years back. In 1917, less than two decades after the school opened its doors, a fire—"

Beep.

"—threatened to burn it down. Thankfully, it began in the spire, and, because it's carved entirely of stone, the fire didn't spread. Open flames in the Lilith, as you might expect, now require supervision from library staff, and today the spire houses heirlooms from the Radcliffe family themselves."

Beep.

Toward the front, someone raised a hand and asked, "Can we go up there?"

"Unfortunately," Dr. Kirk said, leading them between narrow shelves, "access to the spire is prohibited. For the protection of the collection, you see. However, you'll find plenty of resources among the Lilith's main floors if you're—"

Beep, beep, beeeeeep.

"Can you lower the volume or something?" Este whispered, harsher than intended.

"No way. The readings are off the charts in here." Posy pulled the EMF reader from her vest and smacked it against her hand, trying to still the rapidly rising number on the scanner's dim screen. "You know some scholars think the fire was started on purpose."

Este dragged her fingertips along the rumble strip of book spines. The thought of losing even a sentence of this collection made her stomach knot like a yoga class.

To say the Lilith was impressive would be the understatement of the century. Hollow in the center, five sweeping stories rose around them. A vaulted glass ceiling glittered hundreds of feet above them, drenching the library in saffron sunlight. Jutting out of the east wing, a stone spire loomed overhead, braided into the whipped clouds. Night was creeping in quickly, but through the peaked windows, a soft September glow clung to the oak trees' first golden leaves. Vermont in the fall was something striking.

Shelves that stretched to the soffits lined each wall, and every section boasted a rolling ladder to reach the highest books. Layer after layer of bookcases sat laden with leather-bound texts that promised the dusty scent of old books and fading ink. A crooked banner hung from the second-floor banister and read Welcome, Students!

One day, she would know every inch of this library like the back of a well-worn cataloging card, but tonight was her first time treading hallowed ground. She'd imagined this library a million times, but nothing compared to finally pacing the polished floors.

"Why would anyone try to destroy this?" she asked, realizing Posy was next to her, staring up at the spire curiously like she was thinking about fires and phantoms.

"I don't know. What motive does anyone have for arson? Destroying evidence, amateur witchcraft, a desperate attempt to stay warm in a Green Mountains winter before the invention of central heating." Posy pocketed the EMF reader and retrieved a silver laser pointer. "Sixty-seven degrees, but I'll have to keep an eye on it."

That last part she said mostly to herself, but even whispering, Posy snagged the attention of a few students around them. As Dr. Kirk guided them up a polished staircase, a boy with warm brown skin and a head of tight curls that had been bleached at the tips poked Posy's fancy thermometer with a painted index finger.

"Can that really find ghosts?" he asked.

Not in a million years, Este thought. She walked faster, craning an ear to hear Dr. Kirk announce that the Lilith's hidden passageways are "technically off-limits to students, but great if you need a shortcut to class, as long as you don't get caught," and how they're "easy enough to find if you know where to look," and "no, I won't show you, but there's a suspicious-looking painting on the fifth floor you might find interesting."

"Find ghosts? Absolutely," Posy said to the boy. She'd clearly lost all interest in Dr. Kirk. "Shadows, ghosts, wraiths, fades, poltergeists, ectoplasm, *and* apparitions all create cold spots. You'll know it when you feel it."

A towheaded boy twice Este's size butted in, saying, "Dude, I didn't think this place was actually haunted." Pale with ruddy cheeks, he wore a wide-strapped tank top and had a lacrosse stick looped over a sunburned shoulder like he'd just run off the field from practice.

"I'm Arthur Wilhite," the first boy said. "This is my roommate, Shepherd Healy. He knows nothing."

Posy took the liberty of introducing them. "I'm Posy, and she's Este—like the Estes Method."

"The what?" Este asked.

Waving a hand dismissively and turning back to Shepherd, Posy said, "Of course this school is haunted. I thought everyone who applied to Radcliffe knew that."

She looked toward Este for encouragement.

"Well . . ." Este scrunched her face up. "Not everyone."

"You, too?" Her roommate's initial shock was quickly replaced as she plastered on a grin like a morning newscaster. "Oh, my god. Okay, get this: eight students have gone missing while they studied at Radcliffe. Eight. That's not, like, a small number. Every ten years, someone came to school, and they never went home."

"What happened to them?" Shepherd asked. Este didn't miss the way his grip tightened around the hilt of his lacrosse stick, knuckles white.

"No one knows for sure," Posy said, shrugging. "There hasn't been a disappearance since the eighties, but the energy doesn't lie. Some scholars think Radcliffe was built on a ley line. Some think whatever was responsible was much, much worse. Something ancient, evil, and out for blood."

Scholars, evidently, was a loose term. Este could think of a hundred things more likely than paranormal activity. Tuition costs, family emergencies. Some students probably couldn't take the pressure of a curriculum that only scheduled twenty minutes for lunch.

"And you all seriously believe in this stuff?" she asked.

"Me? No," Shepherd whispered, stretching his ham hock of a neck. The way his eyes shifted back and forth, scanning the shadows for stray movements, said otherwise.

"You sure about that?" Arthur reached around Shepherd to tap his opposite shoulder, and the lacrosse player nearly jumped out of his skin. The twisted look on Shepherd's face made Este think he was considering knocking Arthur over with a single flick on the forehead.

Este rolled her eyes. All it would take was one wrong look and the EMF reader would start shouting. Posy's theatrics might have worked on the boys, but she was going to need a little more concrete proof before she started salting her door.

She'd been thirteen when she stood next to her mom, head angled toward the cemetery's patchy grass. Este couldn't watch as they dropped the first clumps of dirt over her dad's casket. Of course, she learned all the signs of spiritual encounters—how ghosts could sift through walls, how the lights would flicker and the floorboards creak. How much time had she wasted trying to believe that whispers on the wind might have belonged to her dad?

Ghosts hadn't been real then, and they never would be.

Her thoughts were interrupted by the *click, click, click* of high heels on old floors. A pale woman sidled up to Dr. Kirk. Black hair dripped over the shoulders of an ironed pantsuit, silken and straight, and she held herself with the kind of Ivy League prestige Este hoped she could someday grow into.

"I won't take up much of your time—Dr. Kirk gives an excellent tour—but I wanted to introduce myself as we kick off the 2027 academic year." The woman's smile was practiced, perfect. "I'm your head librarian, Aster Ives."

Arthur's eyes went wide, and he muttered, "She looks like she could be a student," as if high schoolers in Vermont frequently donned pressed blazers and stilettos.

Ives let loose a good-natured laugh. Was preternatural hearing a prerequisite for becoming a librarian? "Being here keeps me young."

"Not me," Dr. Kirk ribbed, raising her wrinkled hands.

Posy's EMF reader chose that exact moment to let out an ear-piercing beep like a sitcom dad after stubbing his toe. She didn't even have the decency to look remorseful, instead immediately scanning the nearby shelves while Este silently wished she could have had an ordinary roommate, maybe one who liked jigsaw puzzles or collecting Funko Pop! figures.

Ives narrowed her eyes, a blue as sharp as the sapphire on her ring finger. "It's my privilege to continue Radcliffe's tradition of excellence and preserve this collection in Lilith's honor.

If you need help with anything this year, don't hesitate to let me know. And next time you're here, put your phone on silent."

That got Posy to click the off button.

The tour continued upward, Ives joining them, and curios dotted the second floor, a maze of collected relics. Treasures lined each row of books, curated through the years: Greco-Roman marble busts, naval instruments for navigating harsh seas, ancient silk textiles. Dr. Kirk made a point to emphasize that all the best antiquities were hoarded at the top of the spire. These were the disposable valuables, the ones that could afford to be ogled at and fondled by high school overachievers.

Frankly, Este was pretty sure most students were too busy ogling at and fondling each other to pay attention to the artifacts.

While Posy quietly informed Shepherd about some 1960s hippie named Aoife who vanished ("With eyewitnesses!"), Este found herself fruitlessly searching the stacks for a glimpse of the boy she had seen in the window as they neared the alcove over the main entrance. With an enrollment of fewer than two hundred students, it wasn't like she would never run into him again.

The third floor was noticeably quieter. Ceilings dipped lower, and the shelves were lined with thick, dusty tomes. The deeper they wove through the stacks, the darker it grew. Light barely reached this part of the library.

As the aisles narrowed, she imagined her dad pacing down

the corridors, a pile of books held steady beneath his chin. He must have scanned the same call numbers, browsed the same books that she would.

Everything you need to know, you can find in your library, her dad used to say. Este clung to the defiant hope that she'd find a piece of him in this one.

"Here are the school's archives," Dr. Kirk said as she stalled in front of an impressive arched double door. "Completely windowless, this collection is protected from sun damage, and you'll need permission to enter since the texts are incredibly delicate. Our highest-achieving students have the opportunity to become archiving assistants and help us maintain these records, some of which require twenty-four-hour care. Although, would you want to work overnight in the most haunted place in the most haunted school in the country?"

"*Third* most haunted," Posy corrected under her breath.

"Now, don't run off all my volunteers with your ghost stories!" Ives chided playfully, conjuring a wave of hushed giggles from the crowd.

Surveying the doors, Este's pulse quickened beneath her skin. An ornate trim cased the archives' entrance, carved with delicate flowers. Flowers that looked familiar. She traced her fingers along the key around her neck. It weighed heavier now, somehow.

With Dr. Kirk ruminating on best cataloging practices and Posy distracted by her new entourage of ghost hunters, Este slipped away unnoticed. She lifted the key out from underneath her sweater, the teeth biting into her palm. Had her dad worked in the archives? She imagined him holding this key and took a step closer. It wouldn't hurt to peek. Just one look.

Slotting the key into the knob, her hands shook. But the key caught halfway.

It didn't make any sense. The keyhole was the perfect size, and the etchings matched the door. By all accounts, the doors should've swung open with ease, but when she tried the lock again, she had as much bad luck.

"You know, Ives will give you detention for trespassing. In fact, I've seen her give it to students just for looking at restricted sections of the library."

Este jumped backward. Leaning against the bookshelf was a familiar set of shoulders. The buttons of a collared shirt led to the smooth planes of the window boy's face. Her brain misfired at the kaleidoscope blues of his eyes.

Typical.

The most attractive human specimen this side of Burlington, and he caught her attempting to sneak into the restricted section.

She clamped the key into her fist, guilty red fanning into her cheeks. "You mean this isn't the exit?" she asked, trying the lie on for size.

His smile flickered, a contained flame. The boy stepped closer. "I don't think we've had the chance to officially meet."

His velvet-soft voice chafed every nerve. "I'm Mateo."

"And I'm leaving," Este said. She looped the key back around her neck, resigning to try again when there wasn't an annoyingly cute hall monitor on the loose.

"That's a terrible name."

Este ignored the boy and pivoted toward the distant drone of Dr. Kirk's voice. She wove between the stacks, shelf after shelf of yellowed pages, until, when she looked back, Mateo had been swallowed up by the library, tucked away behind the stacks. But when she turned the corner, he was waiting for her.

There was a sparkle in his eyes, rimmed with heavy lashes, and the smug remnants of a smirk on his lips when he said, "There's only one door that key unlocks."

Este couldn't help herself. "Where is it?"

Mateo grinned, a lopsided thing that made Este's breath shorten. "Only if you tell me your name."

She sighed. New England boys were persistent. "I'm Este."

His eyes dipped to her toes and dragged up the length of her. It sent sparks under her skin, and she tried to squash down the color rising to her face. "The door you're looking for leads to the Radcliffe heirlooms."

"The spire?" All the moisture wicked from her mouth. "We can't go up there."

His eyebrows raised, line of sight dipping to the key in her hands. "With that, we can."

"No," Este said, backtracking down the stacks. "*I* can go

up there. *We* aren't doing anything together. Plus, how do you even know?"

He scoffed at her. "You would've spent the entire year trying to break into broom closets if I hadn't told you." Mateo followed her down the aisle. "We could be the first ones to see the spire in thirty years. Don't you want to know what's up there?"

The thing was, she did. For some reason, the spire key had been hidden in her dad's picture frame, and she wanted to know why. However, and maybe more importantly, she also wanted to not get kicked out of school before classes even started.

"Why should I trust you?" she asked, twisting to face him.

"If my dashing good looks and my winning personality aren't enough," he said, amusement darting across the lines of his face, down the long slope of his thin nose and the dimple in his chin, "because I'll tell Ives you took the key. And rumor has it she's been looking for it for quite some time."

"I didn't—" The outrage burst out of her.

"And yet you have it," he said with a shrug. "Who do you think she'll believe? This is your only chance."

Este chewed on her lip and tasted vanilla ChapStick, deliberating. Mateo's penchant for eye contact made her skin crawl. All crystalline blue with nowhere to hide. He made a good point. And exploring the spire . . . it was what her dad would've wanted, right?

"Let's go," she said, and she hoped she wouldn't regret it.

THREE

If this is the part where you axe murder me," Este said, hands braced against the stairwell's clammy walls, "promise me you'll donate my organs."

The entrance to the spire was an arched door on the fifth floor across from Ives's office, and they'd slipped inside with absolutely no fanfare—it hadn't even been locked. The real door, Mateo assured her, was at the top of a spiraling staircase as pitch dark as it was narrow. Este's feet kept slipping off the steps, and her white-finger grip on the walls was barely enough to keep her upright. Apparently, the Radcliffes hadn't believed in handrails.

Ahead of her, Mateo huffed, "I'm not going to do either of those things." He marched, sure-footed and swift, up the stairs without sparing her a look back.

As soon as they'd pried open the spire's fifth-floor entrance, a damp quiet had surrounded them. Here, there was no residual library soundtrack—no chime of the circulation clerk scanning library cards for checkout, no quiet chatter and whispered secrets, only cold stone walls that soaked up the sound of their voices. Trailing a boy she barely knew into a secluded tower wasn't her best idea, but with her dad's key warming in the palm of her hand, she knew she had to see where it led.

If only she could see her own feet.

"Is there seriously not an elevator?" Este whined.

"Oh, there is." Este didn't need to see his face to know Mateo's lips were twisted into a skewed smile. She could hear it in his voice, the way it lilted with a laugh. "But it's in Ives's office and a bit of a tight fit for two."

"Could you at least put on your phone's flashlight?" she asked. "I'm pretty sure I'm going to break my neck, and I left mine in my dorm."

"I don't have one."

Who didn't own a phone? Este tracked the shape of Mateo, his outline muddled in the black. She hadn't pegged him as an off-the-grid hipster. "Not even a flip phone?"

"Nope."

Finally, gray-blue light sifted through the stairwell as they approached one arched window after another. A sliver of waxing moon cast silver streams over the limestone staircase, guiding them up and up and up. Through the streaked glass stood the pointed tops of pine trees, coated by a layer of evening fog rolling down the hills. Este lost track of how many flights they climbed, but she was certain she'd done enough cardio for the entire semester. And they were only halfway up.

"Why not?" she asked.

"Everyone I know is around here." Mateo spun on his heels, taking the steps backward so that she had nowhere to look but up at him. It would take an hour to unravel the stitch in Este's side, and he hadn't even broken a sweat. "I was born and raised right here in Sheridan Oaks."

Sheridan Oaks, Vermont, wasn't much more than a pinprick on the atlas. Este and her mom had careened through the countryside for miles before she glimpsed the wrought-iron gates and brick perimeter that separated Radcliffe from the rest of the world. And a library like this? With its ornate exterior and sprawling collection of antique texts, the Lilith exuded a permanence unlike anything else in Este's life. She couldn't imagine having it all right in her backyard.

"Do you ever think about leaving? Going somewhere else for college?" she asked.

Mateo shook his head in a single, taut stroke. "This place is all I've ever known. I don't know if I could leave it behind if I tried."

That kind of constant was a foreign language Este hadn't heard in years. After her dad died, her mom uprooted everything—sold the house, packed the Subaru, and strapped Este into the back seat for a three-year road trip. They'd eaten ice cream for breakfast and drank Slurpees for dinner, nursing the stomachaches that came with it.

When Este got her license last summer, she and her mom had taken turns driving while the other chose their next destination. She learned how to say goodbye over and over again. It was so much easier than holding on too long. She'd seen what heartbreak could do. She'd watched her mom cave in on herself beneath the weight of grief, caravanning across county lines searching for something she'd never find.

Now, with her hands clawing at timeworn stones in a desperate attempt to find some connection to her dad, Este wasn't sure she was any better. The staircase widened until they reached a curved onyx door cloaked with streams of ivy pockmarked by dainty purple flowers. Each blossom stretched its petals when moonlight slanted on its bulbs and shied away when fog shade drenched the staircase back into darkness, winking closed.

"The honor is all yours," Mateo said, stepping aside on the wide landing.

Este braced herself against the wall, dizzy from the nectarine scent radiating from the flowers, the anticipation of stepping through the threshold, and how closely Mateo stood. She couldn't tell which was the most responsible.

Thick twines of ivy circled the brass knob. Roots wedged inside the keyhole. She'd imagined the Radcliffe collection tucked inside a pristine vault, something with tufted velvet chaises and polished gold—not an overgrown attic.

Suddenly, a wave of nauseating anxiety crashed against her

chest, threatening to pull her into the undertow. She raked her nail against a petal, and it shrunk into itself. If Este walked through the spire door, there would be no turning back.

"Are you sure we should do this?" she asked, scrunching up the bridge of her nose.

"Don't tell me you're getting cold feet already. We haven't even seen what's inside," Mateo crooned. His voice was hushed and harsh at once. Este wasn't sure if it was his words or the hallway's damp chill that grew goose bumps on her neck.

Taking the key from around her neck, Este held it out to him. "You should open it. Coming up here was your idea."

"Ladies first," he said. "I insist."

"No, I do." She dangled the key by its cord, bait for the taking.

His voice dropped. "I can't."

Este barked a laugh. "What do you mean you can't?"

Mateo thinned his lips into a firm line and leaned his head toward the shallow ceiling. With his eyes pinched closed, he said, "I can't touch the ivy, Este. I'm allergic."

"Actually, you're an asshole, you know that?" Este didn't try to warm the cold snap in her voice. "You really dragged me all the way up here just to give me an earful of lousy excuses?"

She coiled her arms around her ribs as she dipped down the stairwell. Maybe she wouldn't see the spire tonight, but she also wouldn't have to spend another moment with someone as irritating as him.

Este was halfway around the first spiral by the time Mateo said, "I guess that's my mistake for expecting more from a Logano."

She paused, frozen between steps. The blood drained from her face. Her eyebrows pinched so closely together, she wondered if they'd fuse permanently into one. How did *he* know *her* last name?

Turning back, Este barked, "What did you say?"

When she faced him, he leaned against the stone wall, ankles hooked together and a hand slipped into the pocket of his trousers, with the graceful ease of a grand master who moved the rook into checkmate. "Dean Logano," he said. "Is he of any relation to you?"

"What do you know about my dad?" Este stalked back to the door, fists clenched. A shadow blotted out the light from the moon, and every purple flower on the doorframe closed its blossom—too afraid to watch.

"The whole school's heard of him. You must know that he was the last person in the spire."

Este's mouth hung open, wordless. When she didn't say anything, Mateo leaned closer. He smelled like a sun-drenched memory—like well-worn book pages and Vermont's white cedar groves. "Unless, you didn't."

Not a question. A realization that he had the upper hand.

"Legend says that while Dean Logano was working on a research project, he took the head librarian's key—some say stole, some say borrowed, you decide—and snuck into the spire. Whatever he found up there, no one knows. He transferred schools, and the door was left locked."

"So, what?" Este huffed, hoping he couldn't hear the frantic way her heart was beating.

"So, no one has entered this section in thirty years, and now you have the key." Barely louder than a whisper, he said, "I saw your scholarship announcement, Este Logano. You've got a legacy to fulfill."

In that moment, Este hated Mateo. She hated that he lured her up here, all eyelashes and arrogance, and she hated that he was right. Underneath the rhythmic pounding of her heart and the storm of worry brewing behind her sternum, there was a magnetic pull to the spire that Este couldn't resist. Her dad had been the last person to see the heirlooms. Her footprints would leave tracks in the gathered dust, right next to his.

As she pulled the key from her pocket, Mateo grinned, and if her curiosity didn't outweigh how much she loathed his incessant cockiness, she would've left him standing there. Instead, she scraped away leaves from the lock with a polished fingernail and fitted the key into its slot. Ivy curled away as she twisted the groaning knob. The door hinges whined, one long syllable, as Este nudged it open with the flat of her hand.

Taking a steadying breath, she stepped up and into the spire's archives.

Oh, my god. She'd need the next seven to ten business days to recover emotionally, mentally, and physically.

Window after window dotted the perimeter of the circular room, and hazy moonlight poured through the veiled sky. Cobwebs strung from the ceiling in lazy silver loops. In the center of the room, bookcases behind iron cages wove a maze of one-of-a-kind texts. Forgotten Shakespearean soliloquies, Italian sonnets drenched in unrequited love, playbooks and philosophies, ancient parables on ink-drenched parchment. Glass cases housed twinkling diamonds and fountain pens, a blade with a ruby hilt, portraits and sculptures, jewels and jade.

And ivy clawed through all of it. Vines wept over the window ledges, the bookcases, the cedar rafters. They crawled down the walls and dug deep into the stone flooring. Those petite, purple flowers speckled the greenery, opening and closing like watchful eyes.

Seeing the same forbidden collections her dad had, every heirloom gem and preserved parchment, sent shivers over her skin. Este couldn't take it all in at once.

Mateo, on the other hand, clearly didn't harbor the same kind of awe and reverence. He unceremoniously breezed past her and veered into the stacks. She scrambled to catch up with him, and he dropped a scrap of notebook paper into her hand.

"I helped you," he said, "and now you can help me find this book."

Unfolding it, Mateo's handwriting was as slim and precise as he was. "How are we supposed to find it with this?" she asked, cutting close corners to keep up with his breakneck stride. "BL293?"

Mateo stifled a curt laugh. "Don't you know how to read a call number?"

"What? No," Este fumbled. He was a spade digging under her skin. "That's—no, *of course* I know the Dewey decimal system."

"Academic libraries use Library of Congress classification." He forged ahead, zipping between narrow rows of artifacts and precious artworks.

Mateo's head didn't swivel side to side at the sight of every relic the way Este's did as they looped through the shelves' crooked corridors. Publications were densely packed behind intricately carved, diamond-paned doors, and she trailed her index fingers across the bars as they passed. He barely gave them a second glance.

Finally, he stalled in front of a case close to the center of the room, and Este took her place next to him, shoulders nearly touching. Their reflections stared back at her, warped in the glass—the round curve of Este's chin, the sharp bow of her lips, a triplet of moles on her cheekbone, all of it framed by a long swath of brown hair, and Mateo's jagged features mismatched with the soft gleam in his eyes. On the shelf inside, a single tome stood centered on a bookstand, with knotted ivy binding the text in a living casing.

Stamped on a gold plate over the cabinet: BL293.

Este's hand covered her mouth in disbelief. "That's the book you want to look at?"

Mateo nodded, his eyes trained against the greenery and the hardback beneath it. "The one and only."

"It's absolutely ancient," she said, breathless. "We should use gloves or something. Did you bring some?"

"Honestly, Este, if the ivy hasn't hurt it, nothing you do will." He ran a hand through his curls and offered her a half smile. Not exactly the encouragement she needed.

A groaning sound billowed through the spire, a vibrato baritone. Este couldn't tell exactly where the sound came from—a northern wind rolling down the Green Mountains or inside the walls of the spire. Either way, an echo of Posy's ghost stories ricocheted through her mind, suddenly too close for comfort. It spurred her into motion.

Este jerked the cabinet's handle, but the door caught, its hinges unoiled and untouched for too long. Three decades of dust and grime sealed it shut. She waited for an alarm system to blare and blow their cover, but when the spire stayed silent, she pulled again, harder this time. The gated cabinet flung open, and the force knocked Este into the shelf behind her. A wave of sweetly scented air breathed into the spire, rich as primrose and sharp as pine.

"It doesn't even have a title?" she asked over her shoulder as she plucked one of the leaves.

"It's called *The Book of Fades*."

Este's hands stilled. Hadn't Posy said something about Fades earlier? She groaned, "Not you, too. Is everyone here obsessed with dead people or what?"

"Just—" He pressed his index finger to his temple. Tension rippled through his shoulders. Este had to admit that she kind of enjoyed riling him up like that. "Just grab the book."

Mateo's fingers rapped against the cabinet's glass pane as she pried away the ivy. Her hands tingled, coated in the sap from the greenery. With each vine removed, another wove snugly around the ancient binding, alive and angry. She curled both hands around the text, casting out any guilt twisting in her gut about what the oils on her skin might do to the antique leather, and the book broke free from the last vine with a final pull.

The book was horribly ornate, with a glimmering stitching around the perimeter and corners capped with scalloped, golden pieces. It must have been at least six hundred pages, each painted with a dainty metallic edge. Before she could flip the front cover open, Mateo stripped it from her grip with a quick hand.

"*You're the best, Este,*" she said, dropping her voice as low as she could in a flimsy imitation of him. "*Thank you for all your help.*"

A shade of a smile grazed his lips as he fanned through the pages, but Mateo slammed the cover shut when Este tried again to glance over the book's head. "Este Logano, I could kiss you right now."

"You could?" she stammered.

He leaned down so that they were eye to eye, and Este didn't dare breathe. "But I'm sure Ives will be up here soon. If I were you, I'd make a run for it."

Este heard it, then, over the adrenaline swirling in her head—the click of high heels echoing from the staircase chamber. Quick, purposeful, and definitely bad news. "We have to get out of here."

But she quickly realized there was no *we* anymore. Mateo had vanished.

"Mateo?" she called.

Este's voice tapered off, answered only by the pearly moonshine, the night silence. Her hummingbird heartbeat pulsed in her ears. He'd used her, and he'd disappeared around the corner cabinet as if he'd never been here at all. Probably jumped into the elevator he'd conveniently deemed unusable on their way up.

She whispered his name again. No use. Tiptoeing to the end of the aisle, the only trace he'd been here at all was an oxford footprint in the dust. The shelves wove together, labyrinthian, and she couldn't find him in them. Este's fingernails carved divots into the soft of her palm.

She needed to find the elevator—and fast. Without it, there was only one way out, and she'd never make it back downstairs without getting caught.

Panic roiled in her stomach, acid burning up her throat as

the head librarian turned the corner in long, lithe strides. Este's hands were slicked with dust and sticky with sap, the spire key hung around her neck, and the case swung open on uneven hinges, *The Book of Fades* missing.

She was totally and completely screwed.

Ives rested both hands on her narrow hips, and a slice of moonlight illuminated half her face—her pointed cheekbones, her red-painted lips. With a flash of white teeth, she said, "Este Logano. I should've known it would be you."

FOUR

❧

Este was going to kill Mateo if Ives didn't kill her first.

She stood in the head librarian's office, several stories below the scene of the crime. The door to Ives's office was tucked into an alcove adjacent to the stairwell's entrance, and she'd wasted no time ushering Este inside. The room would have been spacious if it weren't for the monoliths of ancient tomes leaning against the walls. A few low-wattage bulbs hung from sconces, casting blooms of golden light up to the rafters. Beneath them, shadows curled at Este's feet, as yawning as the pit growing in her stomach.

Mateo should have been standing next to her with a crooked smile on his lips, a hand shoved in the deep pockets of his wool pants, and a bounty on his head. He hadn't only abandoned her—he framed her.

In here, there was no evidence of Mateo's escape elevator. A photo of the school founders, an unlevel shelf spilling over with potted plants, and a small wooden hatch that resembled an old-fashioned book drop, but no elevator. Maybe he'd lied about it being in Ives's office to throw Este off his scent.

Ives went to sit behind her cluttered mahogany desk, the top of it pen scratched and ink stained, marred by the years. She pushed aside a few waxy candles and a lopsided stack of papers and replaced them with a crisp white sheet. The Radcliffe Prep seal was stamped in the corner.

Oh, god. Not the formal letterhead.

As Ives dipped a slender fountain pen into a well of black ink, Este couldn't peel her eyes from each deliberate stroke. When she was finished writing, Ives dropped her pen, folded the paper in half, and batted heavy lashes up at Este who had been too nervous to sit in one of the cracked leather armchairs.

"I have to admit, Este, that I didn't expect to see you in my office quite this early in the school year." The head librarian stood with an easy grace, drifting her fingers along the desk's grooves. "But I suppose it's only right we get acquainted since you're here as a scholarship recipient."

Este's blood rushed through her body, hot. There was no way she could pay for tuition if Ives rescinded the generous scholarship that got her here in the first place, and her dreams of staying at Radcliffe were suffocating with every passing second. Like how she was going to smother Mateo if she ever saw him again, *Othello*-style.

"I didn't mean to—" Este started, but Ives smacked her lips

together, so the rest of the sentence shrank back inside. This close, Este noticed the fine lines drawn into the corners of Ives's face and the sparse silver streaks speckling her glossy curls.

"Take a seat."

Cold leather pricked Este's skin as she dipped onto the armchair on command. Coming to the front of the desk, Ives leaned against it, hooking one ankle over the other. Pinched between her fingers was the folded sheet of paper.

She was getting kicked out. Of course she was. At least, Este had barely started to unpack. It would make the whole *losing her scholarship and getting kicked out of school* thing easier to choke down.

"I've heard your father was an interesting student— unforgettable, really. It was a shame he couldn't finish his learning here, as a diploma from Radcliffe is renowned worldwide. Although I never taught Dean, it's always heartbreaking to hear of a former student's passing. Offering you a full ride to continue his journey at Radcliffe was my honor."

The day the mail came, Este had been sunbathing on Florida's Atlantic coast, and she'd spent all afternoon sneaking sips from her mom's piña colada. When they got back to their room in the breezy Fort Lauderdale motel, housekeeping left the forwarded letter and a bill for the poolside bar on the kitchen table. Only one was sealed with a dollop of maroon wax bearing the Radcliffe Prep crest, two crossed quills.

What Este's haphazard homeschooling lacked, she made up

for in reading. Every town they drove through had a library they could stop in for the afternoon. While her mom worked, writing clickbait pieces for online magazines primarily perused by middle-class, middle-aged women with nothing better to do than read about "14 Types of Pantyhose You Need for Date Night," Este pored over whatever she could find in the stacks. Some days it was metrical poetry and muddling through *Beowulf*'s archaic English. Others, she fawned over egg tempera Renaissance paintings and studied the light in Monet masterpieces.

She had filled out the Radcliffe Prep application months ago on a computer from the last millennium in a Wyoming library and had worn her dad's old Radcliffe crewneck for good luck. Tuition for an elite, private boarding school was an ungodly number Este could scarcely imagine, but she'd studied hard in the hopes of a merit scholarship. It was a long shot, sure, but her dad had talked about his time at Radcliffe so often that she needed to see it for herself.

Every time she checked her application portal from there to the shore, the status read the same noncommittal word: *pending*. But when her finger slid under the lip of the stock envelope that afternoon in Florida, sand still sticking to her fingers, she had known it would be good news. No one wax sealed a rejection.

The scholarship paid for everything—room and board, tuition, her books and fees. It was the only reason Este ever had the chance to walk inside the campus gates. And the thin ice she'd been standing on had cracked with every hot-footed step she took up the spire's staircase.

"At Radcliffe, tradition is everything." Ives tapped her nails against the desktop, any trace of levity evaporating from her voice. "We take special care to protect what was entrusted to us by the founding family. Their collections are the cornerstone of our academics."

Something sharp wedged itself in Este's windpipe, making it hard to breathe, so she nodded.

Ives's jaw clenched with a twinge in her cheek. "It's my duty to protect the Radcliffe heritage. I trust you understand that I do not take my position lightly."

"I know," Este blurted. "I know, and I'm sorry, and——"

Outstretching a hand, Ives said, "The key, please."

Este dropped the brass key into Ives's palm, hands shaking. Her voice cracked when she said, "I'm so sorry. It was a mistake I'll never make again."

A shadow darkened Ives's blue eyes. "No, you certainly won't. This level of blatant disregard for school policy calls for immediate expulsion. I've just signed your letter of removal."

"No," Este gasped. She was on the brink of sobbing or blacking out or both in short succession. Her time at Radcliffe Prep was about to be over before it ever started. The revelation was a hot coal in Este's stomach. The kind that might burn right through her.

Her mom could be anywhere—Boise or Beaufort or the

backwoods of Colorado, cruising down the interstate with the windows down and the radio up. Her dad was buried six feet under in California. And she had nowhere.

"Don't make me go," she said, blinking back stubborn tears. "I'll do anything."

The head librarian's laugh was cold, lifeless. "You acted in blatant insubordination, and you want me to let you stay? What kind of example would that set for the other students?"

Rooting in the corners of her mind, Este reached for anything that could help. Whatever it took to stay, she'd do it. "I'll work hard. I can, um, do the late-night shift in the archives. You said you needed volunteers, right?"

At this, Ives paused. She slid the letter and the spire key onto her desk and then leaned forward, hands steepled beneath her chin. "It is a privilege to discover what is in those archives, not a punishment. Archival assistant positions are typically reserved for second-year students. Students who show promise."

"I know, but I—"

"The door to the spire has been locked for three decades. Somehow, you ended up with the key, and now *The Book of Fades* is gone. Forgive me if I'm a bit skeptical about your intentions."

Este gripped the clawed arms of her chair. "Going into the spire tonight wasn't my idea. I promise."

"Tell me where you put the book, and maybe I'll reconsider your options." Ives flicked up a perfectly arched eyebrow as if waiting for Este to challenge her.

Este's chest rose and fell in quick bursts, her last chance slipping from her fingers. "I don't know where it is."

Cresting forward, Ives said, "That book is the single most prized text in the Lilith, no other one like it in existence, and now it's missing. You were the only one upstairs. I'm trying to be reasonable, Este, but you must work with me."

"I wasn't alone!" Este choked down a few gulps of air in a feeble attempt to slow the rampant rhythm of her heart. Each word came out jagged. "This boy, Mateo. He said the key opened the spire door. I thought we'd just look around, but he wanted that book. I don't know what for. And then, he left me there. I don't know where he is, or where the book is, or anything. But if you let me stay, I'll find it. I promise."

Ives's hands curled around the lip of her desk, and she pushed a forceful breath through her mouth. Standing, she trailed around the desk, tapping her nails against the wood with each step, letting Este steep in her agony.

She'd lost all dignity, begging the head librarian not to throw her out on the streets. Meanwhile, Mateo was probably downstairs, with his stupid dimples, drumming up new lies to feed to some other wide-eyed junior.

Yeah, he was dead to her.

"Ancient texts are not forgiving. One mistake could ruin an entire legacy, and *The Book of Fades* needs to be returned to me in one piece," Ives said, peering down the slender bridge of her nose. She sank into her chair on the opposite side of the desk.

From the top drawer, she pulled out a heavy stack of parchment, a few crumpled sticky notes, and a worn Alighieri print. *The Divine Comedy* in its original Italian ink. Vaguely, Este wondered what circle of hell she'd land in for losing an irreplaceable artifact.

"You'll need proper training to ensure you don't damage something priceless." Ives cracked open the spine and leafed delicately through the pages of *Inferno*. She smoothed something that looked like an ivory tongue depressor down the seam between pages. "You received your scholarship because the school believes your attendance is vital. And so do I."

Este's chest squeezed, something caught between pride and panic.

Ives dabbed the page bindings with a bottle of glue and then carefully pressed a loose page back into the middle seam. Repairing it. Then, she bound the text with wide bands of cotton and tied them to hold it tight. She didn't look up at Este when she said, "For now, I'll allow you to continue at Radcliffe as expected. Tomorrow night, I'll train you here at the Lilith. Starting next week, you'll work school nights from ten to two at circulation. Dusting shelves, repairing books, scraping gum from the bottom of study tables. And, when needed, you'll assist in the archives."

Nodding, Este was grateful she was sitting down. Her knees felt like a plate of green Jell-O.

"I trust that will give you plenty of time to locate *The Book of Fades*," Ives said. "On Tuesday mornings before study period, we will hold weekly meetings so that I can monitor your progress. The nighttime hours cannot affect your studies. Make sure your grades do not slip below a 3.5 GPA."

"They won't," Este rushed to say. Not if it meant she could stay.

Ives slid *The Divine Comedy* back into her drawer and retrieved, instead, a box of long-stick matches. Striking one, she cupped the flame as she lit a desk candle. Prying up the signed expulsion letter, she watched Este, a smile curling onto her painted-red lips. "I expect nothing less than excellence from you, Este. If *The Book of Fades* is not back in my possession by the end of midterm exams, I won't hesitate to remove you from the program permanently."

But for now, Ives touched the parchment corner to the beveled flame, and it faded to ashes. A second chance Este didn't deserve.

FIVE

The Safety and Security office was its own special circle of hell, buried in the basement of the administration building. The air was thick and musty, a smidge damp. Something dripped in the distance, a faucet or a leaky roof tile, but no one in the office seemed to notice or care, instead opting for willing ignorance as the gray room succumbed to rot.

The rest of campus was an immaculate postcard, but the tucked-away corner was a more accurate portrayal of how Este felt this afternoon.

She was still a student at Radcliffe Prep by some miracle, but that miracle hinged on convincing Mateo to give her back the book he stole. And to do that, she had to find him.

Students snaked through a roped maze as if they were in line for a new steel roller coaster rather than to speak to the disinterested clerk, and after twenty minutes of waiting, Este was finally third to the front. Then, the smoked glass door at the entrance whined on its hinges, and a flash of sienna hair barreled into the otherwise quiet office.

Este ducked her head as Posy veered for the back of the line. Something a lot like guilt twined between her rib bones, but she shook it away. Posy would be thrilled to see her because Posy was thrilled to see everyone. She was a human golden retriever. Este was a crab, all pinchers and an exoskeleton shell.

They hadn't spoken since the campus tour. Posy's door had been shut when Este got back to their dorm last night, still covered in spire dust and cobwebs, and that was fine by Este. She preferred to keep the number of classmates who knew she was a delinquent at risk of expulsion at an absolute minimum.

"Do you want to know the truth about what haunts campus?" Posy asked now, peddling flyers to tired students just trying to get their student ID photos taken or find something lost in the move-in day shuffle.

Este trained her eyes forward, straightening her spine. She focused on the buzz of the fluorescent bulbs, the pattern of bricks on the walls, and the clerk's neon-green acrylic nails as they tapped on her keyboard. She willed herself invisible as Posy's voice drifted closer and closer.

"If so, join the Paranormal Investigators! We're Radcliffe's first school-sanctioned ghost-hunting club." Posy held out another flyer before she registered who she was speaking to. "Este! What are you doing here?"

"I'm looking for something," Este said, reaching for the

flyer. On the page, there was an illustration of a navy flashlight with a bright yellow beam, and the words Paranormal Investigators had been printed in a dripping, ghoulish typeface. "You made all these last night?"

Posy bounced from foot to foot. "You know that huge printer in my room? Over the summer, I self-published a magazine exploring local mysteries, so my parents bought it for me. It's, like, a million years old, and sometimes I think it's possessed, but that's fine."

The girl in front of them was the pinnacle of private-school poise. She'd paired a plaid skirt with knee-high socks, and when she stepped up to the counter, she said, "My name's Bryony Pritcher, and I'm in room Vespertine 204C. The lights flickered all night."

"Oh, you definitely need one of these," Posy said, thrusting out a flyer. To Este's surprise, the girl took it, folded it neatly, and slipped it into a pocket between the pleats of her skirt. Posy reeled back to Este. "That's ghosts if I've ever heard it."

Este was beginning to piece together that *everything* was ghosts with her roommate.

"Anyway, yeah. I convinced Dr. Kirk to advise the club last night after the tour, so I stayed up and made these," Posy said, beaming. "Where'd you run off to?"

Este plastered on a flimsy smile. While Posy was speed printing propaganda, Este had also barely gotten any decent sleep. Every interaction with Mateo replayed on a loop through her dreams. She hated him just as much in REM.

Before she could answer, the clerk's tinny voice called, "Next!"

"Hi," Este said sweetly. "Could you help me find something?"

The clerk reached below the countertop and plunked a plastic bin in front of her. Someone had written Lost and Found on the side. Inside, there were phone chargers, someone's desk calendar, and a stray tennis shoe, but no books with gilded edges.

"Something else, actually. I'm trying to find a boy named Mateo." Este leaned onto the linoleum counter. "He stole a library book, and I really, *really* need it back."

"Last name?" the clerk asked.

A stone sank in Este's chest. "I'm not sure. He didn't say."

The clerk—Tammy, according to the name embroidered on her lapel—rolled her beady green eyes. She gnawed on a wad of bubble gum that threatened to slip out of her mouth at any moment. The computer's fans whirred as her search loaded. "No students on the roster with that name."

"Maybe it's his middle name?" Este asked, but her reservoirs of hope were quickly depleting.

Tammy typed, waited, shook her head.

"Nickname? Short for Matthew, Matthias . . . Mattholomew?"

This time, Tammy didn't even bother searching the roster. She blew a hot pink bubble and popped it with the taloned point of her acrylic.

A groan parted Este's lips. "Dammit, Tammy. He has to be around here somewhere."

"Try spelling it with one *t* and two, just in case," Posy said, wedging herself next to Este. "You met a cute boy and didn't tell me?"

"You really don't have to stay," Este said. Once Posy learned what she'd done, there would probably be an exposé in the school paper—*Rogue Student Sneaks into Restricted Spire, Ruins Reputation.* "I've got this. I'll meet you back at the dorm."

But Posy grinned, determined. Her sunshine made Este's shadows starker.

Tammy's nails tapped as she typed, and then she licked the tip of a ballpoint pen and shuffled a stack of papers. "Nothing on file. Would you like to make a formal incident report?"

Este slumped lower, dropping her chin in her hands. Everything Mateo had told her had been a lie, even his name. She shouldn't have been surprised, but maybe she'd wanted to believe him. "If I do, will you hang up Most Wanted signs around campus?"

Tammy blinked, unenthused. "No, but I can let you know if we find your book."

Even if the thought of having her mistakes in writing made her stomach churn, Este conceded. She answered a stream of preliminary questions like her name and year of study before Tammy asked her to explain, in as much detail as possible, the incident. She held herself upright with a tight grip around the counter and prayed no one behind her was eavesdropping. "Yesterday, I went with Posy—"

"That's me," her roommate chirped.

"—to Dr. Kirk's campus tour, and I met this hot jerk allegedly named Mateo."

The pen in Tammy's hand stalled. "You want that on record? *Hot jerk?*"

"Yes." Este's frustration bubbled to the surface. "A senior. Tall, obnoxious, walked around like he owned the place. The very definition of hot jerk. He wanted to show me the spire—"

"Is that a euphemism?" Tammy asked, a bored lilt shifting into her voice.

"No, it's not," Este said flatly. "He asked me to help him look at a book in the spire collection, and I did."

Posy gasped. "You went *inside* the spire? How?"

Este didn't think. She clamped her hand over Posy's mouth, anything to get her to shut up, and continued like everything was totally normal. "Ives came upstairs to, um, see how we were doing, but by then Mateo and the book were gone. *Poof.* Missing in action. So, Ives wants me to make sure it gets returned."

"What's the title?" Tammy asked, blowing another bubble.

"*The Book of Fades.* I need to find *The Book of Fades.*"

Posy's eyes peeled wide open, and her arms flailed. She tried to say something, but with her words muffled, it just ended up with a lot of saliva on Este's palm.

Gross. Este yanked her hand off and wiped it on her jeans.

Posy offered Tammy a wide smile, sounding surprisingly calm for someone who had just taste tested a hand. "If you'll excuse us, we'll be leaving."

Este didn't have time to protest because Posy jerked her away by the straps of her backpack. She didn't let go until they pushed through the heavy glass doors at the mouth of the administration building and stepped into a sheet of midday sun. Tawny light doused campus in a warm glow that dripped from the branches and splashed onto the cobblestones. Wisps of cotton clouds spilled over September's otherwise blue sky.

"Let me get this straight," Posy said. "You disappear from the library tour, meet a hunky upperclassman, somehow go into the single most haunted part of the entire library that has been super locked since before we were born, are looking for *a book about Fades*—hello!—and you didn't tell me immediately?"

If she'd had it her way, Este never would've told Posy. She'd messed up big time. One wrong move was all it would take for all this to be over.

She'd tried all day to hold it together through hours of mind-numbing syllabus lectures and classroom icebreaker games to get to know her classmates, but her brittle veneer was cracking. She took the stone steps two at a time to hide the red that rimmed her eyes, that crawled up the column of her neck.

Este could practically hear Posy's thoughts whirring behind her skull. Her roommate buzzed. "How did you go to the spire? Was there a secret passageway? Tell me you saw a ghost."

If Este didn't respond, Posy would probably just keep talking.

They ducked beneath the canopy of sweet birches and sugar maples, their deep green leaves still clinging to the last few drops of summer. A couple people tied hammocks between the trees or wandered through the floral courtyard surrounding the Lilith. Despite the sun, a chill seeped through the thick knit of Este's sweater.

As they walked, Posy's fingers flew over her phone's keyboard, and Este scanned the grounds for a gleam of black hair, but Mateo wasn't here. He wasn't at Radcliffe at all. He said he grew up in Sheridan Oaks—maybe there was a public school nearby that he went to, only trespassing onto campus to ruin her life.

"Actually, can we back peddle to *poof*?" Posy stopped typing only long enough to grab Este by the shoulder. "Oh, my god. Maybe he's a ghost. Was he see-through?"

"No, Posy. He was perfectly solid, I promise. Just a normal, seventeen-year-old asshole."

Posy's shoulders sank, but she recovered quickly. "Do you think he'd want to join the Paranormal Investigators?"

It took every drop of Este's willpower not to roll her eyes. Instead, she nodded toward Posy's phone. "What are you doing?"

A text message riddled with all caps took up most of the screen. Now, she added ghost emojis and more exclamation

56

points than Este had used in her entire life. Posy was nothing if not enthusiastic—she had to give her that.

"Calling an emergency club meeting, obviously. You just went into the most haunted part of campus. Arthur isn't going to believe this."

Este had to laugh. Her entire world was shattering, and Posy only cared about ghouls and goblins. The message sent with a *whoosh*. They'd been here twenty-four hours, and Posy had already founded a new club, forged a new friend group, and gotten in the good graces of their teachers.

All Este had gotten was a migraine and an ultimatum.

They rounded a corner, and the limestone columns of their dorm, Vespertine Hall, came into view between the maples. Something deep in Este's chest panged at the thought that she might not get to call her dorm *home* again after the end of the quarter if she couldn't find *The Book of Fades*.

Este barged into their dorm and kicked her sneakers off by the door. Tufts of deep green suede cushioned her as she flopped onto the couch, letting out a long, miserable moan. "I really don't have time for paranormal conspiracy theories right now, Posy."

The air in Posy deflated, and the couch shifted as she settled next to her. "I get it. Classes are about to start, you're looking for the book, you want to canoodle with the hot jerk."

"No one is canoodling anybody." And *definitely* not Mateo.

Seconds later, there was a knock at the door, and Shepherd

and Arthur barged into the living room. Shepherd ditched his lacrosse bag by the counter with a clunk. *Sure, just make yourself at home.*

Posy leaped up to welcome them, accidentally spilling flyers all over the floor. "Our inaugural meeting! Thank you for coming on such short notice."

"We live on the third floor," Arthur said, choosing to curl onto the window ledge like a cat even when there were perfectly good chairs. "It's not like we had to go far."

Este stood to leave, but Posy grabbed her by the sleeve. "Where are you going?"

Caught off guard by the way Posy's eyes rounded, big and hopeful, Este hesitated. *She only wants you to stay so that you can tell them about the spire*, she reminded herself coldly, trying to snuff out the flicker of friendship that had sparked. Still, she let herself be tugged back down to the couch as Posy launched straight into her opening remarks.

"Let's start by sharing any supernatural encounters we've had. I'll go first." For dramatic effect, Posy dropped her voice to a stage whisper. Never mind the fact that it was still broad daylight. "When I was twelve, I found a Ouija board at the consignment shop, and I held an entire conversation with Sylvia Plath."

Shepherd scrubbed the back of his neck, crooking his head the way a dog does when it's thinking. "One time, I heard footsteps in my attic when I was home alone. Does that count?"

"Basically every theater I've ever performed in has been haunted," said Arthur.

Three sets of expectant eyes turned to Este. "Oh, um, I . . ."

When she and her mom left Paso Robles for good, they first went to Montana for the wide skies and too-blue lakes. Este had locked herself in the bathroom stall of a Glacier National Park campsite, said her dad's name three times in the mirror, and accidentally singed off half an eyebrow with a citronella candle waiting for a response that never came.

Was that what they wanted? For her to excavate that part of herself, to put it on display like a museum art piece with a gold plaque? *Portrait of a Girl Grieving*, oil on canvas.

No, she couldn't. Shepherd and Arthur, they hung on to Posy's every word, drinking up the scary stories. They belonged in a way she didn't, even if she wanted to.

"I've never had one." Este shook out her hands. She hadn't realized she'd clenched them into fists. "Tell the spirits I say hello, but I think I saw a coffee maker downstairs, and there's a nonzero chance that unless I get some caffeine in my blood-stream immediately, I'm going to have a headache for the rest of eternity."

If anyone protested, they didn't do it fast enough. The front door locked behind her with a separating click. Running from her problems was kind of her specialty.

SIX

By the time Este left for archival training that night, she had enough caffeine in her system to keep her awake until high school graduation. The sky above the Lilith faded into blues as the first pinhole stars poked through. Each of the library's peaked windows glowed from within. Este drew toward them like a moth to flame. Ivy clawed up the Lilith's facade, and her gaze followed greenery toward the stone spire. An arched roof capped the circular room where the heirlooms were stored.

She still felt like she needed to pinch herself. She'd been so certain Ives would ask for her room key and request for her immediate removal. Was she excited about spending every weeknight working the late shift? No, not really. But it was better than the alternative.

If Mateo had a self-preserving thought in his head, he'd never come back to the Lilith, but for her sake, she hoped he would. The thought of seeing him again kept her on edge, blood simmering on low. How she'd convince him to return

The Book of Fades once she found him, though, she didn't know.

She peered over her shoulder for a head of inkblot curls or a pressed collar. What kind of teenage boy even owned an ironing board anyway? Only someone as pretentious as him.

Inside, the library had lulled into an amber quiet, still as if fossilized and wrapped in a lamplight glow. Tonight, there were no chatty campus tours or electromagnetic field readings. Classes wouldn't start until after the weekend, but a few students sprawled across tufted chairs, their noses tucked inside the assigned summer reading as they scrambled to finish the last few pages. Walking up to the circulation desk, Este had expected Ives to be waiting with her features pinched in severe lines, but the head librarian was nowhere to be found.

Instead, striped through the bookcases, stood a familiar white button-down.

He walked down the other end of the stacks, and Este slinked behind him. No way was she letting him get away again.

The Roman mythology collection separated them, so Este lifted on her tiptoes so that she could see Mateo over the tops of shelved books. He crooked his arm on the bust of some old, dead white guy. A leather bag hung off one of his shoulders, and a smirk toyed at the edges of his lips. But he wasn't alone. Around him huddled three other students—how a leech like him had friends was beyond her.

A tall boy with deep brown skin rocked Mateo by the shoulders, and Mateo elbowed him in the ribs, playful. A redhead in a silk dress giggled at something he said, and a shorter girl with straight, black hair faked a yawn at their antics. The sound of it all got carried away, whisked up into the stacks and dissolving like dust in the moonlight. They were a silent film she couldn't look away from.

When they passed a sign for books on eighteenth-century French philosophy, Este crouched lower, crooking her head around the bookcase, but they weren't there. *Not again.*

She doubled back, row by row by row. Empty. Empty. Empty.

Mateo had pulled another disappearing act. This time, his friends vanished with him. This had to be some kind of cruel joke, right?

Este marched down the aisles until she stood where they had. All that was left was the faint scent of cedar, this time mixed with something sweet—one of the girls' perfumes maybe.

Dr. Kirk had mentioned the hidden passageways, but how was she supposed to know what to look for if they were, by nature, hidden? Este dragged her sneakers along the hardwood, feeling for a loose floorboard like she might spring open a secret hatch. When that didn't work, she tugged books off the shelf, Voltaire and Rousseau, in case they turned out to be levers.

Behind her, someone cleared a throat.

"Should I have provided directions to the circulation desk?" Ives asked by way of greeting. Her face was just as pinched and severe as expected. Like Este was a stinging canker sore she couldn't get rid of.

"Just familiarizing myself with the library."

"Familiarize yourself instead with these." Ives handed her a stack of stapled papers riddled with letters and numbers. "You'll need to learn the Library of Congress classification system because—"

"Academic libraries don't use the Dewey decimal system," Este finished. Did she imagine it, or did Ives look kind of impressed?

Never in a million years would she admit she learned that from Mateo.

Ives trailed back toward the circulation desk, a U-shaped, hand-carved behemoth with about six hundred tiny drawers, and Este followed, peeking back toward the French Enlightenment section, but the stacks stayed empty. As Ives plucked a book from a pile collecting dust, Este tried to suppress the regret slithering around her chest. She'd find him again. She had to.

"Nothing here can be loaned or returned without a borrowing card." Flipping the book open, Ives tapped her manicured nails against the back cover. Glued inside was a cardstock pocket holding a stamped paper slip. On the left side, the names of students who had borrowed the book were listed. On the right, the due date. The top had been covered by a barcode. "We've largely moved to online cataloging, but some of our oldest circulating items still require stamps. Others aren't meant to circulate at all."

In the distance, there was the unmistakable tenor of Mateo's laugh. Este squinted through the shelves, searching, searching. The sound had to come from *somewhere*.

Ives asked, "Am I boring you?"

When Este spun back into attention, the head librarian's eyes had narrowed.

"No, sorry. It's just . . ." Este tugged on the ends of her sweater. "You must spend a lot of time here, right? Do you ever hear things?"

Ives let a sort of amused breath out of her nose. "Many. Some more interesting than others. Weekend plans, study sessions, *how many marshmallows do you think we can stick in our mouths at one time*. I think sometimes the choir director Mr. Liebowitz tells the chorus line to practice arpeggios on the fourth floor." Back to business, she yanked open one of the desk's endless drawers, revealing hundreds of thin plastic cards. "Lost library cards. We'll need to clear this out sometime this century. Are you taking notes?"

Este swiped a scrap piece of paper and a pen from the desk, painting on a quick smile. She was now.

Over the course of the next hour, Ives trained her how to keep the shelves straight, how to find books in the computer system, and how to stop the fax machine on the second floor from banshee screaming when someone pressed the wrong buttons. (Also, Este had learned what a fax machine was.) By the time they stood in front of the archives' doors, Este could easily win Double Jeopardy! with *What is Types of Tape Used for Book Repairs?* and her legs ached from hiking up and down the Lilith's floors.

The double doors felt bigger now than they had last night. Flanked on either side were two candlesticks, pilled wax clinging to the sides. Cold seeped through the threshold, and Este made a mental note to bring a cardigan next time.

From inside her blazer pocket, Ives retrieved a silver key ring, heavy with ten or fifteen keys in different shapes and sizes, and the box of matches from her desk. She hesitated, sizing Este up. It made Este hold her spine straighter.

"I heard from some of the other faculty members that your roommate has shown a special interest in certain aspects of school history," Ives said finally. "You might find it difficult to work overnight in the archives if you're prone to believing childish ghost stories."

"I'm not."

"Good, because this collection is temperature controlled, and recent studies have proven that ultraviolet light decays print materials. For the protection of the archives, we now store them in absolute darkness." Ives handed her a candlestick and dragged a lit match over the wick. Very *Wuthering Heights*. "Keep in mind, this is a restricted collection. To prevent any unwanted damages, the door will continue to be locked from the outside while we're in the archives."

Este wouldn't ordinarily consider herself claustrophobic (she'd spent the last three years folded between a Subaru dashboard and a back seat filled with every one of her earthly belongings, after all), but the thought of being locked inside a glorified walk-in refrigerator made her skin itch.

Ives must have registered the panic in her eyes because she added, "You can leave at any time, but others will not be able to access it from the main floor. Safety and Security officers and I have keys to enter in case of emergency." Her voice softened. "It's the safest place on campus."

The doors swung open with the force of Ives's palm. Light from the main floor seeped inside, a single path in an otherwise invariable black, and blotted out when the doors locked behind them.

As they entered, the archives creaked, their old bones moaning. Este kept expecting her eyes to adjust to the low light, but every time she blinked, the shadows came back. She took a few tentative steps forward, led by her solitary orange flame.

"There are a few basic ground rules. Don't bring guests into the archives. Don't leave candles unattended or drip wax onto the materials. And don't, under any circumstances, turn on a light." Ives's voice lowered, hardened. "I trust you won't disobey this time."

Este nodded. She pressed a palm to her chest to keep her

heart from beating straight out. She really should've skipped that last cup of coffee.

Abandoning her in the darkness, Ives retrieved a metal book cart with a shaking wheel. It rattled and clanged as she pushed it, abrasive in the silence. A wobbly pile of books had been balanced on top. The shelf underneath held boxes of tape, glue, and whalebone folders. "I've pulled a few texts I'd like for you to repair and reshelve so that I can check your work."

As Este went to grab the first text, Ives clicked her tongue against the back of her teeth.

"Gloves, Este."

"Of course," Este said with a forced laugh.

Ives excused herself to pull something for one of the other teachers, and Este worked through the first book, taping down loose edges and smoothing wrinkled pages. When she finished, she and the candlestick paced down a narrow corridor, the bookcases edging in on both sides. Somehow, the archives were more cramped than the spire.

As far as she could see—which wasn't very—there were endless rows of tomes stacked ceiling high. Occasionally, she brushed past a rolling ladder, but she imagined the tracks would stick, caked over with rust. This deep in the archives, the air was too still, stiff as if it had been trapped for too long. It was easy to believe nothing had changed since Lilith herself wandered through these halls.

The distant drone of a baritone warbling shot goose bumps

down Este's arms. The sound dissipated, and a shaky breath parted her lips. Mr. Liebowitz and the chorus, obviously. These floors couldn't have been that thick. Their vocal warm-ups must have seeped through the whole library.

Shoving the book where it belonged, she didn't waste any time getting back to the cart. There were more books to be shelved. Maybe it was better to do them in batches. She could work more quickly and spend less time getting lost in the stacks.

Not that she was afraid. She was just being practical.

When she stuck her hand out to grab the tape, she came up empty. Hadn't she *just* set it down there?

Huffing a breath out through her nose, Este scanned the aisle for any trace of the tape roll, peering under the cart, around the bookends, until a silver glint on the shelf caught her attention.

The hairs on the back of her neck shot up like a cat who'd seen a cucumber. She certainly hadn't set it there. Este stretched onto her tiptoes, but it was just out of reach. Her palm grew slick around the candlestick as she lifted it.

"Ives, did you come back?"

Nothing and no one answered.

"Mateo?" she said, hating the way her voice wavered. "This isn't funny anymore."

With a cursory look around, Este couldn't shake the feeling that shadows pooled heavier.

When the archives stayed quiet, a sharp laugh cut out of her chest. She dragged over the nearest ladder and lifted herself up rung by rung. This was ridiculous. Posy's ghost stories were getting under her skin.

"What are you doing?"

A shriek tore up Este's throat.

Then, the voice registered. Ives stood at the base of the ladder with her arms crossed against her chest. Wholly unamused.

"Sorry," Este muttered. Her nerves were totally fried.

Ives said, "I beg of you to keep your feet on the ground for the time being. Neither of us needs to worry with an incident report tonight."

Este grabbed the tape dispenser and skidded back down the ladder. She went back to work, and Ives trailed behind her, correcting her when she misplaced a first edition behind a third or used too much binding glue. Faint hums sifted through the stacks. Low, rasped. Este steeled herself, ignoring the way her stomach knotted and her hands shook. It was only the sound of shadows.

SEVEN

❧

Este smelled the séance before she saw it.

It was her first shift alone, the whole night stretching in front of her, and she'd been shelving paperbacks on the third floor when she found them. All three of the Paranormal Investigators were crammed into a study that glowed beneath the flames of ultrafragranced candles and smelled like the lair of an eighth-grade girl.

"What are you doing? Trying to summon the dead with the entire Bath & Body Works Semi-Annual Sale?" she asked, leaning against the doorframe.

Posy's head whipped up, a smile fanning across her face. "Yes!"

Great. Este was one vanilla candle from being possessed.

She didn't really have time for Posy's antics tonight. What if Ives dropped by the circulation desk to see how her first night was going? But, even if it was all pretend, they looked like they were having fun. Arthur nudged a candle into her cupped hands and closed the door behind her. Open flames needed to be supervised by a library worker, after all—Ives would understand.

Around the room, windows stretched from the beamed ceiling to the creaking floorboards. Any trace of moonlight had been swept behind a cloth of bloated clouds. A storm brewing on the horizon crept closer with every passing second, the cold front swelling beyond the paned glass. Shepherd and Arthur scuttled around the room, pushing aside desks, and placing candles on every open surface.

At least if the power went out, they'd still be able to see.

"We just need to finish the summoning circle, and then we can start." Posy pointed over her shoulder to a canvas bag spilling open with an assortment of things that looked like Arthur must have raided the theater's prop loft—fake cobwebs, sparkly confetti, a Styrofoam tombstone. "Can you grab the snow globe for me?"

Este plucked the snow globe from the tote and shook it, watching the glitter swirl. She handed it to Posy, who placed it in the center of a confetti circle. It was a horrible excuse for a crystal ball.

"Are you sure you know what you're doing?" she asked.

"Holding a séance is an art," Posy said as she flattened a shag bath mat over the polished hardwood to use as a carpet, "and I am an *artiste*."

71

"I think I prefer oil pastels," Shepherd mumbled at the back of the room.

Este lifted a hunk of black plastic from the bottom of the bag. "I'm afraid to know what this is."

Posy didn't have to look at her to answer. "A fog machine."

"Why do you have a fog machine?"

Arthur perched onto one of the tables next to Este. "For the vibes."

Este laughed a little too hard for a little too long before she realized she was the only one.

Posy stood and stripped the box from Este's hands. When she plugged it into an outlet, it sputtered to life. White mist spooled from its mouth and hovered around their ankles. "It's symbolic for the veil between life and death. I learned it from my favorite podcast, *Ghost with the Most*. Shep, hit the lights, and we're ready."

He doused them in darkness and joined them at the center of the room. They lowered to the ground, sitting cross-legged, wreathed by flickering flamelight. Posy clicked a button on the side of a tape recorder, the cassette inside spinning, and she straightened a few extra gadgets: the infamous EMF reader, something with about ten antennae, and a compass that Este could only assume was a special Limited-Edition Ghost Compass that Posy had fallen for. Then, she grabbed Este's hand, who grabbed Arthur's, who grabbed Shepherd's, and he closed the circle.

Why were Este's palms so sweaty? "Don't you need to salt the doors or something?"

"Salt is for keeping ghosts out. We're trying to bring one in," Arthur said, clipped. As if it were the most obvious thing in the world.

"Anyone in particular?"

Shepherd's voice was barely audible when he said, "Lilith Radcliffe."

Este's eyes could've fallen straight out of her head, they were so wide. "No offense, but if I were the long-dead ghost of Lilith Radcliffe, I really don't think I'd want people prodding into my personal life."

"We could ask her if she knows anything about the boy you're looking for." Posy squeezed her hand. Gentle, affirming. "If she's haunting the library, she would've seen where he went."

Este hadn't seen even a glimpse of Mateo since her training. Ordinarily, she'd have hunted him down the old-fashioned way. You know, Facebook stalking. But Mateo didn't even have a cell phone. Ghost communes weren't exactly her first choice for investigative work, but she didn't have a lot of other options left.

It wouldn't work. She knew that. The gleam in Posy's eyes was convincing enough to play along, and the fact that they wanted to help at all . . . she hadn't had that in a long time.

Fog shifted over Este's skin, and she shivered. She might as well get this over with. A few harmonic chants around well-placed candles and she'd be back downstairs before Ives ever found out she'd left.

"Okay, how do we get started?" she asked.

"Close your eyes," Posy instructed them, "and follow my lead."

Instead of focusing on the words Posy recited, something that sounded like it had been stripped from a Halloween storybook, Este counted her breaths. In through her nose, and then out through her mouth. A constant, steady rhythm. Practical, dependable, physical. A trick her dad had taught her years ago when her ribs felt too tight. It grounded her in reality and did a half-decent job of staving off the memory of the archives' depths.

She filled up every corner of her lungs and released a jet stream, imagining inside of it were all her worries. The missing book, Ives's ultimatum, ditching her shift so that her roommate could dabble in dark arts like it was a sideshow circus act. In and out. In and out. In and—

"Este, stop," Posy groused. Este pried one eye open. "You blew out the candle. Now we have to start over."

The storm's first thundercrack rattled the windowsills, and Arthur's grip tightened around hers. The rain came next. Wind howled, brushing tree limbs against the building.

Once the candle was relit, Posy began the ritual again, this time going until the EMF reader blared. She grinned. "I think she's here."

A quick look around the room confirmed that no ghosts had, in fact, entered the study room. The EMF reader was probably thrown off by the lightning storm happening outside.

"What now?" Shepherd asked.

"Este, you think about Mateo. I'll try to talk to her." Posy held up one of the antennae like Lilith's ghost was on Dish TV. She rattled off question after question, each more invasive than the last.

When Este closed her eyes, she was back in the stairwell, tracing the slender lines of Mateo's body in the darkness. The chiseled edge of his jawline caught in the moonlight. A hand half-tucked in the pocket of his pressed pants. The curl of his lips matching the curls of his hair. He moved with an easy, well-worn grace, a soft confidence. As if he'd roamed the halls a hundred times and a hundred more.

"Is it working?" Este whispered.

Posy shushed her. "Maybe you aren't thinking hard enough."

Este blacked out the background, picturing only Mateo. The dimple in his chin, the lilt of his laugh and the way it followed her. She envisioned the buttons on his shirt, the width of his shoulders, the broad span of his chest beneath as he guided her into the spire. He was magnetic, tugging on the iron in Este's blood, a pull she couldn't resist.

No, no, no.

She pinched her eyes tighter. He was a lying, thieving pain in the ass who almost cost her everything she was working toward. Who still would if she didn't find him, if he didn't cooperate. It didn't matter how handsome he was—she would never forgive him.

"Nothing's happening," Este said as she yanked her hands out of Posy's grasp. This needed to end now. The room was exactly as it had been when they started—a forgotten classroom at the end of the hall, drenched in fog. No specters, no spirits. She dabbed her thumb against her tongue and snuffed out a flame as she stood up. "That's enough for tonight."

Posy's jaw dropped open, and Este could practically see the defiant argument waiting on her lips, but her words were drowned out by whipcrack thunder followed by a resonating hum, like the skies were singing. Everywhere and nowhere at once, a bellowing tenor thrummed. Este heard it inside and outside her as if the vibrations absorbed into the Lilith's walls and floors and then through the soles of her feet.

Crossing her arms against her chest, Posy said, "We can try again tomorr—"

A trill of high notes trickled in from somewhere above, cutting her off.

Arthur reached for the tape recorder. "What was that?"

"Mr. Liebowitz's choir practice," Este said, rolling her eyes.

"This late at night?" Her roommate's face scrunched up, eyebrows wagging. She was really milking this. "Sounds like it's coming from the computer lab. Let's go check it out."

Packing up, Arthur shoved the fog machine back into his tote bag, grumbling something about how if they found out he stole—*borrowed*—from the props department, he'd be under-study until he died. Este offered to shelve the books they'd pulled and pack up the candles because the wax needed to cool. Shepherd trailed behind, shaking the snow globe like a Magic 8 Ball, and nearly rammed into the others when Posy skidded to an abrupt stop.

Looking back, she asked, "Are you sure you don't want to come?"

"I'm on the clock. You're looking at Radcliffe's newest archival assistant." Este shrugged to cover up the way her throat constricted around the words. It should've been an achievement.

Something like hurt or pity flashed behind Posy's eyes, but it disappeared as quickly as it came. She nodded and ushered the boys out.

Alone again, Este collapsed into the nearest chair. She could use a few moments to herself. Between Posy's unshakable belief in life after death and the nauseating scent of twenty lit candles, a headache bloomed behind her forehead.

She stacked up the history books Posy had placed in the center of the summoning circle. As she thumbed through the pages, Este stopped at a photo of Radcliffe's front entrance. With his back turned to the camera, a student looked through the wrought-iron gates. He stood with a familiar self-assured posture, one hand in a pocket, and the other wrapped around one of the metal beams.

Below, the text read: *The land had been in the Radcliffe family for generations but remained untouched, the mountains too steep and the forests too wild to build until Robin Radcliffe first cleared the school grounds. Constructed at the end of the nineteenth century, Radcliffe Preparatory Academy opened its doors in 1901. Sixteen years later, Robin and his wife Judith died from tuberculosis, leaving behind two children: Lilith and Mateo.*

She read the last sentence again, just to make sure she wasn't hallucinating.

Mateo?

No. It didn't mean anything. There were probably hundreds of Mateos in the state of Vermont, thousands between now and 1901. Not a chance was *her* Mateo a ghost. He'd leaned against the bookcases, rested against the marble statue, and stripped *The Book of Fades* from her hands. He had been there, right beside her, completely and irrevocably real.

But if Posy was right and ghosts were real somehow, then her dad truly might be out there somewhere still listening. And god, she needed someone to talk to.

She reached across the desk for a lavender candle, cradling it beneath her chin. That kind of hope was like a flame lolling on its wick, as likely to light her path as it was to burn the whole library down.

Was she really about to hold a freaking séance all by herself?

She drew a shaky breath. "Look, I know this is stupid and useless and that I should be getting back downstairs so that Ives doesn't expel me, but I really wish you were here, Dad."

Este spoke to the shadows at the corners of the room, the way they ebbed beneath the candlelight and grew back deeper, darker. Each word was slow, precise. She knew her dad wasn't listening. Somehow that made it easier to speak.

"I miss you." She clutched the candle tighter. "I'm still mad at you for leaving. I still want to make you proud. I'm not really sure how I can feel both those things at once. I didn't mean to get in trouble, I promise. And I really don't want to mess this up. Any of it."

Jagged lightning illuminated the room in electric blue, and in the span of three breaths, thunder crashed. The storm was getting closer.

"I wish you could tell me everything. Why you hid the keys to the spire in your old picture frame. How to convince that jerk to give back the book he stole. Maybe even the answers to the first precalc quiz if you've got them."

Talking out loud softened the calcified layer around her heart. If her dad could hear her beyond whatever veil Posy had been talking about, she wished she had a way to know. If only the dead had cell service.

Then, a pulsing wind wrenched one of the window latches free, and the glass pane swung back and forth with the tides of the storm. Gooseflesh rose on Este's arms as a damp draft swirled through the leftover fog machine mist. Like a stiff exhale, every candle extinguished, plunging the room into darkness.

Licks of rain splashed against Este's hair as she reached for the pane. Straining against the gusts, she tugged the window to its latch. The cold clawed through her sweater, but she tried to shake it off by rubbing her palms down her arms.

The wind had shuffled through the pages of the book, and she thumbed back to the photo at the gates. Beneath the shimmer of the candlelight, she noticed something new. It was a low-res copy, largely reduced to grain and grit on the page, and the faded writing had been easy enough to miss at first glance. Tucked in the corner of the scanned image was thin script, nearly indecipherable but there nonetheless—someone had written "September 1917" in the same lopsided lettering she'd seen on the call number Mateo handed her in the spire.

Holy shit. Este's blood pounded through her head, black edging her vision.

It was probably a coincidence. People's handwriting looked similar all the time. Mateo Radcliffe in the photo from 1917 *couldn't* be the same Mateo who led her into the spire with a sparkle in his stupid, blue eyes.

But maybe she'd show Posy. Just to be sure.

Through the walls, the singing she'd heard in the archives returned, its own rumble of thunder. Different, now. Closer.

Este scrambled to pick up the books and cocked them against her hip. She flipped the overhead light back on, evaporating the shadows on the floors. She pressed her ear to the seam between the door and its frame, listening. There was the distant tap of a few scratching pencils, the swish of pages turning as students got a head start on their studies. The century-old staircases groaned, settling.

She let out a slow breath. Ordinary library noises. All this ghost talk made every shadow sinister, every sound despairing. She was just imagining things.

But when the winds rose and rattled the windows, she backed away from the door. The light from the chandelier fizzled out like a cigarette butt in the bottom of her mom's Diet Coke. Este barely had time to scream as the door burst open and Mateo barreled into the classroom.

EIGHT

Este staggered backward so that she wouldn't get knocked over as Mateo clicked the lock into place, bolting them into the study. Her entire body went stiff, elbows jammed into her sides to keep from shaking and palms slicked with sweat.

In the darkness, the details of his face were fuzzy, but he certainly didn't *look* like a century-old spirit. Although he did still wear a collared shirt and tailored pants suspiciously similar to the ones she'd last seen him in. His satchel hung across his torso, heavy. Half of Radcliffe's student population looked like that, while the other half wore mixed-and-matched lululemon leggings and copious amounts of plaid. It was hardly enough evidence to convict him as a ghost.

Este opened her mouth to reprimand him and demand he return the stolen book, but he pressed a firm finger against his lips. He met her glare for only a moment before slouching forward to listen through the keyhole.

"Don't *shush* me." She took a step toward him but then faltered. Not even the hot blood pounding in her ears could drown out the distant hum of song as it surged again. "Give back the book, you thief."

With his ear still pressed to the door, he whispered, "Now's not the time for name-calling. Keep it down."

"It's not name-calling if it's true." She refused to whisper on his behalf. Let whoever he was hiding from find him. He probably stole from them, too. "And trust me, there are far worse things I'd like to call you. For starters, you're a lying, scheming, son of a——"

A feather duster smothered her words.

Mateo reeled back, shaking out the duster, while Este spat clumps of feathers, her lips matted with grime. He was unbelievable.

"What is wrong with you?" she hissed.

He kept his voice low and level, scarcely louder than a whisper. "I'm trying to avoid some unwanted company, and if you were smart, so would you."

The singing subsided again, ebbing and flowing like the wind. Only once the third floor was completely quiet did Mateo's posture loosen. He moved deeper into the room and rested against the study tables. He pointed the feather duster around the room. "Are you taking candle making as an elective?"

There was not a single, minuscule chance in hell Este would

admit that she had briefly tried to talk to the dead via three-wick candle.

"This isn't about me," she said instead. "This is about how you used me as collateral damage in your plot to steal a first-edition text."

He flipped the feather duster through his fingers, sending motes into the air. A flash of lightning illuminated them like glitter in Posy's snow-globe crystal ball. Thunder knocked against the windows, and every nerve in Este's body went on high alert.

"*The Book of Fades* is better off missing," Mateo said, tucking the duster into his back pocket. "Trust me."

Este could've choked on the venom that coated her tongue. It was his fault she was in line for the academic guillotine, his fault she might have to leave the only place she thought she could finally feel at home. And he didn't even care.

"Trust you?" she spat. "You're the last soul on Earth I'd trust."

The clock on the wall was moments from striking midnight. She'd wasted too much time upstairs chasing ghosts. She didn't have time for more mind games, and she certainly wouldn't give him an opportunity to absolve his guilt with sweet nothings and a smirk. He'd talked his way into this, but Este would make sure she had the final word.

Adjusting her grip on the history books, she marched toward him. "Hand it over, and I'll never speak to you again, okay? I need to get back to the circulation desk in case there are more books to be shelved or repairs for the archives or—"

"You're working in the archives?"

Something in Mateo's voice stopped her, the way it caught in his throat like a belt loop on a kitchen drawer. His eyes dipped to the place where the key had been looped around her neck.

The hollow singing returned, resonating through the third floor's patterned walls. Not one, but three, in perfect harmony. Would they ever stop singing?

"All thanks to your little disappearing act upstairs. I'm lucky I didn't get thrown out immediately." The sopranos' song surged. A nerve in her eyebrow was about to start twitching— she could feel it. "Now I get to listen to the world's most devoted a cappella group every night."

She unlocked the door and hauled it open only for Mateo's palm to slam it shut again. "Este, don't leave."

He stood over her, arm outstretched around her. His chest nearly touched her back. This close, he smelled like wet ink and cedar smoke. She twisted to face him, craning her neck to look him in the eyes. Had he always towered over her like this?

Shadows spilled down his face in stark contrast with the blue-tinged light from the storm. Lightning struck. In the brightness, his body flickered, faded. Transparency lapped at his features, like he was a theater projection when the lights turn on, there but unseeable.

One moment, he was standing in front of her, solid in the shadows.

When she blinked, he was across the room, leaning against the windowsills.

Este flattened herself against the door, one hand on the doorknob. She needed to get out of here, but she couldn't think, couldn't breathe, couldn't move. She sucked air in through her nose and pushed it out through her mouth, but even her dad's breathing techniques couldn't slow the white-hot adrenaline pumping through her veins, telling her to *run, run, run.*

Mateo was a ghost. The same boy in the photo from September 1917 traced his eyes over the shape of her in the darkness. Sizing her up. Wearing her down.

She was paralyzed as he stalked back across the room. All she had to do was open the door. But he knew where *The Book of Fades* was. So, shaking, she held her ground as his hand hovered over hers. The shape of it was staticky and only half opaque. She could still see the silver rings around her knuckles, the crooked notch in her middle finger where she'd broken it years ago.

When he wrapped his hand around hers on the knob, a night-cool wind grazed her skin, but nothing else, nothing more.

She didn't feel him at all.

"You're him, aren't you?" she whispered, and her mouth was dry as sand in an hourglass. His hand had gone through hers—*through.* "You're Mateo Radcliffe."

"So, you *do* know that anything in the spire is rightfully mine for the taking." There was a *click* as he spun the lock. Trapping them here. Together. He lowered until his lips were only millimeters from her ear. "I know you're mad at me. Stay mad if you want. But I promise you, I'm not the worst thing haunting this school."

She sucked in a breath of stale library air, filling her lungs to the brim just to feel alive. It reignited her resolve. She'd never met anyone as infuriatingly insufferable as him before— dead or alive. "If you're a ghost, couldn't you have just floated through the walls to get the book yourself? Instead, you had to drag me into this?"

Mateo slipped his hand back inside his pocket, but Este still felt the remnants of an ancient cold where his fingers should have skimmed her skin. He vanished and reappeared at one of the study tables. "I can't walk through walls."

Narrowing her eyes, Este asked, "What kind of self-respecting spirit can't do that?"

"For someone who doesn't believe in ghosts, you sure have a lot of opinions about them," Mateo scoffed, scrubbing the back of his head. "I didn't lie. The spire was overgrown with rivean ivy, remember? I can't touch it—no ghost can. Things that aren't alive are perfectly real to us, but we can't touch anything living."

"Allergic," she said, remembering his shitty attempt at an excuse.

"Exactly. Even if I'd had the key, I still needed the help of someone living to get inside." His gaze ran the length of her body. "And you are incredibly alive."

Este ground her heels against the floorboards. The rightful heir to the Radcliffe legacy didn't need to know the way her stomach had bottomed out at the sight of him. The things that would do to his already monstrous ego were unimaginable. Thankfully, in the dark, he might not have been able to recognize the pink flush that swept over her cheeks when he looked at her like that—like *she* was the ghost, and he could see straight through her.

In the hall, a familiar *click* tapped along the floorboards, and Este recognized it instantly as Ives's high heels. She could end this now.

Este was about to holler for her when Mateo cleared his throat. "What's your big idea, Logano? Let Ives catch you slacking on the job? Tell her a *ghost* stole her precious book?" He dipped into his satchel and retrieved *The Book of Fades*. She recognized its black binding and metallic embossing immediately. "If you call Ives in here, I'll vanish and take the book with me. You need me just as much as I need you."

Something sharp jammed in her windpipe. Unless she wanted another lecture, she needed to get back downstairs before Ives realized she had gone MIA, but none of it would matter if she didn't have the book. She couldn't let Mateo out of her sight again.

Mateo trailed his thumb down the gold-edged pages. With

every flash of lightning, the shape of him vanished, leaving the book floating in midair until the darkness returned. He reappeared in front of her, holding the book so that she could see the gilded pages.

Nothing was printed on them.

Her throat was sandpaper, chapped with raw anger. "You nearly sacrificed my entire academic career for a book filled with blank paper?"

"It's not blank."

"I'm looking right at it. There's nothing written in this book, Mateo. I'm not an idiot."

"Neither am I." When he rolled his head back, stretching the tense planes of his neck, a grin crept up Este's lips. She had to admit that she kind of liked getting under his skin. If he even had any. "The language of the dead does not belong to the eyes of the living."

"What?" she said with half a laugh. "What sort of cryptic bullshit is that?"

Este reached for the book, but he jerked it above her head.

"Chapter one: embalming the spirit," he recited, eyes scanning the page as if there were words pressed into the parchment, index finger skimming along imaginary ink. "Bearing the Fades' touch, fragments of life cling to Earth and cannot traverse the lasting path. These, we call ghosts. When damned—"

"Cut it out!" Este snarled. "Tell me the truth, or I'll tell Ives you have the book."

"I think it's best we keep the head librarian out of this."

Este couldn't believe him. "You're the one who brought her into this in the first place."

"While that may technically be true," Mateo said as he fanned through the pages again, "it's not wholly accurate."

He stopped toward the end where a jagged seam split the book, a crease where pages had been torn from the binding. Simply imagining the shredding sound the paper must have made was enough to raise goose bumps on Este's arms. A note had been written on the previous page, circled and with an arrow drawn to the ragged edge.

Consider it a loan. DL97.

The blue ink had been smudged; crooked letters looped together like an afterthought. The ink had seeped into the page, like it had been written and dried eons ago.

"DL97, what does that mean?"

"It means someone decided it was a good idea to vandalize school property." Mateo closed the book with a snap and tucked it back into his satchel. "You think Ives would readily accept a book with missing pages?"

There weren't enough adjectives in the English language to describe him. Incredulous, presumptuous, pretentious. Este squinted. "What did you do with them?"

"Wrong again," he said with a pretentious inflection that made her roll her eyes. "If I knew where they were, I wouldn't be here right now. This book is the reason I'm a ghost, and it isn't complete without the missing chapter. I've been trapped at this school for a hundred years, but if we can find those pages, I can come back to life."

"We?" Este balked.

"When I'm alive again, I'll give you the book, and you can do whatever you see fit with it. Turn it in, burn it with hellfire and brimstone, I don't care." He leaned a forearm on the door over her head, a little too close for her liking. She tilted her chin to look up at him, coiling her arms against her chest to hold herself together. "Or don't, and I'll keep the book. You can transfer back to your old high school, right?"

It was blackmail. And it was working.

Before she could answer, black mist spilled beneath the door, streaming through the cracks in the seal and putting Posy's borrowed fog machine to shame. Darkness shrouded the study like a thick, wool shawl. The temperature plummeted so fast Este's breath could've spooled in silk white strands, and she wouldn't have been surprised.

"Hold that thought," Mateo said. "As much as I'm sure the Fades would like to meet you, we should go."

Este's gaze flicked toward his bag, *The Book of Fades* inside. Her voice cracked when she asked, "The Fades? *Those* Fades?"

"Lovely girls when they aren't harvesting student souls." Mateo plucked the lavender candle off the desk. He produced a box of matches from his pocket—the same kind Ives had in her office.

"Did you steal those, too?"

91

Strike and spark, he lit the wick. Mateo's form wavered in the dancing candlelight. "Honestly, Este, is now the time to condemn me for my past transgressions?"

The mist swirled until she couldn't see the floor beneath. It sucked the oxygen out of the air. Heart hammering, Este could barely think straight. "Right, so, how do we get out of here?"

He offered her a sly smile. "We?"

God, he sent her blood pressure through the roof. "I swear, if you disappear on me again."

"I won't," he said, and the gleam reignited in his eyes, "if you promise to help me."

Este backed away from the door as the wood turned frigid behind her. The Fades must have been desperate to get in. "And if I don't?"

Mateo sliced his hand across the vulnerable skin of his neck, sucking air between his teeth. Este pressed her lips together, flattening them into a fine line, but Mateo wasn't finished. His tongue sagged out of his mouth, and he rolled his eyes until their whites flashed.

"Not the time," Este snapped.

"Is that a yes, then?"

The word spun through Este's mind.

Yes would mean risking her chances of staying at Radcliffe Prep, but her hopes of continuing her archival studies were already dissolving like sugar on her tongue. She had gone MIA for long enough during her shift that Ives could reject her on truancy alone. The thought was like a bricked ankle, sinking her to the bottom of Lake Champlain.

Yes would also mean lying to the head librarian, dodging Ives's questions about the book's whereabouts. But maybe Mateo was right. Wouldn't it be better returned with all the pages intact? Wasn't that what an archival assistant was meant to do—preserve priceless tomes and ancient texts?

Mostly, yes would mean avoiding whatever unholy thing lurked beyond the door's bronze hinges, and that was enough at the moment.

The syllable hung heavy on her lips, the way stolen sips of whiskey coated her tongue. Sweet and burning all at once. "Yes."

"Excellent choice, Logano." Mateo paced to the far side of the room and counted his steps out loud. Este trailed close behind. At twelve, he nudged a bisque panel with his shoulder, and it sank deeper into the wall. A hidden door.

He pushed the paneling to slide it open, but the new door got stuck on its tracks. Jammed.

"Can't you hurry?" Este asked, climbing onto a chair so that the ink-black fog couldn't reach her. Her ribs cinched tighter. Her breaths came quicker.

Mateo pushed against the panel with a groan. "Believe it or not, I could use some assistance."

Este scrambled down. She kicked her foot against the paneling, and the plaster gave with a groan. Mateo scrolled it sideways like a pocket door, revealing the open maw of a dark passageway.

He handed her the candle, and she held it like a lifeline. Not even lavender essential oils could calm the dread surging through her as the study room door blew open. A tempest brewed as three shaded figures stormed into the room.

"If you don't want to die tonight," he said, prodding her forward with the feather duster, "you can't let them touch you."

NINE

❧

The Fades looked like sorority girls at alpha pi ohmygod.

A plume of sweet-pea perfume mixed with the stench of their decaying bodies—patches of papyrus-thin skin peeled off to reveal the bone-white below. Each of them wore ponytails at a migraine-inducing slope. Shadows clasped around their necks like cloaks, but beneath the shrouding black, Este glimpsed a swatch of velour, hot pink and shimmering with rhinestones. A vision of true horror.

When Este didn't budge, Mateo ducked into the hidden corridor without her. She couldn't look away from the Fades, no matter how much she wanted to.

Three sets of prying eyes, coated in milk white as if they had cataracts, zoned in like heat-seeking missiles to her beating heart's bull's-eye. The Fades drifted through the maze of desks and wooden chairs. They wielded the darkness, lashing tendrils of black mist obeying their command.

As they sang, their mouths didn't form words Este knew, none that she had heard before. Latin, maybe? Ancient, definitely. It chained her at the back of the classroom, transfixed. The rising tang of panic slicked her throat until it felt like she couldn't breathe.

The Fade dead center matched Este's hypnotized gaze. In a stripe that slanted down the Fade's face, receding skin cracked and curled like paper under a flame. The rest of her face remained unblemished, cheeks smooth and lips slathered in what Este could only imagine was coconut-scented Lip Smacker.

Flanked on either side of the frontwoman, the other Fades were in equally terrible condition. Their skin, different shades of weathered tan, sagged off their limbs. One of them swung a Birkin bag from her crooked elbow because apparently even walking corpses needed a place to hold their cell phones with the grim reaper on speed dial.

From the passageway, Mateo called to her over their singing. "It's like you're trying to get killed right now."

The Fades upped their tempo, moving closer with every downbeat. Only a few study tables stood between Este and their outstretched hands. The realization was enough to launch her into motion.

Este darted into the corridor, and Mateo said, "Look who decided to show up. Help me shut this."

She pressed her shoulder against the paneling as she hugged

the candle closer, begging for the doorway to close as she pushed, but the tracks were as old as the library, rusted and stubborn.

"Why do they look like Paris Hilton knockoffs?" She couldn't bleach the terror from her voice. Each breath was a pointed dagger, slicing through her ribs. Her shoulder was going to have the gnarliest bruise from all the times she slammed it against the plaster, but it had to be better than whatever the Fades would do to her.

"They look the same way they did the last time they came around. I guess they didn't get the memo on the latest trends," Mateo said, bracing his hands against the door. "Are you even pushing?"

"Obviously I am," Este ground out.

She pressed her back into the door, trying not to think about the black clouds inching around the doorframe. With one final push from the two of them, the door slotted back into its track and rolled closed, right as one of the Fades' hands was about to slip through.

Once it was shut, Este didn't stop moving. She raced down the hallway and cupped her palm around the candle holder to keep the flame from blowing out. It did little to light their way. She could still feel the Fades' darkness on the back of her neck.

The only thing standing between her and certain death was a semicorporeal asshole of a ghost who had made it perfectly clear he was capable of disappearing at any moment, which would leave her trapped in an abandoned service corridor with three spirits dressed like 1990s B-list celebrities.

To Mateo's credit, he didn't vanish. He kept her pace, step for step, even as his image faded in and out in the candlelight like television static. He angled his head toward her, probably waiting for some snarky remark, but she couldn't shake the hollow feeling in her chest. Instead, she focused on the striped beige walls, on each footstep forward, on the way her lungs still rose and fell, alive.

As they reached the end of the hall, where the passageway forked into equally cobwebbed stairwells, a wintry gust blew in behind them. Fear clawed behind her rib cage as the Fades' song swelled, a funeral dirge. A cloying dampness sapped the warmth from her skin, and the smell of wilting flowers gave Este's gag reflex a workout.

"Which way?" she managed to ask as the Fades' chill crept up the stairwell.

Mateo looked both ways and shrugged. "Both great options. Manet or mathematics?"

Este fought the urge to glance behind her, to see how close the Fades were. Their melodies echoed between the walls, urgent and insatiable. They sounded everywhere at once. She had to raise her voice above their harmonies to say, "Manet."

Mateo pivoted left, and Este followed him around the corner, feeling heavier with each step upward. The Fades' mist billowed after them, and the longer she ran, the harder Este had to fight not to give in. To let them take her.

Salvation was a hidden door at the end of the hall, and Este focused on the gilded ring of light coming from the other side. Mateo reached it first, vanishing and reappearing at its hinges. The Fades' black tendrils curled around Este's ankle, trying to drag her back into the fog.

Mateo extended the feather duster like a hand, and she grabbed on. He tugged her forward, and lunging through the opening, they landed with a thud in the dimly lit alcoves around the archives. Out here, the passage was disguised on the wall by a framed copy of Manet's painting, *Music in the Tuileries Gardens*. Mateo latched the door shut behind them, and only then could Este finally breathe again.

Every echo of the Fades' singing had dissipated, replaced by an uneasy silence in the main stacks. It had gotten late enough that the study carrels on this floor had been abandoned. No one had been around to hear them.

Despite the lights overhead, Mateo was whole next to her. Not some flimsy apparition, but as solid as ever. If her body weren't fully engaged in fight-or-flight mode, she'd have asked him to explain a few pressing questions like *why aren't you invisible*, and *how is any of this possible*, and, kindly, *what the fuck just happened*.

Instead, Este slumped to the floor, her legs giving out underneath her, and she counted her breaths to quell the quicksand panic bubbling up. If she moved too fast, it would swallow her whole. "They were singing, and I couldn't even understand them, but it felt like, like I couldn't breathe, like I was—"

"Dying?" Mateo propped himself against the bookshelf next to her, ankles crossed. Entirely unshaken by the last fifteen minutes. "The language of the dead can be exceedingly convincing."

Her voice wobbled beneath the weight of the words. "Like the one the book's written in?"

Mateo swiped a paperback from the shelf and tapped Este's head with it. "You're smarter than you look, Logano."

So, he wasn't bullshitting her.

Or, she thought callously, *he still is.*

There was no way to trust someone like him, and the worst part was that she couldn't even decide which made him less trustworthy: the night's realization that ghosts were real and he absolutely was one, or the privileged private-school glint in his eyes. He'd saved her tonight, but ultimately, he would use her to get what he wanted and then he would leave, exactly like he had in the spire.

"Oh, my god. I need to get downstairs," she said, prying herself upright and blowing out the candle. The night had slipped away from her. "If Ives is still here somewhere, if she thinks I'm not taking this seriously—"

"Hey, hey, hey," Mateo said, zipping around so that he stood in her way when she turned. "I thought we had a deal. I want to introduce you to the others."

"Other *what?*" Este barked. "More Fades? I think I've met enough of your friends for one lifetime."

"No, there are only three of those, and they came right from the pages of this book." With one hand he tapped the binding of *The Book of Fades* through his bag. The other arm slotted sideways against the bookshelves, creating a barrier.

As if that could stop her. She slipped through his body like it was a sheet of rain. On the other side, she shook out her limbs. Walking through a ghost had not been on her junior-year bingo card.

No faster than she blinked, he was in front of her again. "These are friends, and I promise it'll only take a few minutes."

His dark hair curled like ink in water, and his lashes cast slender shadows across the sharp edge of his cheekbones. She traced the veins on the backs of his hands to where they disappeared beneath the rolled sleeves of his button-down. He looked so, so solid, but she'd felt the truth.

"No, I have to get back to work. I'm not letting you mess this up more than you already have." Este pinched the bridge of her nose. Was this a joke to him? "As much as I hate to admit it, maybe you were right. What am I supposed to tell Ives? That I got chased by a demented glee club, and *that's* why I missed half my shift? There's no way."

"I take it you're bad at group projects." Mateo paused along the balcony railing. From here, Este could see the entire library—including the empty chair at the circulation desk where she was supposed to be. "Listen, Logano. We're a team now, you and me. You can't expect someone to do all the work for you, but you can't do it all alone either."

For someone who died before using a toaster, he sure thought he was the coolest thing since sliced bread.

Este crossed her arms, clenched her jaw. Ives hadn't given her a *group project*—Este had begged for a chance to prove she wasn't a troublemaker. And yet trouble was exactly what she'd gotten herself into tonight. Thanks to Mateo. Again.

But now Este also had a grocery list of everything that was at stake, and her eyes betrayed her by swaying toward his leather satchel and the tome inside. Ives wouldn't let her keep studying at Radcliffe Prep unless she returned *The Book of Fades*, and Mateo wouldn't let the book out of his reach until the missing pages were found.

Not to mention that the rules of her reality had changed, and Este no longer had the playbook. Mateo knew that, and by the looks of the well-worn smirk playing on his lips, he knew that she knew it, too.

Mateo said, "If you don't keep your end of the deal, I won't keep mine either. The book technically belongs to me anyway. I am a Radcliffe, after all."

Taking exaggerated steps, he backtracked down the aisle, leaving her speechless in his wake. He looked over his shoulder with every slow-motion movement. Waiting for her to stop him.

Mateo feigned a cough to keep her attention. "I said I'm *leaving*."

At least with him, she had a chance. Someone who knew the ins and outs of the Lilith. Someone who was around when the blueprints were first sketched, who could help her avoid the wrath of the Fades, and who might have seen her father when he was a student.

There were so many questions that she couldn't answer herself—had her dad ended up in the wrong places at all the wrong times like her? Did he know, just like her, what lurked around the historic buildings? And, quieter, an acrid question, stale and unspoken on the back of her tongue: was the ghost of him here somewhere?

"You'll never see *The Book of Fades* again," Mateo crooned. He rounded the corner of the shelves, lost behind well-loved editions of classics like *Of Mice and Men* and *Waiting for Godot*. He shuffled a few steps before sticking his head back out to say, "It'll be gone forever."

But if she and Mateo worked together, she could learn why her dad stole the key to the spire and retrace his steps through the Lilith. Even if it meant working with someone who was sure to make her grind her teeth into a pulp by the end of the quarter.

Este pushed down the metallic taste of pride and self-preservation and said, "You've got twenty minutes."

"Welcome to the team!" Mateo said, launching a triumphant

fist into the air. He didn't wait for her, breezing around the stacks. "But if you can't keep up, I'll have to demote you to junior varsity."

Este frowned and punched an alarm on her phone. She'd give him twenty minutes. Not a second more. "Don't make me regret this."

Mateo grinned, a widespread thing that crinkled the corners of his eyes. "Wouldn't dream of it, dear."

They turned a tight corner toward a collection of dictionaries, words from every corner of the world bound and kept safe. The shelves were wider here, the books thicker. A tacky layer of dust coated everything in gray. Este peeled it up as she ran her fingers along the bound spines and jotted *dust dictionaries* onto her mental to-do list.

Mateo rolled to a stop in front of an arched green door marked Senior Lounge on a burnished plaque.

"Look decent, everybody," he said with the gusto of a circus ringleader as he nudged open the door. "We've got a live one."

TEN

❧

Este was the only one in the study who didn't look like her outfit had been ordered out of an old Sears catalog.

The senior lounge was cozy, walls lined with texts in varying shades of timeworn brown and woven carpets layered over the splintered floors. In the middle, a sitting area had been arranged with mismatched furniture that somehow all looked like they belonged: a tartan armchair with carved claw arms, a deep blue velvet chaise, a love seat upholstered with scuffed leather. Draped over the pieces were the three students Este had seen Mateo with.

Except this time, she knew to look for their blurred edges.

The far wall was lined with shelves that flanked both sides of a smoldering fireplace. When you were the son of the school founder, apparently the *no open flames* rule didn't apply to you. The ghosts feathered out at the edges as the firelight crested.

One of the ghosts cleared her throat with a petite *ahem.* She sprawled out on the chaise's tufted cushions, long and lithe as a matchstick flame with red-hot curls flaring out around her shoulders. "Aren't you going to introduce us, Matty?"

"Este, meet Luca van Witt," Mateo said. The amusement in his eyes made her think he relished seeing Este like this— stunned silent. "She's been at Radcliffe since 1927."

Luca popped to her feet, her toes tucked inside a pair of T-strap heels. She'd shawled herself with the same heavy mink coat Este had seen her in before, despite the embers flickering in the fireplace. Este wondered, then, if she didn't have a choice. Luca moved with the same ancient grace that Mateo did, comfortable in an ageless body, but on the outside, she was still sixteen. She circled Este like she was a contestant on a makeover show, her ice-blue eyes squinting and scrutinizing as she scanned from her sneakers to the staircase spiderwebs still clinging to her hair.

"Este, you say?" The way she said it—mouth puckered, eyebrows pinched—made Este iron out the kinks in her spine. Suddenly, she was entirely too conscious that she was the only one in the room with hot blood pounding through her veins.

Finally, Luca asked Mateo, "*This* is the one you won't stop talking about?"

Mateo rubbed his palm across the back of his neck. "Yes, this is Este Logano."

Her name in his mouth sounded like a threat and a promise. Este wasn't sure she wanted to be either of those things to any of them.

"Oh, right. Dean's girl." Luca touched a wine-colored nail to her lips as if to swipe any lipstick smudged by the severity of her sneer.

The mention of her father's name sent alarms clanging through Este's head.

"Dean? My dad, Dean?" she asked, stifling the whispering part of her that begged her to stop fraternizing with the dead like it was normal. "You knew him?"

"All of us did. Knew of him, at least. I don't think he wanted much to do with us." This ghost had a stack of books balanced on her cross-legged lap. She perched on the plaid chair, with a deluge of impossibly straight black strands draping to her waist. Her skin was so pale she might as well have been transparent. Apropos, given the whole ghost thing. "Aoife Godrich. Fall of 1967."

Ee-fuh. Two syllables, and Este could still hear the way Posy said it last week on her impromptu ghost tour. While Dr. Kirk paraded them around the Lilith, Posy had rhapsodized about these spirits with her EMF reader screaming the whole way.

Aoife's eyes were haunting pools of pale gray, but her face showed no signs of age. Este eyed her old-school outfit: an oversize T-shirt with a gaudy stone pendant resting on her chest. She didn't have to stand for Este to recognize the denim fabric bunched by her ankles as the hem of bell-bottoms.

"The Radcliffe disappearances," Este said, the cogs fitting together. "A student every ten years, like clockwork. That's you." She peered around the room, scanning their timeless faces as she went: "1917, 1927, 1967 . . ."

The last ghost sat with his back against Aoife's armchair, all laughter and long limbs. He drummed his fingertips against the floor like he needed to keep them occupied. His deep brown skin and warm eyes made him look more alive than Este knew he must have been for decades.

"1987, baby. Daveed Hewitt."

She should've guessed as much, given his flattop haircut and his neon windbreaker.

"My roommate is obsessed with you," Este blurted, soaking them all in. Vignettes of Radcliffe Prep's past. "I mean—with ghosts."

And she'd been right.

Este could tell Posy everything. About Mateo, the ghosts, the Fades. Her roommate probably already had some kind of Fade detector or a sachet of Fadesbane or *something* stashed away to make sure Este wouldn't get her soul scooped out like a serving of stracciatella gelato while searching for the pages.

Or maybe it would be better to keep this to herself. She couldn't, in good conscience, let Posy poke her gadgets into the Lilith's every corner and cranny—not while the Fades were on the loose. She might get into the kind of trouble Este wasn't sure she knew how to get her out of.

"I remember her," Luca said, easing back onto her chaise with the grace of a classical goddess. For a moment she paused, drawing in a deep breath she didn't need, and Este wondered if she expected to be fanned with palm leaves and hand-fed grapes. "That cute little redhead with the gizmos. She and her friends were snooping around the study rooms earlier. If she wanted to be friends, she should've just asked."

Okay, it was official. There was absolutely no way Este would open that can of worms with Posy.

"Who'd want to be friends with you?" Daveed prodded. His laugh was as light and fleeting as soda bubbles.

Luca zipped a string of pearls around her neck and clicked her tongue behind her teeth. "Everyone knows I'm the life of the party."

Este fought the smile that threatened to spill onto her lips. Seeing them like this, so lively, so genuine, made that permeating nauseated feeling come back with a vengeance. She wasn't supposed to be making friends with them. She was here for answers, and that was all.

"Shouldn't there be a few more of you?" Este dared farther into the room, settling on the lip of the leather sofa. "Lilith—is she here?"

All eyes turned to Mateo, and he shook his head. "She didn't become a ghost, no."

"What about my dad? After he died, did he ever come back here?" The sound of her question was small but somehow still too loud in the quiet study, competing only with the crackling firewood.

"Not everyone becomes a ghost." Mateo's voice was down-feather soft and warm, his gaze didn't waver, and his words were measured as if expecting each syllable to shatter her. "Like the book said, the Fades took our souls and trapped us here. Only those of us who died at the hands of the Fades are ghosts, just a trace of who we'd been."

Este gulped down the bitter taste of disappointment. She'd always known it was too much to hope for—that her dad was out there, somewhere, waiting for her. But she'd seen a lot of things tonight she would've sworn were impossible a week ago.

"So, what?" she asked. "You have to stay here? Forever? Haven't you ever tried to leave?"

Mateo shook his head. "Henry did. 1937. He walked right out the front gates. Didn't make it past the bend in the road before we watched him disappear, and he never came back."

"It worked? He was set free?" Este scrubbed a hand over her forehead, checking for a low-grade fever that would explain why she was here debating the existence of ghosts.

"Darling," Luca said, somehow patronizing, "if I walk out those gates, I'll cease to exist. And I cannot become an unmarked grave."

"Oh, yes, you deserve a shrine." Aoife huffed a stiff sigh.

Luca stuck out her tongue.

Mateo dropped his satchel and joined Este on the couch. "Once Henry left, he *couldn't* come back. To keep our physical forms, we have to stay at Radcliffe. We're tied here to the Fades." He curled his hands into circles, one in front of the other. "Imagine your body and soul are two rings. When you're alive, they're together in one perfect circle. When you die, they separate. Your soul leaves this world for the next, and your body stays behind. Cremated, buried in a casket—"

"Fed to sharks," Daveed offered.

Este nodded, focusing on the shape of Mateo's hands—now held on either side of his face—rather than the darkness edging her vision like she might pass out at any moment. This was all too much.

"But when the Fades attacked us, they took half our souls as sacrifices." Mateo overlapped his hands so that they were neither wholly together nor apart.

"They killed you." Este blinked, processing. "But no one ever found you. Your bodies, I mean."

"You're looking at them," Aoife said.

Mateo nodded. "What's left of both our bodies and souls are tethered here, trapped between realms. Shadows of who we used to be."

"That's why you can't touch anything living." Este rubbed at her temples, trying to sift through every crooked piece of the puzzle. "Your bodies are dead, but what's left of your souls is still alive. Like, you're stuck in the center of the world's worst Venn diagram."

Aoife flipped another page in her book, barely glazing over

the words. Este could only imagine how many times she'd read it. "Exactly."

"So much better than the alternative, though." Luca twirled a strand of hair around her finger, bored.

"Everyone else left. All the other ghosts, they moved on like Henry." Este chewed on the edge of a fingernail. She really hated that this was making sense. "But you four haven't. Because you want to come back to life someday."

"By George, she's got it!" Mateo clapped his hands together and pushed himself off the couch.

The faint glimpse of teeth Este flashed was probably more grimace than grin. Her brain hurt. It felt like an ice pick had been jabbed behind her eyes. Repeatedly. She needed to rewire her entire consciousness, reboot her system.

She glanced at her phone's timer: five minutes to go.

There was one more thing she needed to know before she left, one nagging fear clinging like caramel to her molars: "Am I the only one who can see ghosts?"

Luca chimed a stream of lilting giggles, making Este's stomach turn to curdled milk.

Aoife's steadfast voice broke through, saying, "No, of course you're not. Anyone can see us if we want them to."

A layer of pressure evaporated off Este's chest. "Haven't people noticed you haven't graduated? Don't people come up here to study?"

"Not many, no. Rumor has it, the senior lounge is haunted,"

Mateo said with a wide smile and a wink.

It happened all at once, like a flame being snuffed out. One moment, the ghosts were there, and the next Este sat alone, surrounded by an empty velvet chaise, a vacant tartan chair, and a leather love seat. All that remained was a fading fire desperate to be stoked.

Even though she couldn't see the ghosts, the air was thick with their presence, the hair on her arms standing on edge. Electric, almost. Daveed laughed from nowhere. Aoife's book fanned to the next page, seemingly floating above the seat of her chair. Squinting, Este could make out the slightest silver outline of Mateo's shoulders in the firelight.

She was definitely going to hurl.

"Alright, alright. One thing at a time," Mateo said, flashing back into view. He commanded the room, understated but respected. Like whatever he said, they'd do. "She's had a lot to process since our little run-in with the Fades."

The rest of the ghosts flashed back to reality, and Aoife's eyebrows had raised precariously high. "They really are back?"

Mateo nodded. "They haven't changed a bit since the nineties."

Luca made a disgusted grunt. "Someone should really tell them that brown lip liner is *so* out."

The book in Aoife's hands closed with a snap. She stood, pacing, and said, "I'm pretty sure the Fades don't care that they look a little outdated, Lu. They haven't taken a sacrifice in thirty years. They're out of practice."

Luca flashed Mateo a saccharine smile, sweet and light but sour underneath. "Your parents, may they rest in peace, can kindly kiss my round behind when I finally make it out of this purgatory. I don't care if they never opened *The Book of Fades*; they should've never brought it here."

Mateo ignored Luca's harping and returned his sights to Este. His gaze was so pointed it ran shivers down her arms. "The last time the Fades appeared was the year Dean Logano locked the spire door. Since then, nothing. Until now."

"But now that we have the book back, it could almost be over, right?" Daveed asked. His face turned to stone, hardened around the edges. "Do you have any idea how much I miss french fries?"

Este picked at her cuticles, worry spreading through her body like a windstorm. A migraine clawed at the corners of her mind. Whatever her dad had done in the spire, maybe he had accidentally stopped the Fades, sure, but he had also stopped these ghosts from finding their way back to the living. How had he gotten wrapped up in all this? And how on Earth was she supposed to know how to fix it?

Before she could say anything else, her phone's alarm sang the brass intro to "September" by Earth, Wind & Fire. It was her favorite song, one she inherited from her dad. Hearing it always took her back to the kitchen, him spinning her and her mom around, all of them sliding in socked feet.

"That's my cue." Este thumbed off the music. She pushed up from the sofa cushions and dusted off her jeans. "I'll be here, like, every night, so maybe I'll see you around."

A bloated beat swelled through the lounge. Aoife looked at Luca who looked at Daveed who looked at Mateo, like they all knew some inside joke Este didn't know and probably didn't want to be a part of.

Mateo flashed into view across the room. She would *not* be getting used to that. He hauled open the green door. "I'll walk you downstairs."

"You've done more than enough tonight," she said sourly.

"I insist." He donned a wild smile, a glimmer in his dark blue eyes like gold on the bottom of the seafloor. The kind that made Este's knees feel gooey without her permission.

The door latched behind them, but Este didn't wait for him. She plunged into the stacks, weaving through the shelves toward the cedar staircase as fast as her feet would carry her. She must have had mountains of work collecting on the circulation desk that needed to get done tonight.

"Este, hold on!" Mateo called after her.

Este spun on her heels. She did *not* have time for this. "Look, I get it. We find the pages and get rid of the Fades. Bada bing, bada boom. I get to stay at Radcliffe, and you get a life. Or is getting me fired also a part of your big plan?"

Mateo's hands gripped the shelves on either side of them. "I don't have a plan. If we can't find the pages now, we'll have to wait another ten years for the Fades to return. *If* they return. And if they're gone, the tether to our souls is gone, too. This might be our only chance. The others . . . I can't let them down again."

Este watched for a flinch in his stance, a nervous flicker in his features, but there was none. He stood perfectly still, peering down at her with a seriousness washed clean of performative arrogance. His posture had lost every ounce of pomp and circumstance and replaced it with something a lot like desperation.

"Why now? Why'd they come back?" Este still had over an hour left of her shift, and she knew that every time she closed her eyes, she'd see those gory hands reaching toward her in the dark. "Are the other students in danger? Am I?"

An anvil hit her chest when Mateo didn't protest.

"I'm afraid so," he said, after much too long. "I don't know who or how they attack, but I know they're confined to the walls of the library. Stay out of the shadows as much as possible. If you hear them singing, just run—don't listen and don't look back."

Her voice wavered. "What do I do if they find me again?"

"I'll be there," he said without hesitating.

And, damn it, despite herself, Este believed him. If he wanted to let the Fades have their way with her, he could've left her in the classroom. She was stubborn, but she wasn't stupid enough to think she would've made it out alive without him.

Even the thought of the Fades' song sent fear spiking through her heart like a stake in the earth.

Almost as much as the familiar cadence of Ives's heels currently climbing up the stairwell did. The telltale sign of Este about to get her ass chewed out by the one woman who held the fate of her academic career in her painstakingly manicured hands.

"Don't say a word of this to Ives," Mateo said, dropping his voice so that she had to lean in to hear him. He swiped a few books from the shelves and piled them in her arms. "About the book, about me. Act like you lost track of time shelving books, and that's all."

Then, Este stood alone.

At least, it looked like she was alone. She swiveled her head side to side, searching for any evidence of his presence, a faint outline or the wafting smell of Vermont cedar, like a candle that had just been blown out.

"Mateo?" she whispered.

Only the *click* of footsteps drawing nearer answered. She dragged in a deep breath, ready to face Ives, but Este stepped forward right as Mateo's chest appeared back into reality mere inches from her nose.

"Yes?" he asked with a lopsided grin.

Este skittered backward, yelping, and immediately clamped a hand over her mouth. She peeled her palm away from her lips long enough to hiss, "What are you doing?"

"You called me? Would you rather I ignore you?"

"What? No. I mean, yes, actually. But you—" Este blew a stiff breath out through her nose. He somehow always managed to short-circuit her. "Get out of here."

Mateo laughed, loud enough that Este was terrified Ives would hear and accuse her of having fun when she was supposed to be groveling for her forgiveness.

Instinctively, she pressed a finger over her mouth and shushed him.

He cocked his head with a smile. "You'll make a great librarian yet, Este Logano."

He vanished, and alone again, Este placed the books he handed her back on the shelf where they belonged. She tried to ignore the crescendo of Ives's footsteps, tried to pretend like she'd been doing this, exactly this, for hours.

Ives announced her arrival with a clipped *tsk*. "Remember to straighten the books at the front of the shelf, not the back."

Este gave a tight-lipped smile, scooting the books to the edge. "Right, of course."

"How has everything gone tonight? I wanted to see if you were surviving your first night, since I know a new job can be quite daunting."

Understatement of the century.

Ives nudged a few books into perfect alignment and raised her eyebrows. Waiting.

Oh, right.

"Fine, great. It's been totally, completely normal tonight." Este slotted the last book onto the shelf. "Practically a walk in the park."

Behind Ives, Mateo faded back into her line of sight, hazy around the edges. He lowered both his hands as if to say, *Simmer down, Logano.* Even Ives raised an eyebrow. Este had laid it on way too thick.

"Not that I haven't been working hard," Este hurried to say. "These books don't shelve themselves."

Mateo gave a thumbs-up, and his form fizzled out. Could he mind his own business for once in his afterlife?

"I see. Anything you have questions about before I head out?" Ives asked.

"No, but actually," Este said, riffling through the back of her mind for anything that could convince Ives she wasn't an utter slacker, "I do need to get back downstairs to check in the books from the night drop."

As they wound down the staircase, Este scanned floor by floor for malign shadows and listened for stray voices in the halls, searching for any trace of the Fades' flesh-bare hands reaching for her. At the foot of the stairs, Ives bid Este good night with a yawn, and once the head librarian swept out into the rain-damp night, all that was left was Este and the library and a heaping stack of returned books waiting to be checked in and reshelved. After everything she'd done tonight, this was the easy part. This was where she belonged. No matter what Mateo said, this was her only mission.

Find the stolen pages, resurrect a few ghosts, get the book back, and clear her name.

Easy enough, right?

ELEVEN

"Why are you making this so difficult?" Este whined to the circulation computer.

The program the Lilith used for its circulation records probably predated Este's entire existence, and let's face it, the early 2000s were not known for their phenomenal digital prowess. When the page refused to load, she dropped her head against the desk. It had been two days since her brush with the Fades, but she was no closer to finding the missing pages—and *much* closer to single-handedly filing for a grant to update these dinosaurs to iMacs.

Tonight, the library's first floor was dead quiet. The thing about a college-prep school was that students were supposed to actually prepare for college. The curriculum did not take that lightly. If she listened over the constant whir of the computer's fan, she could hear clicking laptop keyboards and the occasional "Do we cite in MLA or APA format?" between friends.

"Working hard or hardly working?"

Mateo's disembodied voice was the last thing she wanted to hear. She answered him with a grunt, refusing to lift her head.

"A bit of both, I see."

He settled next to her. She could tell only by the way the air shifted and the wisps of hair that wouldn't stay in her ponytail tickled the back of her neck—when she rolled her head to peek one eye open, his body was nowhere to be found.

Fine by her. She didn't care to see him or his annoyingly long eyelashes right now. Even if she'd never admit it out loud, some part of her (deep, deep down) appreciated that Mateo hadn't made himself scarce. He'd crept into her orbit during both shifts since the Fades fiasco.

Thankfully, she hadn't run into the Fades again since then either, but she'd found every excuse not to trek to the third floor. Just in case.

After she refreshed the page, a shoddy HTML version of the program buffered but nothing more. Patience was not one of her many virtues. Choosing the lesser of two annoyances, she said to Mateo, "I'm trying to run the catalog for every book in section DL97."

The stapler, the tape dispenser, and the bottle of book-repair glue from her desk scooted across the table as if pulled by invisible strings. Then, the floating desk accessories began to juggle. Thank goodness her classmates were packed into the upstairs study carrels, too busy with the quarter's first essays to wonder if Este had mastered the power of telekinesis or too sleepy to protest.

"*Consider it a loan. DL97.* Library book call number." Mateo hummed, a thinking sound. "Okay, Holmes. I see where you're going here."

It wasn't a bad guess. And, more importantly, it was the only lead they had. So, here she was, just a girl, sitting in front of the oldest computer she'd ever seen, asking it to show her some answers.

Finally, the computer speakers dinged. Este read the flashing black number at the top of the screen with a sigh she felt in her bones. "2,637 results."

Mateo asked, "Wouldn't it be just as easy to go to the second floor yourself to look through them?"

"If you want to look through all 2,637 books, be my guest." Este clicked on the first book. The computer moaned in response as it loaded the new page. "In fact, I think you should get a head start."

Mateo blinked into view. Even wrapped in a school sweatshirt and a turtleneck, Este shivered as his sudden appearance sent goose bumps down her arms. His existence was an ice-bath shock to her nervous system.

He caught the office supplies he'd been juggling and set them back on the desk. "You can't get rid of me that easily."

Said the boy who could quite literally disappear on command.

Este had finally begun to memorize where everything at the circ desk belonged. Tape dispenser: top-left desk drawer. Recycling can: under the Ellison machine. Flashlight: bottom drawer on the right. She had to shake the flashlight until the batteries lodged into place and the bulb ignited, but once it did, she pointed the beam at Mateo's chest. Nothing happened.

When Mateo laughed, it tugged at Este's seams, daring her to unravel. All these years spent trapped at the library, caught between dead and alive, and he still laughed like it didn't matter.

From his pocket, he retrieved his matchbox and lit a solitary flame. When he cupped his palm around it, his hand faded out of sight. "Nice try, but synthetic light does nothing. It takes the real thing, right from the source. That's what sees through us."

He blew out the match, and Este waved away the smoke.

"The point is," she huffed, "that we have to start somewhere."

Mateo squinted at the computer screen. "And you want to start with Swedish-meatball recipes?"

Apparently, the Library of Congress classification system's code for DL97 corresponded with Scandinavian history from 1900 to 1918. So, technically, they were historically accurate Swedish-meatball recipes.

"I don't see you coming up with any better ideas," Este snapped. They'd spent the last two shifts going back and forth about whether *Consider it a loan* meant the pages or *The Book of Fades* itself, but the pocket for the book's borrowing card was empty, and none of its circulation records had been digitized—if it had ever circulated at all. Which left Este grasping at the second half of the clue, a rogue call number.

"1900 to 1918," Mateo said, sighing. He hoisted himself onto the desk, bending one knee up so he could rest his arm on it. "Those were the good old days."

It was also, conveniently, a time when the Radcliffes could have returned from an overseas trip with an incredibly cursed book. "What are the chances your parents went to Sweden?"

"After the *Titanic*? Zero. Before . . ." He considered this, bobbing his head on his shoulders like a grandfather clock. "It's possible. They'd travel periodically, always leaving us at home and always coming back with trunks of books, these books."

If she wasn't careful, it would be all too easy to think of Mateo as any other classmate instead of the ghost of the founder's son. She had admittedly gotten used to having him linger in her periphery. The same way she'd gotten used to wearing her first thong—she didn't necessarily enjoy it, but it served its purposes.

She tapped a pen against a sticky note, but her eyes glazed over the moment she looked at all the different circ records. Their numbers blurred together. She clicked open a few pages and scanned for any trace of something that would link them to the Fades or the Radcliffes' questionable book-acquisition techniques. Unfortunately, most of the texts focused on Sweden and Norway's separation in 1905 and the correct ratio of bread-crumbs to egg yolks in her favorite IKEA meal. As much as she wanted to believe they were on the right path, this already felt like a dead end. It didn't make any sense why someone would lead them here.

"Maybe it's actually OL97, instead?" she tried, chewing on the inside of her cheek.

Mateo shook his head. "That call number doesn't even exist."

Boy, she really needed to carve out time to study in case Ives gave her a pop quiz on classification.

Around her computer, Este watched Shepherd stampede into the Lilith, a bull in a very quiet China shop. He aimed toward the circulation desk. A midnight weariness clung to his frame, his arms weighed down with textbooks. Este hadn't pegged him as the bunny-slipper type, but his shoe choice proved her wrong.

"Hey, Shepherd," she said when he reached the desk. "Trying to finish up the English essay for Mr. Donohue?"

"Yeah, and I lost my library card, but I need to log on to the computers." He scrubbed a hand over his eyes. When he looked over Este's shoulder at Mateo, Shepherd jutted his chin up in a bro nod that Mateo reciprocated terribly.

Trailing her fingers over the drawers until she found the right one, Este yanked open a treasure trove of lost library cards. Somewhere between fifty and a hundred thin plastic cards jostled inside. New ones with freshly laminated edges, old ones with yellowed corners, and right on top: Shepherd Healy.

Handing it to him, she said, "I think all the desks on the fourth floor are taken, but there are probably a few open on the fifth floor."

"Thanks." Shepherd turned to leave but paused to ask, "Did you ever find that Mateo guy?"

Before Mateo could say anything arrogant and self-incriminating, Este blurted, "Nope. No luck. He's still a criminal on the loose."

"Well, good luck, or—" Shepherd scrunched his face up real hard like he was trying to force neural connections to form. "Break a leg, I mean. Arthur says that's the right way to say good luck."

No number of quick recoveries could spare her from the way Mateo's gaze fixed on her as Shepherd trailed up the stairs.

"You sent a whole search party after me," he said, sounding as pleased as she had imagined.

"I didn't send anyone," she said with a huff. "They insisted."

She preoccupied herself by sifting through the cards, scooping up a handful and letting them waterfall back down. Hadn't Ives said someone needed to organize this? Now seemed like a great time.

"I have to admit, I'm flattered." Mateo vanished from one side of the desk and reappeared on the other, hedging into her line of sight. He cocked his head on a fist, haughty as a man made into a marble statue. "I'm a wanted man."

While the back of her mind debated the pros and cons of reminding Mateo he hadn't lived long enough to qualify as anything more than an honor roll student, Este sorted the cards into stacks for each student's graduating year and set aside anyone who would have already graduated. Clawing through the cards, Este found a set of hazel eyes—the ones she inherited. She barely had time to register them before the card got sucked back into the vortex of lost cards.

"My dad's in here," she whispered.

"I thought we'd established that him becoming a ghost went against the laws of mortality."

Este plucked her dad's library card from the drawer and held it out to Mateo. "No, this."

In the corner, there was a faded headshot that looked like it had been taken with a disposable camera. He wore the outfit she'd seen in his move-in day photo, the same Radcliffe Prep crewneck she wore now, new then, and wire-rimmed glasses that couldn't have been trendy, even in the nineties.

"Does it still work?" he asked.

There wasn't even a barcode on the back, but when Este typed the card number into a system, the computer chugged, spitting out her dad's student profile. With a few clicks, she revealed a paper trail of who he'd been back then.

The screen loaded a copy of his school roster, flashing with a red expiration date. All his coursework, his grades, his class schedule had been logged in some primitive form of technology, like Windows 95.

She clicked to a page of previous transactions. *Poetry Scansion for Beginners*, the complete works of Edgar Allan Poe, and a short list of school yearbooks topped the list, and that was just the first page.

Mateo had leaned so close that his words felt cool against her cheek. "I see the library fascination is hereditary."

Shoving a pad of sticky notes and her pen in Mateo's general direction, she said, "You said my dad was involved?"

"Maybe—"

"Start writing down titles," Este said. "We'll see if any of their call numbers match."

While she rattled off the names of each text, Mateo scribbled until the desk was lost beneath hot pink three-by-three Post-its. Her dad had checked out several periodical loans from the school newspaper *The Radcliffe Register*, almanacs and atlases, *Herbal Remedies and Antidotes*, a horror anthology. A whole slew of supernatural case studies. J.R.R. Tolkien and Virginia Woolf and T.S. Eliot.

"Okay, we've got PR3, G1004, PS3509 . . ."

Este skimmed her thumb across his photo. Her dad sported a goofy grin, the same kind he'd worn when they played Uno together and he'd let her have the winning hand. Next to his headshot was his name and enrollment year: Dean Logano, 1997.

"Wait. It's not a call number at all." Breathless, Este said, "It's him. My dad was DL97."

All the amusement washed out of Mateo's face. "You don't think . . ."

"I mean, if you look past all the normal stuff he was probably reading for class, he'd clearly been doing some digging—all these yearbooks, the newspapers. He literally checked out a book called *How to Know You're Being Haunted*." She could barely squeeze the words out around the hammering pulse in her throat. "So, if you're wondering if I think my dad stole the spire key, tore the pages out of *The Book of Fades*, and locked the door behind him to conceal the evidence . . . yeah, I'm kind of thinking that."

Her voice sounded distant, as if she were two thousand miles away and thirteen years old again, sweating in the central California heat, even as the cemetery's blue canopy hid her from the midday sun. She was digging her dad up, shovel by shovel, and unearthing a part of him she'd never known. For the first time, she wasn't sure she wanted to know what she'd find.

TWELVE

❧

Autumn wrapped around campus like a scarf. Overnight, the trees had shaken the green out of their leaves in favor of their finest golds. The air had a new chill to it, and Este cupped her steaming coffee mug closer to her chin on her way to Mr. Donohue's English class. When she passed the Lilith, she scanned the windows for any trace of Mateo. The midmorning sun slanted through his usually shady alcoves, and she was pretty sure she didn't imagine the way her shoulders sank when she didn't spot him.

Although that could have just been the weight from her backpack. She'd barely been able to zip it shut around a stack of yearbooks they'd found listed on her dad's card.

She and Mateo had made a plan. Este would start at the top of the list, and Mateo and the ghosts would start at the bottom. Together, they'd work their way through every book her dad checked out while at Radcliffe. There had to be an answer in the pages somewhere, and since the ghosts had forfeited their need for basic bodily functions like sleeping and eating when they'd also forfeited their lives, they could cover a hell of a lot of ground.

Este took the steps up to the humanities building two at a time. This part of the school grounds had an overgrown, lived-in feel to it. Ivy coated the handrails, climbed up the bricks. Inside, the floors hadn't been polished, and Este followed them to the last door on the left.

On the first day of classes, Posy waved to Este when she walked in and pointed to the seat she'd saved next to her. Now, Este found herself migrating to the far end of Mr. Donohue's classroom out of habit, a safe familiarity. Posy's seat was still surprisingly empty—while Este had a study period before English (which today she'd used to refuel with stale coffee from the Vespertine Hall kitchen and cram a conclusion paragraph into her essay), Posy came from precalc nearby. Normally, she'd be here, halfway through a cranberry-walnut scone by the time Este walked in.

It was new, knowing the ins and outs of someone. She'd had friends before, girls who would ride the bus home with her and do braid trains at slumber parties, but no one she fought to keep after her dad died. Her grip had turned slippery, and it had been so much easier to let go than to hold on.

Besides, back then, part of Este had welcomed the chance to vanish. Fueled by the onset of puberty, a new pair of Doc

Martens she needed to break in, and the sinkhole caving in behind her sternum, she'd wanted to become anyone but Este Logano, the girl without a dad. Spotty cell service didn't make it easy to stay in touch either. When her mom started whisking her from city to city, her social media derailed into snapshots from D-list tourist attractions from around the country—the world's largest wind chimes, two smiling dinosaurs on the side of an Oregon highway, a wax-museum homage to train robbers.

Letting herself get close to someone again felt like wearing a shirt with a scratchy tag. Her only options were to get used to it or cut it off.

While students trickled in and Mr. Donohue downed the pitch-black contents of his coffee mug like a shot, Este dipped into her backpack. Her dad's circulation history included yearbooks from five school years—1967–68, 1969–70, 1977–78, 1978–79, and 1987–88. He'd had his finger on the pulse of the disappearances, that much was evident. Este went ahead and filled in the blanks, grabbing the decades he had been missing, and she'd tucked 1997–98 in for good measure, just to cover all her bases.

As Este flipped through the yearbook for the 1987–88 school year, she was whisked back through Radcliffe Prep's timeless past. The buildings, the trees, they almost looked identical. There were cringeworthy school portraits, club photos, write-ups on homecoming and the prom. Snapshots that proved, at a finite point in time, the greater population had been convinced shoulder pads were a good idea.

As she scanned the pages, she recognized a wide-rimmed grin: Daveed in the stacks of the Lilith. He stood at the center of a group of students laughing like a bad stock photo. They all had their arms wrapped around each other's shoulders, and he was sandwiched between a boy with glasses that rivaled Elton John and a girl with dark hair and a big, blue costume ring on her finger. A bit gaudy for a study date, but who was Este to judge?

Este's chest constricted with each turned page. Radcliffe Prep had seen so many generations pass through these halls. She could imagine it all as easily as if the clock hands wound backward.

In 1987, Daveed might have skated through the courtyard, a boom box perched on his shoulder. Maybe his peers glared, but he probably wouldn't have noticed.

Aoife could have been coiled onto a stone bench in 1967, lost in another world, one of parchment and pen. She'd have thumbed through the pages as fast as she could.

When the glow from incandescent light bulbs lit the narrow halls in 1927, Luca might have spun through the oiled stacks in her heels and her drop-waisted dress. The tassels at the hem must have fanned out as she twirled, sliding books from the shelves as she went.

Then, in 1917, Mateo probably split his time in half, either needling his professors or parading around campus like the Chosen One. He'd have had an easy posture, a feverish laugh—the kind that was too contagious to ignore. Honestly, he still did.

Posy slammed her books down on the desk next to Este's, rattling her back to the present day. "I think I found your Mateo."

If Este had been drinking her coffee at that precise moment, it would have shot out her nose. "Excuse me?"

"Shepherd told me you still hadn't found him, so between first and second periods I went to the computer lab to do some digging on my favorite forum. Here, I'll pull it up." Posy squeezed down into her seat without even bothering to take her backpack off as she plucked her phone from the side pocket. "The Mateo you met? Totally Mateo Radcliffe. *The* Mateo Radcliffe."

If all but two of Este's brain cells hadn't decided this was the right time to go completely dormant, she would've said anything except for, "*Whaaaaat?* No way."

"Yes way. I can't believe I didn't think of it before. It was right in front of my nose. I knew you saw a freaking ghost." Posy pried up the cover of the yearbook, as if only now registering she'd been in the middle of something when she barged in. "What are these?"

Este snapped the book closed and shuffled them aside. "Nothing. I'm, um, considering joining the yearbook staff."

"Good morning, class," Mr. Donohue said, a yawn behind his words. His head was bald as a cue ball, and, like most of them, he wore a thick-knit sweater to fend off the brisk morning. He dragged his coffee mug with him to the podium. "Pass up your essays, and we'll get started."

When Este twisted to get the papers from behind her, Posy slid her phone onto Este's desk. Judging by the blocky text, the wretched color scheme, and the fact that it was called Ghoul School, there was a solid 95 percent chance that the website Posy referenced had first been coded back when people still relied on dial-up internet.

Este scanned a stream of recent threads with varying degrees of scientific validity. "Unveiling the Ghosts of Radcliffe's Past," "Everything You Need to Know About Radcliffe Prep's Disappearances," "Which Radcliffe Child Are You Most Like?" She clicked the last one, and a series of generic this-or-that questions spawned (early morning or late night, tea or coffee, sweet or salty). She tapped in her answers—for science, obviously—and she handed up the finished essays while her results buffered.

When it loaded, she wished it hadn't.

You are: Mateo Radcliffe.

Underneath, they'd included a photo, and there was no denying it was him. Mateo gripped a book in one hand and the rungs of a rolling ladder in another. He wore a knit Radcliffe Prep sweater with the school's crest embroidered into the chest, and his cheeks creased with dimples. The comments section was riddled with *If he's a ghost, he could haunt me any day* posts that made Este's breakfast turn to toxic sludge in her stomach.

All it would take was one look at the boy Este had been spending nights with at the library, and Posy would know she was right.

"Phones down, Miss Logano," Mr. Donohue said as he pulled down a series of paper maps, unrolling them in front of the chalkboard. The first revealed a topographically accurate portrayal of Radcliffe Prep's corner of Vermont, where Sheridan Oaks was nestled between Montpelier and Burlington. Then, one of the United States at large. Finally, a world atlas blanketed both, and Mr. Donohue jabbed a wooden rod toward the Greek peninsula. "Who here knows how to read ancient Greek?"

Este handed Posy her phone back, pointedly avoiding the way her roommate mouthed, "Is that him?" because it totally was, and Este wasn't ready to say those words out loud yet. Not when her future at Radcliffe hung in the balance, and definitely not when it would mean admitting to Posy that she was right. Then, she'd *really* never shut up about ghosts.

"No one?" Mr. Donohue prompted. He wafted his pointing stick around like a magic wand as if he could *bibbidi-bobbidi-boo* them into paying attention. "Then, how can you read *The Odyssey*?"

"Translations?" someone in the back offered.

"Precisely!"

For the better part of an hour, Mr. Donohue droned about how translation inherently breathed new life into old texts, about the historical significance of the *Oxford English Dictionary* for its lexical bookkeeping, and how, to his dismay, literary criticism often derailed from the source text with every generation and to get to the heart of the story, you need to read the original work. Este only half listened, spending the better part of her hour with a yearbook slotted inside her textbook, scanning spread after spread for any smudge of her dad's handwriting or trace of the missing pages.

Posy glued herself to Este's side as soon as Mr. Donohue dismissed them. "Dr. Kirk's leading our first Paranormal Investigators ghost hunt Saturday at five. I bet we can find Mateo."

"That really won't be necessary because—"

"Seriously, Este. I *want* to help you. Imagine if I'm able to prove the Radcliffe ghosts are real. The forum would freak out."

Este opened her mouth to clarify that she didn't need Posy's help finding *The Book of Fades* anymore, even if she wasn't ready to reveal that it was because she was in cahoots with the thief, but Posy squealed, riled up from her own excitement.

"I bet I could guest star on *Ghost with the Most*. I need to buy a better microphone. Do you think omnidirectional or unidirectional would be better?" Posy's phone was in her hand in an instant, and she asked it, "Best mic for podcasting?"

In her back pocket, Este's phone vibrated, and when she reached for it, her mom's contact flashed on the screen. Her options were simple: listen to her mom harp about gas prices for twenty minutes or pretend she never saw the call.

Her mom could have texted, like any other parent in the twenty-first century, but Este could practically see her: phone cradled between her chin and shoulder, counting change at a toll booth and sipping flat gas-station soda. Phone calls had become her mom's preferred method of communicating since most of her days were spent driving eighty-five in a seventy. She'd ask Este how school was going, and Este would have to lie and say *everything's fine* because she couldn't exactly tell her mom the truth either.

Este let it ring for three buzzes before she sent the call to voice mail.

"Let's wait here," Posy said once they were outside, evidently satisfied with her podcasting research. "Arthur and I are going to walk to history together."

The humanities building sat adjacent to the Hesper Theater with the fountain of the same name standing sentinel out front. Rivulets of water pooled beneath the carved stone feet of Robin Radcliffe. He'd been depicted behind a desk. One of his hands pressed a quill to the pages of a book, and the other outstretched poetically while his eyes gazed upward as if monologuing to the midday sun. The fountain's well was filled with coins, the sanguine wishes of students sparkling like gems. If she dug to the bottom, Este wagered she could find coins from the very first class at Radcliffe Prep.

Posy's eyes glistened up at the statue when she said, "Dr. Kirk said there's this school tradition about how if you kiss someone at the Hesper Fountain, your love will last forever."

Forever, Este neglected to remind her, was an impossibly long time.

Arthur breezed out of the Hesper Theater, dressed head to toe in black, and linked arms with Posy. "Daydreaming about kissing Shepherd again?"

"No!" An undeniable blush bloomed across Posy's cheeks, and she swatted Arthur's arm. "Okay, maybe. We'd make a cute couple, don't you think?"

Este let them walk on without her. Her next class was in the opposite direction—an elective on the basics of library sciences before lunch—and, besides, Arthur was already rambling about disembodied voices he'd heard in the prop loft and how he needed to take the voice recorder up next time.

Este stifled a laugh. The only real ghosts were perched in the senior lounge, probably playing a game of makeshift darts with mechanical pencils or practicing their two-step to one of the Etta Jones vinyl records in the music collection.

Before they drifted totally out of sight, Posy hollered over her shoulder, "Ghost hunt on Saturday. Don't forget!"

And because every good ghost hunt required a ghost, Este invited Mateo to join them—invisibly, of course. If she was going to spend her Saturday night entertaining Posy's antics, then at least they could multitask and search for the pages.

The club met, like Posy had instructed, at exactly five o'clock in the lobby of the Lilith two days later, and Dr. Kirk wasted no time before handing out buzzing gadgets for the club's inaugural ghost-hunting expedition. The look on Posy's face when Mateo's presence sent their machines beeping made it all worthwhile.

As they careened through the library, Arthur, Shepherd, and Posy existed as one unit, clumped together around Dr. Kirk and her tall tales of school legends and ancient hauntings. And Este shifted uncomfortably when she realized not all of them were completely made-up. A few extra faces made appearances tonight, new Paranormal Investigator initiates. Este let them all surge ahead, cranking the volume on her EMF reader down to zero so that it wouldn't go berserk with Mateo next to her.

"That's where I skinned my knees trying to slide down the banister," he said for her ears only. Este found the curve in the staircase—she could practically see a younger Mateo, lip buckled beneath the fright of the fall. "And *that's* where I had my first kiss. Fifteen, Helen Ruth. Scandalous little thing."

"Did you use tongue?" Este goaded, wagging her eyebrows.

"A gentleman doesn't kiss and tell, Logano."

It was a dangerous thought. What Mateo's bowed lips might

feel like against hers. A daydream that had no right to take up real estate in Este's mind. For starters, he was practically a million years old. Secondly, she'd only had one kiss, a terrible, wet thing that scarcely qualified so much as a kiss to begin with and veered closer to the definition of excited Saint Bernard. She wouldn't consider herself an expert.

But from a strictly objective perspective, Mateo was handsome—at least when he was visible.

They turned the corner to a windowed corridor where campus stretched out underneath them, now pooling with dazzling reds and yellows in the evening light. The school was a mosaic of golden knolls and shade-tree shadows, and a layer of fog swept through the courtyards and draped over the brick and limestone buildings.

"This is home," Mateo said, his voice sinking to a whisper. "My father bought the land and built the house before I was born. These have always been the corners of my world. And now . . ."

If only she could see him, search the slant of his mouth for any unspoken emotion. He had died only a year before selective service would've whisked him to the war, but he also never had a chance to experience the fanfare of the roaring twenties, sneaking speakeasy absinthe and dancing to syncopated jazz standards. The school grounds were a hand-blown snow globe, a picturesque miniature of life, protected but confined.

"They always will be," she finished for him.

"Miss Logano, did you find something?"

Este whipped her head toward the group. Dr. Kirk and the others faced her, waiting. She double-checked to make sure Mateo hadn't decided now was the perfect time for his big entrance, but thankfully he had the good sense to stay invisible.

"No, sorry." She wiped on an apologetic smile and scuttled to catch up. "Just recalibrating the reader's solar input for night mode."

"Oh, yes, of course," Dr. Kirk said, continuing to pace down the interlocking shelves, and Este let her shoulders relax. "As I was saying, banshees may roam the Radcliffe halls."

"This is a personal affront to my existence. Banshees, really?" Mateo said, much closer than Este anticipated. She upped the reader's volume back to 20 percent so that it chirped like a personal doppler radar and she knew he was nearby.

Dr. Kirk prattled on, unbothered by the sound. "Some say you'll hear tortured singing coming from study rooms upstairs. Perhaps the spirit of someone who forgot to study for midterms."

That earned a couple laughs.

"What about Fades?" Este asked.

Dr. Kirk twisted the knobs on one of her tools and then traded it for something sprouting with antennae. "Those are a unique type of spirit, typically bound to something physical— jewelry or a sculpture, trapped inside a mirror, perhaps—that belongs to a person who controls them, the Heir of Fades.

They're very rare. It's not likely we'd have any Fades on campus."

Yeah. Right. Este blanched at her nonchalance but nodded, tight-lipped, so that Dr. Kirk would continue spouting off about wraiths or orbs or whatever else it was that she wrongly believed roamed campus while missing the truth. When had Este become the resident paranormal authority?

"We don't have time for this," Mateo muttered. "Follow me."

While the rest of the group trickled upstairs, Este and her chiming EMF reader clung to the shadows. And once they were finally out of sight, Mateo flashed back into vision, equal parts curls and cheekbones.

He trailed ahead of Este with his long strides. For a split second, Este's muscles flinched as if she might grab his hand, tug on his shirtsleeve to pull him alongside her as they drifted through the shelves. That could obviously never happen. She wrapped the bells of her shirtsleeves around her palms instead and clenched them into fists.

"Let me guess," she said when they reached the northern end of the library, desperate to break the silence. She pointed to the tufted window seat in his favorite alcove. "That's where you read Milton for the first time."

Mateo shook his head singularly, focused somewhere in the distance, past the brick walls and the bookshelves toward something even farther away. "'I went to the woods because I wished to live deliberately, to front only the essential facts of life, and see if I could not learn what it had to teach, and not, when I came to die, discover that I had not lived.'"

"Thoreau," Este said. As the first starlight sifted through the stained-glass windows, it was all too easy to imagine Mateo, legs folded to his chest, dreaming of escaping to Walden Pond. To let the water lap at his bare ankles, to lounge beneath the red maples.

"I wish I'd read it sooner."

Mateo dipped into his pocket for a creased sheet of paper and held it toward her. As Este wrapped her hand around the paper, her fingers brushed the place his should've been, and it was like dipping her hand in a wellspring of cool water. Her heartbeat hopscotched.

She unfolded it to find a handwritten list, a floor-by-floor collection of nooks and crannies ranging from the first floor's loose floorboard next to the bust of Oscar Wilde to the trick mirror in the men's restroom on the fifth floor. She thumbed over the writing, feeling the grooves where his pen had pressed into the paper. "Places we can look for the pages?"

"I've been trying to undo what happened a hundred years ago every moment of every day since then," Mateo said, his head craned down toward her. "But I've never done it with you."

Heat rushed toward Este's face, prickly and pink. She rolled her eyes to bat away the cloying bashfulness. "So, your new-found motivation has nothing to do with the three demonic pop stars who have decided it was time for their comeback hit? What was all that Dr. Kirk said about the Heir of Fades anyway?"

Mateo shuffled his weight from foot to foot. "It's probably not important for finding the pages."

"What would they even inherit?" Este wrinkled her nose at the memory of their sweet-pea fragrance, putrid as a funerary bouquet. "Besides bad fashion sense and an even worse stench."

Mateo leaned against the wall next to a draping tapestry, one hand slipped into the pocket of his wool trousers. She'd spent enough time with him in the last two weeks to recognize the stance was his own version of a yogi power pose. A shield to cover up whatever tender thing he kept hidden underneath. "Life. Mine, Luca's, Aoife's, Daveed's. They took ours in exchange for immortality."

"The Heir is real?" Este asked, and Mateo's grimace was enough of an answer. "Do you . . . do you remember who it was?"

"They killed me, Este. Not exactly a memory I tried to hold on to."

Este stepped closer, wanting to be closer to him. "Do you remember anything?"

"Well, I know I was in the spire, everything smelled like smoke, and then I woke up dead. Unless we find those pages, I always will be." He scrubbed a hand through his curls and shrugged away his train of thought. Este got the hint: touchy subject. "The Heir is only human. According to the book, without the Fades spoon-feeding them souls every ten years, the Heir would eventually grow old and pass. They only became like this because of what they summoned out of those pages, and the Fades are bound by ink to the book of their creation, so I think the missing chapter will tell us how to stop them—why else would Dean separate it from the rest of the book?"

Este nodded, throat dry.

"If we don't find those pages, the Fades might never be contained and the Heir never stopped." Mateo twisted a stone in the wall beneath the tapestry, and a trap door slid open on the floor in front of them. When he smiled, it was hard to look away. "Want to start from the bottom?"

She didn't exactly have much of a choice.

THIRTEEN

When Este enrolled at Radcliffe, she'd expected to spend far more time studying and far less time spelunking through secret doors. Mateo climbed down first, rung by rung on a ladder housing who knew how many termites, and she followed him into the dark.

Stagnant air welcomed them at the bottom of the ladder. The narrow hall was cool and damp, much too close to a crypt for comfort. Mateo peeled a candlestick from the wall and dragged a box of matches from his pocket. He handed them to Este to strike.

"Why do you carry these around with you everywhere?" she asked as the matchstick friction turned to flame. She lit the wick and blew out the match before returning the box to Mateo.

"Old habit," he said, pocketing it. He smiled, illuminated, and faded in and out of transparency with the wafting flame. "There's no better way to read than by candlelight."

"Even if it makes you see-through?"

"No one can interrupt me if they can't see me." He tapped his forehead like he had singularly outsmarted Einstein, and Este couldn't stop herself from laughing.

Being around Mateo was becoming a little too second nature. They fell into step with each other, and, in the dark, it was all too easy to believe they could have something they couldn't. Sometimes it was hard to remember he was dead at all.

The passageways were their road map to traversing the Lilith without getting spotted by the Paranormal Investigators. They popped out from behind a statue on the fourth floor right as Dr. Kirk led the tour up the stairwell, and they sank into a hallway disguised behind a bookshelf when Mateo stepped a little too close and Posy's *Ghostbusters* gear started trilling. At one point, Este was pretty sure she overheard Arthur trying to convince Dr. Kirk to team up with Mr. Liebowitz to put on a black-box production of *The Phantom of the Opera*.

They wiggled out a loose brick between the second and third floors (empty), peeled open a wall panel behind an original Rembrandt (dusty and empty), and Mateo dared Este to stick her hand inside an early-Hellenistic clay amphora (not empty—she got a fistful of expired Halloween candy—but also not helpful).

By the time they exhausted the list, Este's feet ached, the moon had risen to its peak, and the pages were still missing. She could've collapsed, both with exhaustion and disappointment.

"Come on. I'll walk you home," Mateo said when they landed back on the first floor.

He angled toward the doors, but Este hesitated in the warmth of the lobby. "Can you, you know. Leave?"

Mateo took a single, definitive step out of the library. And then another. The hold he had on his form must have slipped a bit because he feathered out at the edges. "The farther I get from the Lilith, the weaker I'll become, even in the dark. But yes. It'll be nice to get some fresh air."

Around them, the night was alive. Students roamed from building to building, clinging to what felt like the last warm night of fall. Her boots crunched fallen leaves against the sidewalk, and with every step, Mateo's scuffed leather oxfords faded a little more.

They took the long way underneath the bent boughs of black birches, their bright yellow leaves like stars against the dark sky. Mateo coursed through the courtyards without missing a single stepping stone. He'd had a hundred years to walk this path a thousand times. He must have seen generations come and go, but maybe some of them had seen him, too.

Quiet, Este asked, "Did you ever talk to him? My dad?"

And quieter, Mateo answered, "I did."

It had been three years but past tense still didn't sound quite right. Her dad was supposed to be defined by active verbs. He was the kind of dad who read her bedtime stories and taped the pages back together when she wore the books too thin. A dad who planned scavenger hunts around the house, who made dessert for breakfast and breakfast for dinner.

Instead, all that was left of him were the modals, the woulds and coulds. *Your dad would have loved this*, her mom said when they drove through the wide-open desert, nothing to slow them down but the tumbleweeds. *I wish your dad could be here to see this*, her mom sighed as they toed the ledge of a Cape Elizabeth cliff, snow crunching beneath their boots and a frozen tide lashing against the crags. The worst was Este clutching the Radcliffe acceptance letter to her chest, saying, *It's what Dad would have wanted*, knowing he'd never see her here.

"Only once," Mateo said. "Dean spent a lot of time at the library. I thought he could help me, and maybe I could help him but . . . well, you know how that worked out."

They neared the Hesper Fountain, and the rest of the world dimmed. Mateo had turned half-transparent as they strayed farther and farther from the Lilith, but there was no one else on this side of campus to see. This, he shared with her alone.

Sometimes she felt like the only person in the world who knew the ache of losing someone who couldn't come back, like the gaping hole it clawed out in her chest was a cavern that could never be crossed, but standing in the shadow of the school's founder, Este realized she and Mateo had more in common than she ever thought possible.

She stalled at the base of the fountain. "Do you miss them?"

Mateo glanced up at the carved face of his father. "Oh, yes.

Terribly. But sometimes I think I'm grateful that they didn't have to see what I became."

"A pain in the ass?"

Mateo sighed and rolled his eyes, something like a smile glazing over his mouth. Needling him took some of the tension out of the air. His shoulders hung looser, and Este was able to breathe a little easier.

"My mom passed first, and during those in-between months, my dad spent every night in the spire, writing and reading, counting the stars. He never stopped loving her. That's why it's called the Hesper Fountain." Mateo wasn't looking at her, or even at the fountain, but overhead at the stars. "On her birthday, he points to Venus, the evening star."

Este ran her fingers against the fountain's smooth marble. Chiseled out of the stone, Latin words circled along the trim. "What does it say?"

Mateo inched closer to her. The outline of his hand brushed over hers as they traced the shape of the letters. Her breath hitched as he said, "'There is life, there is death, and there is love.'"

Somehow, Este knew what would come next.

"'The greatest of these is love,'" they finished together.

And for the tiniest fraction of a second, Mateo looked at her with an expression she'd never seen on him before. Surprise and something softer. Like the first time someone remembered your favorite song or ordered you a chocolate shake because they knew you liked to dip your fries in it. The look of knowing someone and being known right back.

Este jostled backward and tucked a piece of hair behind her ear, suddenly feeling far too warm for mid-September. "My dad wrote that to me once. He must have remembered it. I have a photo of him standing here, shaking your dad's hand."

"Really?" Mateo asked.

She slid her phone out of her back pocket and thumbed through her photos until she found a scan of the framed picture in her room—out of focus and with a glaring sunspot in the corner, her dad sported a cheesy grin that made her chest tighten. "It's one of my favorite pictures of him."

A seriousness settled into Mateo's tone. "I need you to go shake my dad's hand."

"That's sweet but I don't really need to recreate the photo. It's so dark right now, and besides, are photo ops really our highest priority?"

"Not for a picture, Logano. For the pages." Mateo's grin was a sunbeam. "And it's a two-person job."

Much to her annoyance, Este hiked one leg over the fountain's wall and then the other. The pennies beneath her feet jingled as she sloshed toward the statue, biting down a stream of curses as the cold water soaked into her jeans, squidged in her shoes. Jets surged and ebbed on a schedule Este couldn't predict. One wrong step, and she got a mouthful of stale fountain water.

When Este's hand wrapped around the stone carving, she didn't know exactly what she expected. An electric shock? To hear her dad's voice boom from beyond the grave? For Robin's mouth to open and shoot tranquilizing darts into her eyeballs? If there was one thing she'd learned about Radcliffe—nothing was as it appeared. She winced in anticipation, but nothing happened. The statue looked the same, Este felt the same, and the water jets sprayed the same.

"Hold it more firmly," Mateo instructed, which was easy for him to say since he didn't have a jet shooting ice water into his spleen.

She tried that, flexing her grip strength until her fingers ached, but nothing changed. "Now what?"

"Pull it down."

On a hinge, the statue's hand crooked downward, and the lever set off a chain reaction like a Rube Goldberg machine—a metallic groan as a drain at the bottom of the fountain slid open, a gurgle as the water whirled down. At this angle, Robin's hand pointed to the cobblestones beneath Mateo's feet.

"The water from the fountain is diverted through a subterranean pipe system," Mateo said, aligning with the tilted hand. "Hold on, it might take a second."

For a moment, everything was still. Then, one of the bricks in the pathway jutted up high enough for Mateo to get his fingers around it.

Este let go of Robin's stone hand to hop down and get a

closer look, but no sooner than Robin's hand slotted back into place did a jet spray her in the face. Sputtering, she felt for the grip again, her eyes pinched closed to keep the water out.

Mateo laughed, open and wild. "What part of *hold on* wasn't clear? You have to keep his hand pulled down or the brick will sink back into the ground. And the water will be redirected back to the fountain."

Strings of drenched hair stuck to her lips. "Now you tell me."

Once again Este shook the statue's hand, and Mateo pried up the stone. Grimacing, Este clambered back down the statue, and it took all her flexibility to keep from getting supersoaked again. A heaviness sloped down his shoulders as he shook the brick and a single, tightly scrolled piece of paper landed in his half-opaque palm.

"Is that it? The missing page?" she asked.

Mateo scowled. "It's supposed to be pages. Plural."

Este pinched the paper's edge—the page was weathered and cracking, like it might spontaneously disintegrate. If Ives found out how much her hands were shaking as she scrolled open the fragile parchment, Este would have gotten kicked out of her gig as an archival assistant faster than she could say *European book cloth*.

Mateo held her phone for her, angling the flashlight so that she could read. Printed in bold ink, there was a headline: *Radcliffe Legacy Goes up in Flames*. Nothing else, the rest of the piece had been torn off, but the article from *Sheridan Oaks Daily* was dated October 16, 1917. In the bottom corner, a handwritten call number was smudged, and a thin stripe of blue ink underlined the title with a miniature arrowhead pointed toward the other side.

She flipped the paper over. Pressed into the back of the article was a trail of blue ink that read:

I've tasted sweet. I've tasted bitter. Life, it seems, is both.
To find the truth, I tasted death to read the words unknown.
What burned, come dawn, will not be lost. What buried roots will grow,
and when the ink fades, we will see what only love returns.

Este laughed, but it was a hollow sound. "Iambic heptameter breadcrumbs. That's what he left us."

"It almost . . . No, that couldn't be."

"You might as well tell me," she snapped. It wasn't his fault her dad was leading them on a wild goose hunt, but her nerves had been exposed. She was a walking root canal. "It's not like we have any other leads."

"It reminds me of something written in *The Book of Fades*." Mateo scratched his temple, looking as lost as she felt.

Este squinted. "You think my dad Duolingo'd the language of the dead?"

"Sometimes you say things, and I have no idea what you're talking about. Do you know that?"

It was her dad's handwriting, his initials. She'd practically almost drowned trying to retrieve it. There was no reason not to investigate it further.

"Show me," she said. "In the book."

As they ran back to the Lilith, ribbons of light streamed through the tree canopy, night silver. When they surged through the senior lounge's green door, Aoife, Luca, and Daveed slumped into their usual seats, reading a text on metaphysics, preening in a handheld mirror, and balancing four books on his head, respectively. Stacks of books she recognized from her dad's circ history were piled in the center of the coffee table.

"Any luck?" Luca asked as Este settled into a plaid armchair next to the fireplace, kicking her legs over one of the wooden arms to dry off.

Mateo stomped his foot on the ground, and one of the floorboards popped up as if it were spring-loaded. He reached inside for *The Book of Fades* and tossed it toward Aoife. "Godrich, will you read the epigraph for us?"

"Can we not fast pitch that book? My entire high school career depends on it," Este huffed, but in Aoife's defense, the book was caught with remarkable dexterity.

While the other ghosts huddled around Aoife's chair, Este didn't bother moving. The words would still be invisible to her. Although she made a mental note to pry up that board if Mateo ever tried to double-cross her again.

As Aoife read the epigraph, no one breathed—but that was normal for ghosts. With each word out of her mouth, Este's jaw dropped a little farther because every line was the same as the poem her dad had written on the back of the news article.

"Thank you for that incredible dramatic reading." Mateo nudged a panel among the bookshelves. Behind it, there was a chalkboard. "Este," he said as he juggled a piece of chalk, "why would your father steal from a book he couldn't read?"

She sucked her bottom lip between her teeth. Her father had died more than twenty years after attending Radcliffe. He hadn't been sick—his devastating stroke was the handiwork of a clot he couldn't have known possible when he was a student. "He . . . wouldn't?"

"Exactly." Mateo scribbled words across the chalkboard, drawing circles around them and lines in between them: sweet, bitter, truth, death. It looked like the evidence board in a harried detective's office. All he was missing was red string. "Dean Logano found a way to read *The Book of Fades* without dying."

"Wish I could say the same," said Daveed.

Aoife, with her eyebrows pinched together, asked, "How do you know?"

"Because my dad wrote that epigraph on the back of this news clipping." Este smoothed the headline on the table. "He must have been able to translate it somehow."

Mateo scrubbed a hand over his face, leaving behind a cloud

of dust. "It just doesn't make sense how he'd been able to do it."

Aoife took his place at the helm, and Mateo opted for pacing the perimeter of the room. While the ghosts analyzed the ancient text's lettering, scanning for any clue, Este read and reread her father's handwriting on the back of the newsprint. His hand had trailed over the words, blurring the ink, like he'd been writing quickly.

Gingerly, Este flipped the paper back over. Her fingertips ran the length of the headline, all the way down to the call number in the corner. "What's shelved in SB617?"

Aoife didn't stop writing on the chalkboard when she answered, "Poisonous plants."

Este lurched out of her seat so quickly Luca flinched. She pawed through the pile of texts on the coffee table, but none of the call numbers matched. "Where are they shelved?"

"Shouldn't you know that?" Luca asked. "Don't you work here?"

Este's frown lines rivaled the Grand Canyon. "Been a little preoccupied."

"Second floor, west wing," Daveed said. "Why?"

She barely squeezed out a quick "Be right back" before she was out of the room and into the hallway and racing down the stairs so quickly her feet threatened to fall off.

As she passed the archives, three ghastly voices stopped her cold. The Fades' song hummed in the shadows. Ice clogged her veins, and she stood frozen. *If you hear them singing, just run—don't listen and don't look back.*

Este crammed her fingers into her ears and darted between the light from the sconces until she made it downstairs to the second floor. The call numbers melted together as she spun through the stacks. In SB617, she pinpointed a thin blue book titled *Herbal Remedies and Antidotes*—she recognized it immediately from her dad's list. The glossary led her to a spread that included illustrations of the vine's anatomy in lieu of any photos.

This genus in the family Convolvulaceae is commonly known as bindweeds. Similar to morning glories, these plants are responsive to light, and once rooted, they will grow persistently. Este flipped the page to follow the paragraph. Rivea asterannis *contains elements now known to be detrimental to humans but had previously been used in rituals. If ingested, an antidote can be concocted from the following herbs and spices . . .*

Este clutched the book to her chest to keep her heart from pounding straight out. This was it. This was the tie she'd been missing. Before she went back to the lounge, she had to make a pit stop.

Let it be known to Mr. Donohue that she did, in fact, pay attention in class. To understand the true meaning of the blooms, she needed to understand their history. She deserved extra credit for cracking open the *R* volume of the *Oxford English Dictionary* and skimming the onionskin pages.

First, she found the entry for its root word—*rive: verb, to cleave, to split, to separate.* Like the ghosts, souls torn from their bodies and stranding them in an infinite in-between. She ran the pad of her fingertip downward over rivea's fine-print definition: *noun, from rive, the new dawn light; the moment when night ends.* Below, there was a separate entry specific to rivean ivy. *Noun,* Rivea asterannis, *vine with highly toxic night-blooming flowers; often used in ancient ceremonies to communicate with the dead, this flower symbolizes life and death.*

The door slammed open as Este burst back into the senior lounge. The ghosts froze, every motion halted midair. Aoife's chalk screeched against the board as her hand slid downward. Mateo's eyebrows shot up so high they got lost behind his curls.

Este tapped her fingernails against the book's hard cover. "I think I know how my dad read *The Book of Fades,* but I'm going to need Ives's keys."

FOURTEEN

Of all the terrible ideas Este had this quarter, this could easily have been the worst.

Her hypothesis was simple. When Este was little, her dad used to hike her up onto his shoulders to pick honeysuckle blooms from the trellises around their house, and if she pinched her eyes closed tightly enough, she could still taste the drop of summer-sweet sap they'd pulled from the blossoms.

So, it really wasn't that much of a stretch to think that her dad might have picked one of the spire's purple blooms, tasted the drop of nectar on his tongue, and then—whoops! Suddenly, he could see the unseeable and read *the words unknown* like the poem said. All he had to do was take the antidote to stop the poison from seeping so far into his bloodstream that it fried his brain into a potato pancake, and he was good to go.

Testing the hypothesis, however, was not as straightforward.

Este arrived in front of the head librarian's office for their third Tuesday morning meeting with an extra cup of coffee in an effort to bribe her way back into Ives's good favor. She'd even splurged and went to the on-campus coffee shop so that the coffee didn't taste like the months-old beans they had in Vespertine Hall. But Ives, as it turned out, was not a coffee person. When she opened the door, the whole office smelled like freshly brewed Earl Grey. Este's worst nightmare.

"Good morning, Miss Logano." Ives eyed Este's double-fisted caffeine fix as she stepped inside. "Late night?"

Este shook her head and resisted the urge to look over her shoulder. "Long day ahead."

She couldn't see him, but she knew that Mateo had made it inside the office when a cool breeze brushed against her hand. His familiar scent of cedar and ink calmed her nerves.

That was happening more and more lately, with and without Este's permission. She was spending less time in her dorm room where Posy, Shepherd, and Arthur huddled on the couch holding horror movie marathons after class and more time in the senior lounge, pretending to study while sneaking glances at Mateo like he might vanish entirely if she looked away for too long. On a scale from irritating to highly anticipated, she'd say his presence had, at some point, veered past *tolerable* and into the *enjoyable* zone.

"How do you feel the first few weeks of school have gone?" Ives asked as she sank into the hardback chair on the other side of her desk.

Este knew exactly which drawer held the spire key. It would

take ten, maybe fifteen, seconds for Mateo to reach in, grab the key, and stuff it inside Este's backpack. Her mission was to make sure Ives didn't notice.

She forced a smile. "Things are going well, I think."

"I have been adequately impressed with your performance as an archival assistant," Ives said with a sip of her tea. Which was probably the closest thing to a compliment that had ever come out of Ives's mouth.

"Thank you?" She'd meant to say it definitively, but the end of her inflection curled up in a question mark.

"Your grades, however." Ives tapped her nails against the ceramic mug in a way that made Este's entire body tense. "I admit that I have some concerns."

The drawer jiggled. Este coughed into her elbow trying to cover up the sound.

Mateo just needed to open it up, slip a hand in, and grab the key—

The drawer didn't open. Locked.

This was not part of the plan.

Este swallowed thickly. "Concerns. Like, what?"

"Mr. Donohue spoke to me after grading your first essay." Ives slid Este's stapled essay across the desk, and there was a circled red C-plus in the top-right corner.

Not bad for a girl who graduated from the Homeschool of Hard Knocks to attend an elite college preparatory academy, but the disdain on Ives's face told Este now was not the time to state that particular case.

"I trust you remember our agreement," Ives said.

Este pressed her palms into the knees of her jeans to steady herself. "Return *The Book of Fades* in one piece."

Another sip of Earl Grey. "And your grades need to stay above a 3.5 GPA. All archival assistants must be eligible for the dean's list for academic honors. Dr. Kirk has expressed concerns about your history scores, and I've spoken to Ms. Eberly in advance of your poetry exam because . . . Well, Este, like I said. I'm concerned."

Este's focus wasn't on Ives anymore, though. Behind her, Mateo must have been searching for something to open the drawer with because a few books floated as if being picked up one by one and piled into his arms. As if Ives would hide the key under a book the way her parents used to keep the spare under the porch mat. As Mateo's stack grew precariously high, Este had to intervene before he toppled over.

She took a quick inventory of everything on top of Ives's desk. A heap of books in various states of repair. A recently lit candle with lukewarm wax drips still clinging to the sides. A staple gun—tempting. Under a stack of papers stamped with the school letterhead, the gold handle of a letter opener caught her eye.

"As for finding the book," Ives said, "have you made any progress?"

Este blinked like she was trying to solve a complicated equation. Sure, she could have told Ives exactly where the book was if she wanted to. End her deal with Mateo right now and be done with him and the ghosts for good. Three weeks ago, she wouldn't have hesitated to serve his head to the head librarian on a silver platter, but now she busied herself with a suspiciously long drink of coffee. One gulp, two, three. It burned the whole way down.

The pile of floating books froze, and Este could envision Mateo's reaction even while he was invisible—on the surface, he'd look calm, almost amused, but she knew how his shoulders went rigid, Atlas beneath the weight of the world.

Ives's eyebrows rose impatiently.

"Some," Este decided on. "My roommate is helping."

That was apparently enough for Este to outrun the gallows at least for a while longer because Ives nodded, her tongue tucked into her cheek. "And your shifts? How do you like being an archival assistant?"

Aside from the whole being-haunted montage?

"It's great," Este said, forcing a grin far too wide.

"Your father was an archival assistant. Did you know that?"

"I didn't," Este said, but pride ballooned in her like she was a kids' birthday party clown with full authority over a helium canister. Every day, she discovered new secrets to his past.

"Before, of course, he left Radcliffe permanently," Ives said, taking an imaginary pin to Este's metaphorical balloon. "It's always curious to see how history repeats itself. I don't suppose that boy Mateo has caused any more trouble for you, has he?"

More than you know.

Just over her shoulder, Mateo balanced ten, fifteen, twenty books—and then, before Este could say, *Nope! No trouble at all*, he wasn't balancing any of them anymore. Books crashed to the ground, toppling over each other and knocking nearby stacks of books down like dominoes.

Ives whipped around. "What on Earth?"

When she crouched to pick up the books, they skittered across the floor away from her. As if someone with a penchant for getting Este in trouble might have kicked them. She reached for another one, and it went sailing the other way. Not an accident. A distraction.

"Here, let me help," Este said.

While Ives's back was turned, Este reached for the letter opener. She gathered a few of the spilled books for the sake of posterity, but as soon as she placed them on the desk, she shimmied the letter opener into the drawer's brass keyhole. It wasn't the most elegant solution, but the pins wiggled and budged inside the lock, each one bringing her closer to the spire key, and Ives was too busy muttering about botched repairing techniques to notice.

Plus, the more books she picked up, the more Mateo knocked over. The office was crammed full of texts in various states of repair—some rubber banded, some annotated with strips of paper where they needed to be glued or taped, some pressed between boards to flatten. An endless supply of ammunition.

The letter opener jammed. Este pushed and tugged, but it wouldn't go out or in. Even if Ives hadn't seen Mateo's floating books in her periphery, there was no way she wouldn't notice the rogue letter-opener-turned-crowbar situation Este had going on.

Mateo must have sensed the panic that radiated off her in tidal waves because she felt a familiar cool touch against her shoulder, gone as quickly as it came, but soft and reassuring.

The lights flickered. Slowly at first, and then full-on Coachella strobe lights. If Ives hadn't been up to her knees in half-repaired books, she might have noticed the light switch flipping on and off, but instead she tossed her hands into the air, exasperated.

"The quirks of a hundred-year-old building," she said as she marched to the switch to investigate it herself.

Every time the lights dimmed, Este jerked the letter opener, begging the drawer to budge, and when they surged back on, she straightened a stack of books. Finally, the lock gave.

Este stripped the spire key from the drawer, but as she knocked it shut with her hip, the head librarian's eyes were on her in an instant like she'd heard code-red alarm bells blaring.

"What are you doing?" Ives snapped.

Startled, the key fell from Este's fingers and clattered against the floorboards.

Este lurched for it, and instead of the key, her hands found a long-quilled pen along the floorboards. *Thank you, Mateo.* She popped back up with the quill in hand. "I wanted to jot down some notes about book repair if that's okay. You were saying something about alkaline buffers?"

Stacking books back into piles, Ives prattled on about the importance of finding the right pH balance for paper, and the spire key skimmed toward the door, hovering over the floorboards without a sound. Was Mateo . . . army crawling? Este bit the inside of her cheek to keep a straight face.

"And that's why we wear gloves," Ives said. She lifted the last of the books onto her desk and blew a strand of ink-black hair away from her face, trying and failing to regain her usual composure. "Any other questions?"

In the stack, a book called *Poetry Scansion for Beginners* snagged Este's attention—she recognized it from her dad's circulation history, and, if she was being honest, Ives had made a few good points about her upcoming poetry exam.

"What are all these?" Este asked, plucking it from the pile.

"I've been restoring a few texts of interest," Ives said as another pile toppled. "Perhaps this is a project I can have your assistance with."

"Can I borrow this one?" Este asked.

"Yes, fine," Ives said, flustered. "Make sure you scan it out, and I'll see you next week for our meeting."

Este walked out of Ives's office like she had an electric-shock collar on, just waiting for the zap. She scrunched up her face in anticipation for the moment Ives realized what was missing, to be reprimanded. It didn't come. Ives closed the office door behind her with a *click*.

In the stacks, Mateo manifested with a sly smile and the spire key in his hands. He dropped it into her palm. "Not too shabby, Logano."

"I couldn't have done it without you," she said, craning her neck to meet his eyes. "Meet me at the spire door at midnight?"

Her heart skipped a traitorous beat when he said, "You've got yourself a date."

FIFTEEN

The spire looked almost exactly how Este left it: moon-steeped and mesmerizing. A deeply floral scent swirled through the air as purple blossoms fanned their petals and stretched toward the bloated full moon.

Mateo was practically glued to Este's side. He kept peering down at her, concern etched into the lines of his face, and Este made a pointed effort not to look back at him as he said, "Drinking nectar from a poisonous plant, Logano? Not exactly scholastic research."

"Mr. Donohue would beg to differ." They waded through the shelves to an east-facing window. A bouquet of blossoms clustered at the sill. "According to him, translation inherently changes the contextual meaning of writing. This is my chance to read the words just like my dad did. And, plus, maybe it's not even *that* poisonous."

"It is," Aoife chimed from her other side. The rest of the

ghosts insisted that they joined Este and Mateo for the spire escapade since their lives literally depended on it, which meant Aoife had appointed herself as director of poison control. She dipped into her knapsack and retrieved the slim, blue text of herbal remedies that Este's dad had checked out. Her finger trailed along the ink as she read. "Rivean ivy is known to cause mild to moderate irritation when coming in contact with skin."

Este raised her eyebrows. *See? Not so bad.*

Aoife turned the page. "It says that the nectar, when ingested, is a virulent poison capable of causing fatigue, increased heart rate, hallucinations, delirium."

"So," Este tried, "like a hangover?"

Aoife snapped the book closed. "And even death."

Okay, she got the point. Her stomach lurched like when she'd finished a bowl of bad clams on Cape May, and she pinched her lips together, biting back the taste of bile. "I guess that's to be expected. Trying to read the language of the dead, and all that."

Aoife faded back toward the others, admonishing Daveed about not disrupting the archives, and Mateo pivoted toward Este. The moon cast his features in a dewy light.

"You don't have to do this." Mateo's voice was cautious, a whisper against the snowbanks to keep from instigating an avalanche.

"I need to know what he saw." Este's resolved hardened as she said it. She couldn't speak the whole truth—that some

172

buried part of her hoped maybe there was something written that would only make sense to her, that she was the only one who could piece together her father's clues. That drinking the nectar would bring her closer to him.

Hopefully in the metaphorical, emotional way and not the physically unliving way.

"What if it's a mistake we can't undo?" Did Mateo's voice crack? He brushed a hand across the skin of his neck, shaking his head.

A smirk crawled up Este's lips. "Are you worried about me?"

Since she couldn't reach out and touch him, to plant a hand on his rising shoulders or smooth her thumb over his cheek, she instead clutched the spire key. Mateo glanced toward its intricate carving, the sharp teeth.

"You're extraordinarily troublesome," he said with a smile that made her heart thud twice as hard.

She had to turn away before she said something she regretted. Like how there was a smaller voice in her head—an intrusive thing she hadn't asked for—whispering that if the nectar thinned the veil between worlds enough to let her read the language of the dead, it might also bring her closer to Mateo. Close enough to hold his hands or loop one of his curls around her finger.

Este took a vine between her fingers, and sticky sap coated her skin, oozing from the ivy's pores as she plucked the blooms off one by one. But when she separated bud from vine, the petals withered into useless brown ribbons.

"You can't pick them?" she asked.

Mateo stepped forward. He rested his palm on the shelf next to Este's head, leaning toward her. "Este, maybe we should—"

There was a bouquet of vibrant purple by his leather shoes, and she lunged right through Mateo's body to reach them.

Mateo shook out his bones. "It's like I'm invisible."

As Este crouched down, she dug Ives's letter opener from her back pocket. She'd swiped it from her desk this afternoon so that they could return the key again once they were finished with it. Using the sharp end of the gold tool, Este sliced through the greenery and uprooted the cluster, vine and all.

She and Mateo met the others in the middle of the spire where the bookcases created a space wide enough for a desk with a high-backed chair. Este cradled the flowers in her palm. Eight petite blossoms with their mouths open, a well of ambrosia in the middle. "Someone brought the antidote, right?"

Luca laughed, a sound like cut glass. "This is preposterous. Let us read the book to you."

"She's right. You could die," Daveed said.

Este scoffed. "Says the literal ghost."

"I'm with them." Aoife moved a piece of hair behind her ear so that Este had to look into the hardened steel of both gray eyes. For emphasis, no doubt. She gripped the pendant at her neck like a crystalline safeguard. "The energy is all wrong in there."

"The antidote?" Este asked again.

Daveed shrugged, tapping an envelope in the side pocket of his JanSport. "I had to sneak into the cafeteria to get it all. Even with it, I still think this is a terrible idea."

Este shifted toward Mateo. She raised her eyebrows as if to say, *Back me up, Radcliffe.* If he went along with it, they all would. It was evident in the way their feet and shoulders angled toward him—the sun to their summer blooms.

He wrung his hands out. "We don't know how long the effects last or how quickly it'll work."

If she tried a drop of nectar now, she'd still have plenty more chances.

"We shouldn't even be up here," Aoife said sternly. The voice of reason. "At least wait until you're in a controlled environment."

But the blossoms' honeyed scent pulled Este in. If she didn't try it now, all her bravado would evaporate. Mateo must have read it in her eyes because he sighed and said, "Hand her the book."

Aoife huffed as she pried *The Book of Fades* from her backpack but made a point to hold on to it for the time being. Like raising a glass for a champagne toast the way people did at weddings in the movies, Este lifted a bloom in front of her. "To my father."

And the ghosts echoed, "To Dean."

Este pinched the dark purple nodule at the center of the

flower. As she extracted it, a globe of golden nectar gathered at the end of the stem.

It happened all at once. Heat flared on Este's tongue where the sap dripped. Citrus and rich vanilla, a taste unlike anything she'd ever had, spread through her mouth and sent static through her limbs. A flush climbed her neck, her cheeks. The tips of her fingers tingled.

"Do you feel anything?" Luca asked, her round eyes growing wider somehow.

Aoife's nose was back in her herb book. "Temperature rising? Heart racing? Impaired vision?"

"D," Este said, the word trailing from her lips too slowly. A dreamy haze edged her vision, casting everything in an ethereal glow. "All of the above."

She put her hands to her mouth, feeling the stretched skin of swollen lips, and her eyes sank half-lidded. When she looked at Mateo, he was wreathed in opalescent light despite the dense clouds outside. An ember glowing in the night. Her torchlight out of the darkness.

"Her pupils are dilated," Aoife said, scribbling something. Her voice was a message in a bottle, floating away.

Mateo was the only clear thing in a world of star-webbed wonder. If she focused on the architecture of him—his pointed arch brows, his starched white shirt and the barrel vault curve of his shoulders beneath—she could stand steady.

Luca asked, "Este, can you check your pulse?"

Este dutifully put two fingers on her wrist. "One, two, three . . . four . . . eight, ten, twelve, um, seventeen. One hundred."

But her gaze didn't move from Mateo, and his eyes didn't leave hers. He was handsome, so handsome. Was that the ivy talking? No, she definitely thought he was cute. Why try to deny it? Maybe she'd kiss him. She wanted to feel his hands on her. Why did he have to be *soooooo* dead?

Este reached for him, and when she moved her arms, they were weightless. Her hand caught on a bookshelf beside him instead. She blinked once, twice. That wasn't where she meant it to go. A confetti giggle lifted out of her. Sweat clung to her body, burning her up from the inside out.

More. She wanted more. Another drop of ambrosia. Another taste of eternity.

"I think you've had quite enough for one night," Mateo said, handing the ivy blossoms off to Daveed, who tucked them in his backpack. Had she spoken? Her lips were hot, smiling. She couldn't stop laughing. "Why don't you sit down and try to read?"

Este aimed for the desk chair. The bookcases she bounced against kept her upright. "Thank you," she said to them, bowing to their sturdy mahogany.

Her swirling thoughts were interrupted by a *click, click, click* that struck a Pavlovian spear of fear through her heart, even as it trampolined around her chest.

"It's Ives," she breathed, pressing her hands to each side of her head to stop the pounding. "I'm dead I'm dead I'm dead."

"You gotta get her out of here, chief," Daveed said, shaken. "We'll make a distraction."

Mateo nodded in slow motion. Or maybe that was Este's brain working in slow-mo. His mouth was moving, but she couldn't hear him. She couldn't listen past the tide of blood in her ears, like she was wading through her own mind to reach the shores of consciousness. Next to him, the other ghosts vanished one by one until he, alone, stood in the doorway beckoning.

A crash echoed through the stairwell, and Ives's clicking heels stopped. When they resumed, they grew farther and farther away with each resounding step.

"Nice work, Daveed," Mateo whispered.

Este closed the spire door behind her, locking it after a few missed tries, and stumbled down the stairs once Mateo confirmed the coast was clear. Which would have been way easier if she weren't kind of drunk right now.

Out on the fifth floor, the study carrels were empty. Light poured from beneath glass green table lamps, all of it streaking together in one long-exposure blur as Este whipped around corner after corner, following Mateo.

A pantsuit stopped them in their tracks. Ives stood against the balcony railing, her arms crossed and steam practically pouring out of her ears. The look of a woman who knew the spire key was missing. Again. No one was coming or going around the fifth floor without her seeing them. And they had about thirty seconds before she spied them at the base of the spire, guilt written all over their faces.

"If she finds out I stole her key—" The rest of Este's sentence was swallowed up by a hiccup.

"This way," Mateo said, yanking down a copy of *Wuthering Heights*, and it opened a door into a hidden hallway. "Left, down, down, right, up. We'll come back up to the fifth floor closer to the senior lounge, so she won't see us, okay?"

Este had become so used to plunging into dark corridors that she barely stopped to wonder if she'd get a face full of spiderweb. She chanted his directions over and over in her head, and Mateo was back by her side as soon as he clamped the door closed.

"How do you feel?" he asked.

"Great," Este said, holding on to a rickety banister for dear life as they raced down two consecutive stairwells. "No, bad. I don't know. I can't feel my face."

"Daveed has the antidote. You'll be okay." When they reached a fork in the hallway, Mateo nudged open a hatch that they had to crawl to access. "Stay close," she heard him say, but then she'd lost sight of him. The room was so dark Este couldn't see her hand in front of her. Where were they?

In the back of her mind, a song started playing, crackling to life like a needle pressed to vinyl. Este swayed, eyes drifting closed. She hummed the melody, lazy legato notes. She'd heard it before, but where?

"This is my favorite song," she said, a sloppy string of syllables. She spun and spun, hands lifted overhead. Maybe she could reach the stars, dangle off the crescent moon. Instead, she got swept up in a cold front.

When Este pried open her eyes, she didn't see Mateo, but a candlestick lit in the distance and some blessed part of her brain that hadn't been inhibited by the nectar recognized the dimly lit bookshelves as the archives.

"Este, this way!" Mateo called.

Out of the black formed three ghoulish figures.

She rubbed her eyes as if to scrub away the flower's toxins and blot out the Fades, but it didn't work. They were there, not a hallucination but truly there and wrapped in a haze she couldn't shake.

Nausea churned in her stomach. She lurched down the aisle toward Mateo's voice and the light from the candlestick. The Fades' song cut through the ivy's trance, and this time when their chorus echoed, Este understood. They sang for her.

"The dying light with shadowed hands will spin you in eternal dance."

Este might have been drunk off nectar but hearing their clanging stanzas weave into words she could actually understand was enough to rattle some sense through her thick skull. She'd never live it down if she died at the hands of a few velour-clad sorority girls that doubled as supernatural hit men.

As their black fog swept through the bookcases around her, Este's feet pounded against the splintered floors. She had to reach Mateo, but her feet tangled in themselves. Her knees hit the hardwood first, then her hands. Ives's key scattered across the floor, ricocheting against the bookcases.

Este begged her legs to stand up. Her knees wobbled as she trudged forward, but the black crept closer, too.

"What blooms tonight, a secret sworn, and you are ours until the morn."

The Fades lunged, zagging through the archives. They split up, each disappearing behind different bookcases. Este dragged herself toward the door, case by case, until suddenly, Mateo was next to her, flickering in the candlelight. He held *The Book of Fades* under her nose.

He was saying something, but his face swam in and out of focus. His eyes were ocean deep and wide with panic as the Fades' cold crept closer and closer.

"Este," he pleaded, "grab on to the book and don't let go." Her fingers found the leather binding, and she latched on. With the text clutched between her hands, Mateo dragged the book upward and Este along with it. "Just because I can't touch you doesn't mean I can't help you."

As they ran, cold lashed at Este's ankles, frostbite licking at her skin. An ink-black tendril blew out the candelabra Mateo clutched; their only source of light reduced to smoke.

Beads of sweat dabbed at her forehead despite the plummet in temperature.

Mateo jerked right, and Este's hand slid off the book. Her hesitation was enough. The Fades' frontwoman pounced with her hands outstretched, and even through the haze of the ivy, Este felt a sharp, hot pain under her ribs as those horrible, hot pink acrylic nails clawed down her side. She collapsed, and her breath came in jagged heaves, scraping for air beneath a corpse-cold tide of darkness.

Miles away, Este heard Mateo yell. Her nails dug into the floor, and she pulled herself upright, staggering down the aisle, guided by touch alone. One hand pressed to her side and the other felt along the bookshelves. Mateo must have opened the archives' door because the dim light from the third floor suddenly pooled in front of her. Almost there. Almost there.

As soon as Este barreled out of the archives, wisps of black reached and recoiled. They curled back into the darkness, and Mateo slammed the door shut.

Acid flared where the Fade's hand struck, and Este gulped down air, but it wasn't enough. She burned from the inside out. As everything faded to black, she could still hear the Fades singing, "*You are ours.*"

SIXTEEN

❧

Este woke up with a hangover from hell. Literally.

Her head throbbed and lips burned. When she pulled her eyelids open, they scraped against her dry eyes. Every corner of her body ached. Crashing her mom's Atlantic blue Outback against a tree in the Catskills while she was learning to drive had done less damage.

A few candles had been lit in the senior lounge, but the wall sconces were blessedly extinguished. Her hatching migraine couldn't have handled the extra light. Someone had put the surviving rivean ivy blossoms in a glass vase, and their heady perfume swept through the room.

Este's fingers pressed into the smooth fabric of the velvet chaise, sitting upward despite the protests of every swollen joint. The antidote envelope sat on the table next to her, emptied. Was that why her mouth tasted like month-old salami?

The door creaked open. Mateo nudged through, arms

cradling a tower of bits and bobs like he'd accidentally walked into a Target without a list.

When he lifted his eyes, he flinched at the sight of her. She winced as everything he'd carried crashed to the floor.

"Criminy, Este," he said as he scooped up boxes of bandages and ointment bottles and a stray thermometer that scattered all the way to the fireplace. "Give a man a warning before you rise from the dead."

"How did I get here?" Este asked, smearing her hands over her tired eyes.

Mateo toed a wrinkled Persian carpet heaped on the floor. "Once I got the rug underneath you, dragging you down the hallway was easy enough. Had to get Daveed's help to get you up the stairs, though."

Este cringed. She could picture her body splayed in different directions, mouth sagging open and drooling, as Mateo slid her around the Lilith. Not exactly the most flattering image.

"What's all that stuff for?" she asked as he shuffled across the room. His balancing act almost crashed and burned a few extra times before making it to the base of the chaise.

"Do you remember anything?" Eyes wide, Mateo's line of vision drooped to Este's waist, and hers followed.

Memories waded through a black tide. The ivy nectar, the heat against her cheeks, her eyes the size of moons when she looked at Mateo. *Oh, god.* She made such a fool of herself. She winced at the thought, and her side stitched with pain.

184

Bile climbed up her throat. This wasn't just the worst hangover ever. Her cable-knit cream sweater had been shredded. Crusted rust-colored stains coated the threads. She pinched her eyes closed and reopened them in case the sight was a hallucination from remnant toxins clinging to her bloodstream, but the mess stayed. Whatever adrenaline surged through her veins was enough to mask the immediate pain, but when she actually had to feel those claw marks, it wasn't going to be pretty.

The acrid taste clung to her tongue as she said, "The Fades."

"Got her hands on you pretty good." Mateo dropped his stack of supplies next to her. Suddenly, the pile of gauze made a lot more sense.

The Fade's face, her rotten breath, her bone-bare hands. Este couldn't have done anything to escape. Through the murkiness of her memory, she felt the searing touch pierce her skin, and then nothing at all. The Fades had vanished.

"What stopped them?" she asked.

"I don't know," he said, like it killed him to admit.

The sound of the Fades' singing pounded through Este's head. Each harmony threatened to split her skull wide open. "Please tell me you brought Tylenol."

"Sorry," Mateo said. "Back in my day, all we had was morphine." It only took one sharp look for him to throw his hands up in surrender. "Yes, Este, I brought normal, run-of-the-mill acetaminophen. No leeches, no arsenic. I think you've had enough strange concoctions this evening."

A blush swept over Este's cheeks. Or maybe that was a fever blooming from remnants of rivean sap on her tongue or the infection surely sprouting at her waistline.

"I could understand them," she said, digging her fingers into the threads of the chaise. "The Fades. I knew what they were saying. The nectar worked, Mateo. It actually worked."

"How do you feel now?" His eyebrows tugged together.

"Horribly sober."

"Good to know the antidote works." The chaise gave as Mateo sank into its cushion. "We need to get you cleaned up. You've lost a lot of blood."

"Why don't I go to the health center where there are actual nurses who know what they're doing?"

"Do you want to tell them you were attacked by an ancient, bloodthirsty spirit who tried to kill you?" he asked, drenching a cotton pad with hydrogen peroxide. "Or should I?"

He dropped the pad into her hand, and the solution bubbled against the grime on her fingertips. Maybe he was right. She wasn't even sure if she could walk all the way to the medical building in this condition—let alone resign herself to getting poked and prodded when she tried to explain the truth.

Mateo's voice was feather soft, even shy, as he said, "I'm sorry I won't be able to help more. Just follow my instructions, okay?"

She nodded. Anything to make the pain subside.

He let loose a small cough. "You're, um, going to need to take off your shirt."

Oh. Right. Este fumbled with the hem of her sweater. Her heart raced as she peeled the fabric over her head—half from the frantic way it tried to keep her alive, and half from Mateo's proximity. At the bottom of her vision where her skin met the waistband of her denim jeans, an ugly maroon smudge stained her skin, sticky and still warm.

"I look like I got in a street fight with Freddy Krueger." It was probably the least sexy thing she could say half-naked. "I really don't want to do this."

"Well, I really don't want you to die either." His words were clipped, like he'd bridled himself, afraid of saying the wrong thing.

When she peeked at him, Mateo stared ahead, rod-straight with his fingers digging into the knees of his wool pants. His eyes were trained on the bookcases, modest.

How annoyingly Victorian.

"You're allowed to look at me," she said, mouse quiet.

After a long, winding moment, he snuck a glance over his shoulder. Este pretended she didn't notice the way his eyes drifted down the curve of her bare shoulder and shot right back up to her face. "You need to clean the wound with the peroxide soon before the infection spreads," he said. "It'll probably—"

Este wailed as the cotton skimmed her skin.

"—burn slightly."

She huffed, breathless until the pain subsided. "Thank you for that astute observation."

"Are you okay?" he asked, turning to face her again. Concern and something deeper laced his voice.

She grunted in response and tried the cotton pad again, this time gritting her teeth as the peroxide washed away the blood and dust. The Fade's fingertips carved four gnarled stripes into the soft dip on her waist, halfway to her belly button. The pulped flesh stung with each swipe of medicine.

"What next?" she dared to ask, already fearing the answer.

Mateo slid a roll of beige bandages across the chaise toward her. "I'm so relieved you're alive. You—" Este turned as he leaned his nose toward the ceiling rafters and swallowed, his Adam's apple bobbing. Trying so hard to look anywhere but at her. "You shouldn't be. The Fades don't usually leave leftovers."

A quiet breath wove through the room, stitching them closer together in a way words couldn't. She'd never expected death's gruesome stare to wear sparkly pink eye shadow, but it did. She could have died. Este should've been crying jagged sobs that tore her open from the inside, but the tears didn't come. Even when hot spikes radiated from the gorged flesh in her side, carved by the hand of death herself, Este only clenched her jaw.

It would sink in later, she was sure. But for now, she had adrenaline in her veins, ivy residue coating her tongue, and a ghost at her side who smelled like New England forests and candle smoke and crisp, yellow pages—like home, if she had one.

As if hearing her thoughts, Mateo dragged his eyes away from the ceiling and looked at her again, eyes round as reflecting pools, revealing all the things that scared her most. He followed the curve of her hips to the dip of her waist and upward until her face warmed beneath his gaze. "For a moment, I thought I'd surely lost you. It's a vulnerable thing to have, a body."

Este didn't dare blink, afraid that if she closed her eyes for even a moment, he'd disappear like smoke on the wind. She nudged the roll of bandages back toward him. There was enough electricity humming through her bones to light up New York City.

"Could you hold this while I wrap?" she asked finally.

Mateo spooled out yards of elastic bandaging, and Este wound it around her abdomen, tight enough to stop the bleeding. The wounds were deep and carrying books up and down the Lilith's stairs was sure to be a bitch for the next few weeks, but she probably didn't need stitches.

Este twisted, letting out a small groan when her waist protested. She needed to see him, needed to watch his brows knit together or his mouth quiver with a treasonous smile, his face an atlas to his thoughts as she whispered, "If they hadn't left, I guess I would've spent eternity here. It doesn't seem so bad."

Mateo shook his head. "You don't want that. You don't want to be like me."

The hazy memory of her nectarine daydreams begged to differ. She wanted to feel the calluses on his hands, etched from years climbing library ladders, wanted them to smooth over the broad stroke of her thighs. The ivy's lingering heat burned a pit at her navel.

"I bet I'd have time to read every book in the Lilith," she said, clipping the bandage in place. "I'd read every page in this place. I could spend year after year finding new favorite stories."

"Year after year, after year, after year . . ." Mateo's shoulders sagged. "I'm tired of waiting. I want to know what it's like to grow old, to see the world. Gray hair? The things I'd do to see myself with gray hair."

Este stifled a laugh that cinched her side with pain. "You *want* that?"

"A life? To die and know that I'd lived as much as I could. Yes." Mateo's face softened, and he let out a sighing laugh. "You know, I used to coat my hair in dust and stand in front of the mirror. Just to see what I might've looked like if I'd been given the chance."

The bandages compressed Este's waist, making her lungs feel too shallow. It was almost impossible to imagine him anywhere but here. He belonged the way the cornices and the crown molding did, like he'd been built into the structure of the library, a load-bearing wall.

"I used to think I had everything I ever needed." His laugh

was a lopsided sound—half-humored, half-hurt. "I've had a lot of time to learn how wrong I was."

Sitting next to Mateo felt like looking at a Renaissance fresco. There was something ancient underneath his tough shell, something strong enough to last the ages. From a distance, she could only see the shape of him—hard lines and polished edges, faded over time—but she couldn't help but think that if she let herself get close enough, she would be able to see all his gentle shading.

Her red-stained fingers inched toward his on the swells of blue velvet but stopped shy of his skin. Because of course they did.

Este's chin sank to her chest. She curled her fingers away from Mateo's and slipped her sweater back over her shoulders. "All I've ever wanted to do was make my dad proud, to come to Radcliffe Prep like he did. He always said we could find all the answers we needed in a library." She couldn't help it—a jaded laugh seeped out of her. "We've searched this place up and down, and all I've got to show for it are more questions, a gash on my side the size of Kentucky, and a poetry exam I'm not ready to take."

Mateo touched the tip of the ointment bottle to her chin so that she had no choice but to look up at him. "We'll figure it out. I'm certain Dean would be proud of you for trying, and I can help you study. I've had nothing better to do than audit classes for the last century."

Este could imagine him poring over a typewriter, pounding out papers for classes he wouldn't even get graded on. Perhaps he'd take a few courses and then disappear for a couple years as the professors rotated and students graduated—no one would notice he'd been here all along.

"Thank you," she said softly, picking at the hem of her sweater. In a different life, maybe they could have had a normal college experience together. His arm could have wrapped around her as they fanned through pages of Byron and Browning. Her frame might have fit into the crooks of his body as they trailed their fingers along blank meter pages, figuring out all his stressed and unstressed syllables, the scansion of being known. "But none of it even matters if I can't find those pages. I'm not sure what's worse: the Fades or facing the wrath of Ives if she finds out I broke into the spire again."

It wasn't only her academic destiny in jeopardy anymore. Mateo's resurrection was riding on the line. The ghosts were relying on her. It was all too much—Este was going to let everyone down.

"Your mother's still around, right? Maybe she knows something we don't."

"Barely." She could try to call her back, but she didn't even know what time zone her mom was in these days. Este had ignored every voice mail, silenced all her calls. Sometimes talking to the only person who understood hurt too much. "Who knows where she is? Losing my dad made her lose herself, too. Love just makes things messy, and then it's over. And it's always over eventually, whether you're ready or not."

Mateo looked at her. Really looked at her—slowly blinking, forehead creased, lips split with words he seemingly couldn't decide if he actually wanted to say. Finally, he pinched the bridge of his nose between his fingers and shrugged. "No, I don't believe that, even a little bit."

"You don't?" If anyone was going to be disenchanted by the impermanence of love, Mateo would've been Este's first guess.

He shook his head, eyes scanning the senior lounge's hardback books. "When you love someone, it's like building a library and filling the shelves. It doesn't matter how many years it's been since Austen wrote *Emma* or Fitzgerald wrote *This Side of Paradise.* We can still pull them from the bookcases and dive back into the words, the same as the day they were written. All the years and memories are still right here, cataloged inside us."

Fizzy warmth spread through Este's body, and this time, she was certain it wasn't the ivy. Maybe Mateo was right—she could still remember her dad chasing her into the waves of the Pacific, letting her choose the CD on their drive back through the redwoods, laughing at the kitchen table. If she closed her eyes, she could map the constellations they traced on summer nights camping or make out his scribbled penmanship on birthday cards she pretended to read so that she could blow out the cake candles.

"You're different than I expected," she said to Mateo. The tremble in her voice couldn't be disguised. He was a tether, a trail of crumbs to lead her home. She hadn't realized how long she'd been lost.

He grinned. "Did you want me to be a monster?"

"I did." All Este could hear was the rhythmic echo pounding inside her chest. *I did. I did. I did.* Making him out to be some devilish poltergeist masked the horror of the truth: that he was just a boy, carved out from his place in the world.

Mateo reached toward her, as if he were going to place a strand of hair behind her ear. Este closed her eyes. She didn't want to see his hand turn silvery, cool, and translucent as it washed through her. Could it be enough if all they ever had was almost—almost touches, almost together, almost real?

Warm fingertips grazed Este's skin, and her whole body stilled. Mateo looped a piece of hair around her ear, and his fingertips trailed down the column of her neck, his thumb brushing circles against her cheek. Hesitant. Delicate.

She lurched upward and immediately regretted it. Her head spun with dizzy stars, and her side screeched with pain. She caught herself with one hand on the sofa, and when the black in her vision subsided, Mateo paced toward her.

"Este, dear?"

Panic seized her throat and tears pricked her eyes, her steely resolve broken by the simple brush of fingers. Her words came out strangled, a sound she didn't recognize. "What just happened?"

"I don't know."

"*You don't know?*"

A shaky smile worked its way onto his lips. "I'm a little out of my element here, too."

Este sucked down a deep breath in a feeble attempt to steady the pace of her heart and the shake in her hands, but it didn't work. She backed away from Mateo with every step he took closer.

A horrifying encounter with the Fades was one thing—the makings of nightmares undone by years of therapy down the line if she was lucky. But the touch of Mateo's fingers against her cheek sent electrifying telegram signals to every nerve of her body.

It was worse because she wanted it.

This was supposed to be impossible. He was supposed to be something she could never have—something she could never lose. But Mateo's fingerprints had trailed down her cheek, and she felt them, every groove, every callus. She could learn the shape of his fingers and the way they fit between hers.

No, she shouldn't think like that. Love only ever ended up in broken halves. One buried, one left behind.

Este backed into the lounge's green door, and Mateo stood toe to toe with her. She lifted her chin and searched his wide eyes for a hint of explanation, as if she could read those blue tides for signs of storms on the horizon.

"The ivy," she said, mostly to herself, if she was being honest. Her head was filled with gunpowder and glitter, a hundred bottle rockets shooting off without warning. "It's the nectar in my system. Like how I could understand the Fades."

Mateo lifted his hand palm up. A peace offering. "Maybe it was a fluke. Perhaps I could try again."

Este inhaled, nodded. She shouldn't have, but she whispered, "Do you want to?"

"Very much so," he said, voice gravelly.

Mateo pressed his finger to her chin, thumb running a stripe along her jaw. The touch was careful, cautious, but real, so real. Este cinched her eyes closed, trying to unravel the knotted thing in her stomach, a tangle of fear and desire.

This couldn't end well. This couldn't *possibly* end well. But with one of Mateo's hands tilting her chin up and the other snaking around the safe side of her waist, Este wished she was foolish enough to believe it could.

Instead, she reached behind herself, feeling for the door-knob. She peeled into the hallway, squinting in the blinding light, and pretended she didn't notice a flash of hurt dash across Mateo's face as she ducked around the corner.

"Sorry," she said over her shoulder, breathless from the pain in her side and something else. "I just—I have to go."

The senior lounge faded away behind her as Este drifted through the stacks, the ghost of his touch still warm on her skin. He was just another thing that wouldn't last.

SEVENTEEN

Given the circumstances, the last thing Este wanted to do was go to a party.

"Dr. Kirk said we'll get extra credit if we go," Posy said as she paced around Este's room, picking up scraps of fabric and dropping them back down when she decided they weren't fashionable enough. "And it's not a *party*, it's an interactive trivia night sponsored by the history club."

"Where there will be music and costumes and the need for small talk," Este said. "Sounds like a party to me."

Guilt thrummed along Este's bones. In a perfect world (you know, one where she wasn't actively being haunted), she wouldn't have bailed on trivia night. She'd have willingly dressed up in whatever goofy ensemble costume Posy chose and sipped cider and gotten ten bonus points for attending. But in real life? Her waist ached beneath its fresh bandages, and the last thing she wanted to do was wipe on a smile and parade around the Lilith as if she hadn't seen what lurked in the shadows.

Posy had no idea. She was wasting her time digging through the closet for an outfit Este wouldn't wear. "Please, please, *please* come with us. It'll be so much fun. The Paranormal Investigators are all dressing up as the school's ghosts."

Este's eyes widened. "You're what?"

"Yeah, like, I'm going as Aoife. I found the perfect necklace at a vintage shop in town. I wish you could've come with us, by the way." She clawed through Este's drawers, tossing bras and socks over her shoulders. A B-cup landed on Este's head, and she shrugged it off with a scowl. "Arthur's dressing up as Luca. Bryony's coming too—did you two ever meet? Her costume is going to be amazing. And, there's that ghost from the thirties named Henry, so that's who Shep's going as."

"Tell me you're kidding," Este said. She even laughed because how could it be anything besides a joke, but Posy's set jaw didn't flinch. "You shouldn't be trying to sniff out the ghosts. You don't know what you'll find or how dangerous it could be."

"Yeah, but . . . that's the whole point of being Paranormal Investigators." Posy donned a confused smile. "And what about Mateo? Don't you want to find him? I'm still convinced he's your thief, you know."

A knife twisted in Este's gut. She'd definitely been avoiding him—but in her defense, she'd been avoiding basically everybody. The pages were still missing, her dad's clues had led them to dead end after dead end, and every time she approached the senior lounge's door, she'd turned around. What could she say to Mateo? *Forget the demented a cappella group—the scariest part about all this is how much I miss you when you're not around.*

"Although, if you wanted to, maybe you could—"

"I'm not going, Posy."

Posy stopped moving. One of Este's sweatshirts fell from her fingers. "Seriously?"

"Seriously."

The bleeding from the Fade's touch may have finally clotted, but the radiating pain still spread like dandelion seeds floating through her body. She'd felt a pang in her shoulder, a throbbing in her knee, and a pinch in her head. They'd always subsided as quickly as they came, but her nerves had been a wreck, too. Every motion in her periphery looked like the decaying flesh of a Fade, even in broad daylight.

She kept telling herself that if the pain got worse, she'd tell Posy everything—the ivy nectar, the Fade attack, how she was right and Mateo Radcliffe was her thief, and how she couldn't forget the way his hands felt on her skin. That's what roommates were supposed to do, right? Trust each other? But now, she wasn't sure if Posy would understand or if she'd simply add Este's experience to her list of paranormal encounters without ever taking two seconds to consider the kind of danger she'd be in if she knew the truth. And if she realized that Este had been lying to her this whole time? She'd leave, and Este would be alone again.

Her roommate whined, "You only get two years at Radcliffe, and Ives is just going to trap you in those archives? Like you're a prisoner? Like you're a work mule?"

"Like I'm trying not to get expelled?" Este countered.

"You're a babe who deserves to go to a party."

"So, you admit that it's a party?"

With a groan, her roommate closed the door behind her on the way out, throwing one more pleading glance over her shoulder before giving up, and Este circled her neck to ease the thousand pounds of built-up pressure. She dragged her textbook off the top of the pile. The pages fell open to the chapter she'd been reading—maybe because she'd fallen asleep with her cheek squished to the print at the circulation desk a few too many nights in a row.

The words fuzzed around the edges as Este tried to focus. Her eyes flitted toward the purple blooms on her windowsill yawning in the filtered moonlight. Este had swiped them from the senior lounge earlier this week when it looked like no one was around, and they'd managed to stay perky with their stems dipped in cool water. She hadn't dared touch her tongue to the nectar again.

With their lilac petals outspread, dousing her room with their dizzying scent, Este couldn't help but think of Mateo. They weren't that different, he and the rivean ivy. Both of them held tight to what few threads of life they had left, and both were bound to land her in an awful lot of trouble if she wasn't careful.

A fluke. That was what Mateo called it when his hand skimmed her cheek. The ivy had made him real to her. She could do it again if she wanted. Those honeyed blooms could draw her deeper into the veil between worlds, close enough to death to touch him, and all she had to do was taste another drop. Was the dry mouth, the hallucinations, the fever that threatened to burn her up worth the trail of his fingertips over her arms, her waist, her thighs?

She shook her head. *Pull it together.* Those flowers were supposed to be used for research purposes only, and she'd wasted the first one in the spire. Refocusing on her textbook, her eyes followed her index finger along the path of letters that, if she could screw her head on straight, were supposed to be teaching her about the invention of the Gutenberg printing press.

A knock on the front door jolted Este upright. Posy's distant footsteps padded to the door, and voices faded through the dorm—she must have ushered the Paranormal Investigators into her room. Este eased back down with a groan, favoring her right side.

When she wrapped herself in her blankets, a frozen gust swirled through her bedroom as if her windows had come unlatched and let in the night. Her door eased open with a mind of its own.

The Fades couldn't be here. She had never seen them outside the Lilith, but Este pinched her eyes closed. *I'm fine, I'm fine, I'm fine.*

She waited to open them until the draft passed, warmth returning to her extremities, but when she did, a figure appeared next to her on the bed.

A scream tore up Este's throat. She clamped a hand over her mouth to stifle it as soon as she recognized the slope of Mateo's broad shoulders, the rebellious curls dripping over his forehead.

Posy burst through the bedroom door, and Mateo blotted out as quickly as he'd appeared.

"Oh, you're still in bed," she said, deflating. She'd fastened a long, black wig to her head and now brushed one of the loose strands from her face. "I thought maybe you decided to come and burned yourself with your curling iron or something."

Este forced a feeble grin. "Sorry, false alarm."

Arthur, Shepherd, and a girl Este vaguely recognized from the Safety and Security office trailed in behind Posy. A bloated silence filled the room, pressing uncomfortably against them. Este shifted her eyes to Bryony and asked, "Who are you dressed as?"

Bryony wore a black shirt with a high-neck collar that looked more like Wednesday Addams than any of the ghosts Este had met. Her sleek brown hair had been piled on top of her head and tied with a thin black ribbon, and she teetered in platform heels that looked like a nightmare for waltzing across

Radcliffe's cobblestone paths.

Bryony straightened her shoulders. "Lilith Radcliffe."

"Cool," Este said, training her voice to be even despite the way Mateo shuffled on the sheets next to her. Could they tell? Besides, she doubted the real Lilith frequented glitter eye shadow and a cat-eye liner sharp enough to kill in the early twentieth century. "Well. I'll be here. You all have fun."

When the Paranormal Investigators drifted back into the living room, Mateo reappeared, and his outline had a hard edge—his presence strong, even this far from the Lilith. It was dark in her room, and the remnants of the ivy nectar in her system must have made him look more real. He flashed an easy grin as he sank deeper into the bedding. "She looked absolutely nothing like my sister."

"You know, most people start with *hello*?"

"Hello, Este, dear." He stretched his arms behind his head. Este hated how comfortable he looked on her bed, but she hated worse how she didn't even really hate it at all.

Seeing him here in her bedroom, surrounded by her stuff— her wrinkled photographs and gas-station postcards, her half-empty coffee mugs, and her bookshelf crowded with fables plucked from trips she and her father took to the secondhand bookstore on Twelfth Street—felt like an optical illusion. He belonged to the Lilith's mahogany shelves like dust illuminated in streaks of crescent moonlight, not hogging half the square footage of her twin-size bed.

Este shook out a breath and tried to loosen the worried knot tucked under her sternum. Mateo had to have a reason for showing up unannounced, and reasons like that weren't usually good ones.

"Why are you—"

"I wanted to make sure—"

They both clamped their mouths shut, waiting. Finally, Este cleared her throat with a flimsy cough. "Sorry, what were you going to say?"

Mateo fiddled with the button on his sleeve. Before she remembered he couldn't blush, Este half expected to see a swath of red wash over his cheeks. If she didn't know better, she would have thought he was nervous. "I wanted to make sure you were doing okay." His eyes dragged to the vulnerable hollow of her waist and back up.

Tonight, the nail marks burned low and slow, only registering in the deepest creases of her mind. If she didn't move the wrong way, she could almost forget they were there until a stray twinge spiked. Frankly, she'd had worse period cramps.

"I'm fine," she said as she thumbed through the pages of her textbook. "Just trying to cram in some extra studying since Ives gave me the night off for the history club party."

Mateo peered around her knees to see the cover of her textbook, and he cocked an eyebrow at the title. "If you need help, I know a little bit about history."

Este groaned, leaning her skull against the headboard. "I

could bomb all my classes and it wouldn't even matter if I'm going to get expelled anyway."

"You're catastrophizing," he said gently.

"It is, by definition, a catastrophe." The words were a block of ice in her throat. She didn't want to believe it could really happen, but midterms were coming up quickly, her grades were still shot, and they were no closer to solving her dad's riddles than before.

"Maybe a distraction, then?" He fumbled in the leather satchel he'd dropped next to the bedframe and retrieved *The Book of Fades*. "There might be something else in here that will help us know where Dean would've left the pages. I thought you might want to try again."

The memory of saccharine ivy coated her tongue. "I think we both saw how well that worked out. That stuff is practically ghost booze."

Mateo angled toward her. "I think you mean *boos*."

Este tucked her laugh down inside, folding it neatly against all the other things left unsaid. She pressed her cheeks between her hands to feel the smile on her face, one that didn't care how stupid it was that she actually liked being around a century-old phantom.

It had been easy enough to convince herself that pushing him away was the smartest thing to do when she'd been able to keep him at a safe distance—far enough away that neither of them would get hurt. But here, next to him, it was impossible to want to be anywhere else. Being near him made her heart beat faster and her head feel light—intoxication by osmosis.

"Wait." Este's head whipped toward the moonlit night outside her window. "Maybe there's another way. Osmosis."

Mateo's forehead wrinkled. "You're going to have to be more specific."

Este peeled herself off the bed and drew a single blossom from the vase on her window ledge. The smell alone was enough to make her knees weak, or maybe that was from the soft underbelly of Mateo's gaze as it followed the swing of her hips back to the sea of duvets. She flipped the book open to a page near the back where the rough hem of her dad's stolen chapter lined the spine.

The pages looked gray today, as if a faint wash of ink had spilled over them. Still, the words were invisible to Este, but if she squinted . . . no, she was just tired, her eyes scratchy.

"What if I don't drink it? Like, a contact high," Este said. She pinched the node in the center of the bloom and extracted the droplet of nectar. Maybe the deadly poison in its DNA could lift the ink through the veil for her to read without her ingesting the nectar. This would either go incredibly well or horribly, destructively wrong. Her eyes darted to Mateo's face. "Do you trust me?"

"Explicitly."

The bead of sap seeped into *The Book of Fades*'s ancient pages.

Mateo stifled a surprised gasp with a fistful of knuckles. "Never mind. I take it back."

"Too late," Este whispered. As the nectar's dark trail crawled toward the edges of the page, spreading across the parchment, she hoped she didn't regret it. Even if she didn't flunk out, Ives would never let her stay an archival assistant if she knew she'd defiled the very book she was supposed to be returning safely.

Este splayed her hand against the damp page, delicately turning it to make sure it hadn't stained through. The nectar stuck to her palm, the crevices between her fingers, the skin under her nails, but at least she wasn't hallucinating. Unfortunately, nothing else was happening either.

Her shoulders drooped. "I thought that maybe it would, I don't know, activate the ink or something." She flipped the cover closed. "It was a long shot anyway."

"No, wait." Mateo's finger caught the page and reopened the book, his face somehow paler than usual. He squinted at the pilled paper, heavy brows knitting themselves closer together. "Something's happening."

The wilting blossom slipped from Este's fingers. "It is?"

He put his face mere millimeters from the parchment. "The ink is fading. I can still read it, but it's faint."

Este skimmed the page from corner to corner, searching for a hint of something beneath the ivy's dew. She counted the seconds in Mississippis, the way she and her mom would measure thunderstorms. When nothing happened by the time she reached ten, she was about ready to drip the remnants of the rivean ambrosia into her mouth out of desperation. But then a pen stroke appeared, thin and weak but there indisputably, and Este clutched the book closer.

Word after word manifested on the parchment like morning glories under dawn's first light. The light gray text was tiny, Latin, and pushed aside by diagram boxes with captions and dictionary entries for words she'd never seen before.

"This is it," she breathed. This was what her dad read in the spire thirty years ago. What might have convinced him to steal the pages and run.

Mateo's fingers found hers, and he coiled their hands together. With the nectar coating her palm, he was solid in her grasp. He brought her finger to his lips, brushing the skin of her knuckle gently there.

A match strike lit in Este's stomach, and the embers wound along a wick, one that would explode with either flames or fireworks, but there was only one way to find out. Heat rushed through her body, even from the smallest touch.

"Life and death together," Mateo read, "create the complete human experience—no one without the other. What, then, perseveres? Like an oath sworn in blood, love ties the living to the dead, for you cannot know darkness without first knowing light."

As Mateo translated each line into English, the words were still unfamiliar to her—love was just another dead language.

He turned page after page in the study of shadows, and his thumb traced lazy circles on her hand in time with the cadence of each sentence. Este's eyes locked on the shape of his lips, the vowels and the hard consonants, like she would find all the answers she ever needed on them.

EIGHTEEN

Working the late-night shift would have been way easier if Este didn't have a real reason to be afraid of the dark. Tonight, she walked through the first floor's stacks with a flashlight in her back pocket and a packet of salt in her front. With each step, Este peered through the shadows for shapes that didn't belong.

The salt was technically Posy's idea. She'd mentioned it at one of their Paranormal Investigators meetings, and Este wasted no time confiscating packets of Morton's from the cafeteria. She was pretty sure it was only supposed to work on ghosts, and she wasn't exactly sure what kind of spiritual monstrosity the Fades were by technical definition. All she knew was that she'd begun seeing them in all her nightmares, and she'd never expected the reality of her own futile mortality to come dressed in Juicy Couture.

Este tiptoed down the main staircase, arms loaded with books she'd found in a return carrel, and nearly body-slammed Posy.

Her roommate shuffled a stack of papers in her arms. Tonight, she wore a navy baseball cap that had been embroidered with a flashlight shining a woven yellow beam—the logo for the Paranormal Investigators. And she was . . . dusty.

"Where did you come from?" Este asked.

"The archives." Posy's chest puffed out with pride even as she swiped a layer of grime from her cheek. She fell into step with Este as they walked back to the circulation desk. "Ives escorted me inside for some research I'm doing with Dr. Kirk."

"How was it?" Which was the simplest way Este knew how to ask, *Was it a near-death experience?*

If Posy tried to smile any wider, her teeth would've fallen out. "Amazing! I found so much good information about the library's history. I totally get why you love it there."

Este loved the archives about as much as she loved dog-eared pages. Not exactly a compliment.

"We missed you last night at trivia," Posy said. "Shep carried the team. I swear, no one else in the state of Vermont knows as much about ancient sports as he does."

"Oh. Yeah. Sorry I couldn't go. I just don't have that much free time with this archival assistant stuff, you know?" Este drawled. She skimmed through a few items to check for damages before scanning them in on the computer with a satisfactory *beep, beep, beep.*

"Any luck finding Mateo? I can't believe you haven't seen

him again." Posy slumped into the spinning chair behind the circulation desk next to Este. "I know he's here somewhere. I feel it in my bones."

"Don't you think he'd keep to himself if he knew he had a whole mob with pitchforks after him?" Este focused on skimming, scanning, and *beeping* through the pile of returned books instead of the way her roommate's eyebrows narrowed, determined.

As if sensing her disdain, four students settled into one of the study tables across the floor. Mateo, Luca, Aoife, and Daveed watched Este, waiting with their hands clutched beneath their chins. Not a subtle bone in their undead bodies.

She turned her back to the ghosts, leaning intently toward Posy who was rhapsodizing about the ethics of the afterlife. The words glazed together, and the next time Este glanced over her shoulder, the ghosts had vanished.

Hallelujah.

But then, movement flared in her periphery, and the ghosts reappeared at a closer desk. Posy was too preoccupied with spinning her chair in lazy circles as she talked, thinking out loud about the sociopolitical implications of her ghost-hunting club, to notice the actual ghosts right in front of her. Este couldn't focus on her drifting sentences, distracted by Daveed apparently beatboxing, his hands cupped against his mouth as he bounced to a rhythm Este couldn't hear from across the atrium. Luca danced in practiced steps, swinging her hips like a flapper. Aoife managed to ignore all of it with a book on her lap, and Mateo . . .

Well, Mateo was staring right at Este.

Her stomach double knotted at the sight of him. With his crescent-moon smile and that dangerous look in his eyes. With his arms crossed against the broad expanse of his chest. With his leather satchel hanging heavy, *The Book of Fades* probably tucked safely inside. If Posy saw even a glimpse of Mateo, she'd recognize him faster than Este could say *Dewey decimal system*.

Mateo ripped a page from a notebook and wadded the paper into a ball. Aiming with one eye closed, he cocked his arm back and launched his makeshift missile toward the circulation desk. It fell short, but only barely.

Este flashed her eyes wide, a warning, and Posy's voice brought her attention back to the circulation desk. "So, what do you think about being treasurer?"

"Sorry, what?"

"Of the Paranormal Investigators. Arthur heard from Julia who heard from Dawson who was in choir with Mr. Liebowitz when he said that college apps are prioritizing students who are active in clubs, so now Bryony wants to be VP so that she can get into Yale—which is totally haunted, by the way. And I could appoint Arthur as marketing director, and Shepherd doesn't need a fancy title because he's obviously going to school on a lacrosse scholarship, so he can be secretary. And then you'll be treasurer. If you want."

"Posy, I—" Este fumbled. "I'm sorry, but I can't right now. I really have to get back to work."

For a fraction of a second, something like hurt dashed across Posy's face, but she shook it off quicker than Este could name it. "Totally, yeah. I've got a million old newspapers to read anyway. Just . . . think about it, okay?"

On her way out of the library, Posy walked past the ghosts who were now playing a raucous game of musical chairs without giving them a second thought. Aoife was losing by the look of it. Este found herself gravitating toward them, right as Luca knocked Daveed out of the only remaining seat, claiming her triumph by crossing her legs and her arms like a queen on a throne.

"You cheat every time," Daveed groaned from where he'd landed on the floor.

Luca beamed, as unapologetic as it could get.

"I want a rematch," he said. "Este can referee."

"I don't think so." Este cocked her head toward the pile of tomes on the circulation desk. "If you're going to hang around all night, why don't you do something useful like help me put all these books back. It's going to take forever, but it's not hard. All you have to do is—"

"We know how to shelve books," Luca said with a tut. "I know it's been a while, but we all used to work here. You knew that, right?"

Este's gaping mouth was proof enough that her critical-thinking skills had shorted out. She clamped her jaw shut and pried it open again. Nothing.

"Dusted shelves," said Aoife.

"Stamped borrowing cards," Luca added.

Daveed said, "Raced the rolling ladders. I've never lost."

"Archival assistants," Este said. "All of you."

"It's true. But things are different these days," Mateo said.

For a moment, Este thought she saw sadness flicker behind the deep tides of Mateo's eyes when he looked at his undead cohort, the afterlife companions he didn't choose and didn't ask for. They'd become friends, and they'd become family. What had that first decade been like before Luca had been sacrificed, ten years trapped alone in a place that no longer felt like home?

But then, like a reversal of a drama mask from Melpomene to Thalia, a grin spread across Mateo's face, the kind that made the skin by his eyes wrinkle. "They don't even use cataloging cards anymore. Let's get to work. Everybody, grab a stack of books on your way."

One by one, the other ghosts blinked out of vision. Invisible Aoife at least remembered to push her chair in. At the circulation desk, piles of books lifted from the mahogany table as if of their own volition. Three hefty anthologies rose into the air with a flourish, circling through the air with an expert juggler's hand—Mateo's, most likely.

They manifested again on the fifth floor, and Este trailed them toward the far edge of the library where two rolling ladders rested at the helm of the atrium. Thank goodness Ives's door was closed and locked this late at night, the light inside extinguished.

"Hop on," Mateo said, setting his books on the ground next to the ladder.

Este scanned through the call numbers on her books. "I don't think I have anything that goes up there. Everything's mostly ground level."

"Not to shelve," Aoife said. She tied her black hair back into a ponytail. "To race."

"Oh, no," Este griped. They had work to do. Was she the only one taking this seriously?

Mateo beamed. "Oh, yes."

"Stop buggin'. It's easy," Daveed said. He stretched his arms over his head, rocking from one side to another. "If you're on the winning team."

Mateo pointed upward where the rolling ladders attached to the frame. "The tracks go all the way around the floor, one on the north side and one on the south like parentheses. You and Luca get on, we push, and the first one around the atrium wins."

The heap of books in Este's arms suddenly felt heavier. "There are a million other things we should be doing right now. What happened to shelving the books?"

"It won't kill you to take a break."

"Or looking for the pages?"

"Este."

"There are dictionaries to dust, interlibrary loans to file, holds to pull—"

"Climb the ladder, Logano," Mateo urged.

Este's shoulders sagged. Her tone softened. "Your life's on the line, remember?"

"I'm perfectly aware." Mateo bent forward, hands on his knees, and said, "But have you considered, Este dear, that just once you might try to live a little while you're actually alive?"

She tried to argue that she had lived plenty, *thank you very much*. Had he ever watched the Albuquerque International Balloon Fiesta from the side of the highway or sipped gas station hot chocolate in Aspen? But Mateo rattled the rolling ladder on its hinges, and Luca was already halfway to the top of hers, so Este dropped her books and scrambled upward, knuckles white against the creaking rungs.

Daveed gripped Luca's ladder and bent his knees, ready to sprint. "Hope you're ready to eat my dust, Radcliffe."

Aoife stood between them, wielding a feather duster like a checkered flag. "On your marks. Get set. Go!"

Este's stomach lurched as Mateo launched into a run. "Slow down!"

From the bottom of the ladder, Mateo laughed. "Do you want us to lose?"

The bookshelves were little more than a whirl of colors, their jewel-toned bindings all blurring together as they sped past. Laughter bubbled out of her, and she held tighter to the rungs as they took the first curve. It felt like floating, weightless.

She dared a glance down to where Mateo gripped the ladder, wind whipping through his curls. Seeing him like this—buoyant and boyish—steadied her. He was laughing, his face shining like an Edison bulb. She hoped it never turned off.

They rounded the next corner, sailing toward the finish line where Aoife stood as judge. Daveed and Mateo were keeping nearly identical paces, and Luca's giggles wafted through the air as they sped toward each other. Mateo burst into one final sprint as they neared the finish line, but it wasn't enough.

The duster waved in a figure eight as Aoife proclaimed, "Daveed Hewitt, our undefeated champion, reigns supreme!"

Luca slid back down to earth, but Este clung to the rungs for a moment longer. With her bird's-eye view, she could see the entire library—every chandelier glistening, every crooked corner of the bookcase maze. A new perspective.

From here, she could see the circulation desk and the study tables in the center of the atrium. Shadows webbed over the third-floor corridor that led to the archives' double doors, and a shudder ran the length of Este's spine. She could still feel the biting cold of the Fades' black tendrils around her ankles, her wrists.

The Fades don't usually leave leftovers, Mateo had said. But they hadn't stripped her soul from her body and hadn't left more than a mark on her waist. Their black mist had evaporated when it tried to seep out into the light of the library. That must have been why they hadn't kept chasing her. They'd only ventured out onto the third floor during the storm, when the moonlight had been stamped out by clouds and the candles in the study room had extinguished.

The Fades were contained to the darkest parts of the library.

Posy had just come from the archives—had she seen them? As quickly as the thought entered Este's head, it evaporated. No way could Posy have seen the Fades. If she had, she either would've been shredded like rotisserie chicken, or Este would've gotten an earful about how it was going to be the front-page story on her blog. In fact, she'd still be downstairs listening to it.

Este was about to slide down the ladder when she realized where she'd ended up. Section AY was dedicated to reference texts that ran the gamut from almanacs to yearbooks. "Hey guys, did we finish pulling books from my dad's circ history?"

"Dean Logano was a prolific reader," Aoife answered below. "So. No."

Trailing her fingertips along the spines of almanacs, Este hovered over a title she recognized, an almanac. Poking out of the pages was a crimped corner of cardstock, and Este plucked it out.

At the top, a smudged handwritten title read *The Book of Fades.* Este's breath hitched. It was a borrowing card. Last names lined the left side, dates on the right. The ink was a red so dark, it almost looked black. Almost looked like it had been written in blood.

"Ew, ew, ew, *ew*." Este couldn't drop the paper slip fast enough, and it floated down to the ghosts. When she scrambled down the ladder with the almanac, they all huddled around where it landed, face up.

"Is that what I think it is?" Luca asked. She crouched so low that the hem of her white dress skimmed the floors.

"A biohazard? Yeah." The taste of copper wouldn't leave Este's mouth just looking at the letters. She read down the list, a lilting cursive in shades of dark red. The names were ones she recognized, each belonging to the library's ghosts. Radcliffe and van Witt, and then later, Godrich and Hewitt. The names of the ghosts who had since left Radcliffe to find rest peppered in between.

A final name capped the list at the end. Logano.

Mateo cleared his throat and nodded as if he could read every trace of emotion on her face like the lines in a play. "The Fades are under the command of the Heir and this . . . this must be how they choose the sacrifice. Immortality comes with a cost. A blood oath."

"Talk about unsanitary," Luca said with a squirm.

From the slant of the *L* to the loop of the *O*, there was a finality in the writing, like doing a crossword puzzle in ink, knowing you had all the right answers. Este's dad had been marked as the next sacrifice.

"That's why the Fades disappeared for thirty years after my dad dropped out. He was the only sacrifice they could take, so when he left, so did they." Este's hands slicked with sweat, and her tongue scraped against the roof of her mouth, Sahara dry.

Mateo opened his mouth like he wanted to argue, but the evidence was splayed out in front of them.

"It's me. The Fades came back because I'm here, a piece of my dad's bloodline to complete the ritual, like the book said. It's why they attacked me but no one else."

The silence of the ghosts sealed her suspicions, and the realization left her light-headed.

No one else would get hurt. Posy and the Paranormal Investigators, prodding into things they barely understood . . . they'd be fine. It was her the Fades wanted.

She could still leave. *Should* leave. She could pack her bags and run out the university's iron gates and never look back.

But, for once, leaving had its risks, too. It would mean stranding the ghosts without the answers they needed, the missing pages still at large, thanks to her dad. And if she gave up now, she'd never learn what he'd known. From beyond the grave, he'd led her here. How could she walk away from him now?

Her voice was barely more than a breath. "That means I'm next."

NINETEEN

❦

It was 8:04 p.m. when Este stepped out into the night cold. She'd gotten carried away with the ghosts and should've left sooner. If there were two things her roommate believed in, they were ghosts and punctuality, and the Paranormal Investigators had a strict no-tardiness policy.

October's northern wind frosted every windowsill, and Este buried her chin into her bulky cowl-neck as she veered beneath the amber lamplight toward the edge of campus. Heat radiated through the stained-glass windows as Este bounced up the porch steps, and the whole place smelled like cinnamon and steamed milk.

Half museum and half coffee shop, The Ivy had become their official meeting place. A hundred years ago, the teetering Victorian housed the Radcliffes' groundskeepers, but at some point in the last century, walls had been demolished on the first floor to accommodate age-worn tables, soaked with spilled espresso. The entire upstairs was devoted to small permanent exhibits with black-and-white photos of Sheridan Oaks, Vermont, in the 1900s. Now, it was the school's unofficial study break zone.

Este worked her way through the crowd to the espresso bar in the back where she ordered her regular—black with a pump of vanilla syrup—and snagged a seat in the last booth next to Posy's orange bob.

Shepherd's wide frame lounged across the inside seat next to her, and Este tried to keep her eyes from darting to the place where his hand rested on Posy's knee and retreated. Were they a thing now? How could she have a new thing and not tell her?

Bryony and Arthur sat across the scuffed wooden table that had been carved and painted in the familiar shape of rivean ivy blooms. Their mouths hung silent, the words on their tongues evaporating as soon as Este sat down.

Este's eyes shifted between the club members' faces. They all stared back. It felt a little too much like walking into the room as a kid when her parents were arguing about where to put the dishes or how to hang the Christmas lights. Arthur took a long slurp of his iced latte.

So, she'd bailed on History Buffs, but she hadn't exactly expected to become the club pariah.

"Thank you for joining us," Posy said, words taut as a trapeze artist's line. She'd procured a purple folder seemingly from thin air. "First order of business: our suspect list for the Heir of Fades."

Este's mind spun. She hadn't thought Posy was paying attention to Dr. Kirk's throwaway comment. But Posy always paid attention when it was about ghosts.

"What do you know about the Heir?" Este asked. "And didn't Dr. Kirk say that there was basically a zero percent chance of any Fades actually being at Radcliffe? Aren't they super rare?"

Posy gave her a look and Este gulped, hoping it wasn't too obvious. Unfortunately, lately, Posy was a bloodhound, sniffing out all Este's lies. "I told you I've been doing research in the archives. I'm practically an expert now, and I promise you, they're here," Posy said, her fingers clenched around her papers, but her words stayed even. She skimmed through the folder overflowing with tabbed papers and wrinkled receipts, snippets from newspaper clippings and scans of age-old texts.

Behind those, old photographs of the Radcliffe disappearances had been paper clipped to printouts of forum threads surrounded with the smudged ink of handwritten notes. Este glimpsed the stark contrast of Aoife's pale skin with her blue-black hair captured in 38 mm, a sepia-toned rendition of Luca's curls, and a disposable-camera-lens flare washing over Daveed's face. The next page revealed a familiar, arrogant grin and inkwell curls that sprouted warmth in Este's chest. A red sticker had been stamped onto the corner.

"Mateo?" she asked, reaching for his photo, the same one Este had seen on the forums.

"You recognize him?" Posy asked, her eyes blazing.

"From the website," Este said quickly, as four sets of eyes trained on her. "Plus, if . . . you're saying he's a ghost . . . he *can't* be . . . the Heir."

"Yeah, I thought you said the Heir was supposed to be immortal or something," Shepherd said. He rested his arm along the back of the booth, the kind of thing only a boyfriend did.

Arthur steepled his fingers beneath his chin. A single, sterling silver half-moon cuffed his ear. "In a way, ghosts are. They're not *not* immortal since they're trapped in the mortal realm forever."

Este downed a big swig. At this rate, she'd need to switch to decaf before her heart pounded out of her ribs. "Wouldn't immortality imply not being dead already? Because ghosts are sort of alive and dead at the same time."

"Of course they're dead. That's, like, Ghost 101," Bryony said.

One of Este's nails frayed where she picked at it. She tucked her hands beneath her thighs where she couldn't do any more damage to her manicure and huffed an irritated breath out her nose. "They aren't living, but they're not wholly dead either. Like the middle of a Venn diagram."

"And you're the expert now?" Arthur asked.

"No," Este said quickly. "I just . . . I just thought."

Posy shuffled her papers to regain everyone's attention. "Whoever the Heir is," she said, licking her thumb to preen through the pages, "they've been here for an awfully long time. They'd know a lot of people, but somehow they've kept their secret."

In her squirrelly cursive, Posy had written the rest of the names of the founding family—Robin, Judith, and Lilith Radcliffe—as well as a few of the tenured teachers like Dr. Kirk, Ives, and Mr. Liebowitz.

"Or someone's keeping it for them," Arthur noted.

"What's the point in protecting someone immortal?" Este asked.

"They might not be protecting the Heir," Posy said. "Maybe they're protecting something else. Everyone has something they can't stand to lose."

Este scooted Mateo's photo away from the rest of the suspects. "Well, it's not Mateo, so mark him off your list."

"He's a suspect. If you did see his ghost, then we already know he's a thief." Posy riled through her notes until she found a newspaper clipping from the early twentieth century and slapped it on the table. An obituary. She'd scanned it and then taken the liberty of annotating the article with a pink gel pen. "It says right here, *Robin Radcliffe is preceded in death by his wife, Judith Radcliffe. He is survived by his daughter Lilith and the heir to the Radcliffe legacy, Mateo.* And since you've seen him—"

"That doesn't mean anything." Este crossed her arms, fingers clawing deeper into the elbows of her turtleneck with every passing second. "I wish I'd never even mentioned anything about the Mateo I met."

"This kind of groundbreaking research is my life's work, Este."

"It's my *life*!" Hot tears welled in her eyes. Maybe they'd spill. Maybe she wouldn't even wipe them.

"If you didn't blow us off every two seconds, maybe you'd see that I'm right."

"I'm not—"

"You are! You've missed everything." Posy's voice cracked, and she shook her head, red crawling up the column of her neck as her eyes rimmed silver. "We barely even see you anymore. You're just, like, disappearing, and you don't even notice."

The bell at the front door sounded, and a sweep of cold air pulsed through the bar. No one bustled in with it, shrugging off their scarf or folding their gloves into their pockets. Este didn't need a thermal camera to know a ghost when she saw one. Or, in this case, didn't see one.

A few crisp leaves trailed toward the bar as if following in the wake of someone's steps, and while the rest of the coffee shop gossiped and laughed, no one noticed two drinks being scooped off the countertop, floating back toward the entrance in invisible hands.

"You're seriously not even listening right now."

227

"No, I am. I am," Este stammered, turning back to the table. "Please, all of you, stay out of this. I know you're trying to help, but I promise you it isn't Mateo."

"How can you be so sure?" Posy asked.

"Because I know him."

Posy's gaze turned dagger sharp. "You *know* him?"

"You mean you know *of* him?" Arthur asked.

"You mean *saw his ghost once*?" Bryony suggested.

"No, I mean . . ." Her throat constricted around the words. "I found him. After he stole *The Book of Fades*. And you were right, Posy. He was a ghost—is a ghost."

Posy blanched. "So you can see ghosts, and you didn't even tell me?"

Este shook her head. How could she sum up everything the last few weeks had been? "Ghosts, they aren't like what you think. And Mateo, he's not the Heir. He saved me from the Fades."

Uncapping a gel pen, Posy jotted down a few notes in the margins of her scans. "You saw the Fades, too? What were they like?"

"They're . . ." Este faltered. To Posy, this was a game, but Este knew that what waited in the archives was so much worse than a scary story. "You know what? I have to go actually."

Posy blew a stream of bubbles through her straw. She slouched her cheek onto a bed of knuckles when she said, "The meeting just started."

"I know, but Mateo's going to help me study." Este packed up her things. She had one more ivy blossom, one more chance to unveil hidden secrets in *The Book of Fades*.

"You shouldn't be hanging around him," Posy huffed, but there was something serious in her stare that said she meant it. "I've done the research and . . . and I don't trust him."

Este swallowed. "You won't even know he's there. You've never noticed him before."

The bell at the door chimed as Este surged into the frost-bitten evening. One of the Lilith's windows must have nudged open because the Fades' velveteen melody caught on the wind, a harrowed hymnal that carried her forward. Waiting for her in the shadows was Mateo, his hands holding two coffee cups and his smile broadening with every step she took closer.

"So, how was investigating the paranormal?" he asked as he handed her one of the confiscated drinks, and his form grew more and more solid as they walked.

Standing next to Mateo felt safe, warm, a respite from the night cold. Her fingers twitched, wishing she could clasp his hands in hers, but those sap-sticky, stolen touches never lasted. Instead, she clutched her drink closer, the heat seeping from her palms into her arms, all the way down to her belly. "Fine."

A few dried leaves swirled as Mateo's breezy figure slid through them. "I don't believe you for even a second."

Este shook out a breath that spooled in front of her in gauzy white ribbons. "Posy's dating Shepherd, I drank a little too much coffee a little too fast so now I kind of want to throw up, and also Posy thinks she knows who the Heir is."

They drifted into a grove of hemlocks, a pocket of darkness between streetlamps, and Mateo was cut in such sharp contrast that she could see every detail, every muscle, as his spine went rigid. "She does?"

Here, moonlight was trapped between evergreen boughs, only dripping to the sidewalk in slivers. Each footfall crunched against a layer of frost, and Este nodded, kicking a pine cone down the cobblestones.

Posy wanted her to believe it could be Mateo, but he'd protected her every step of the way. He'd been by her side in every shadowed corridor, every lightless place. Without him, she would have been lost. She swallowed his name like a key in a magician's trick.

Instead, she tugged her sleeves down over her palms, crossing her arms tight as a shield against her chest. "She thinks it's Dr. Kirk. Can you believe that?"

Mateo stared over her shoulder, down the path to the Lilith, where the Fades haunted the halls. He ran a hand through his mess of curls and refocused on her. The blues of his eyes faded. "Not a bad hypothesis, but as long as we find the pages, it doesn't matter who the Heir is. Let's grab our books and get to work."

TWENTY

If she didn't get a good night's sleep soon, Este might actually be able to read the language of the dead without rivean ivy.

Her throat scratched every time she spoke, and her eyelids grated with every blink. A sheet of fog scrolled across campus as dawn's first light lifted above the sycamores. Este and Mateo still had their research splayed across her bed. She didn't mind spending their nights like this—together, *The Book of Fades* between them, and searching for clues in the pages of the books her dad had checked out. Tonight's reading? *The Old Farmer's Almanac 1997.* She'd made up most of her sleep during class, drooling onto wide-ruled composition notebooks and blushing when her teachers called her name.

But this morning, she had the added joy of a leftover caffeine headache, throbbing with each beat of her tired heart. The windowsill vase was empty of blossoms, every chance she had for glimpsing the language of the dead dried up. Their pale petals littered Este's bedroom floor.

"What'd my dad need an almanac for anyway?" She covered her mouth, cutting short a wide yawn. The haze of sleep made her wonder if her thoughts were even coherent anymore. They'd been grasping at short straws for hours. "It's not like he was a farmer."

Mateo, who was no longer indebted to his circadian rhythm, looked bright-eyed as ever, shockingly solid as long as he avoided the beams of early-morning sunlight. He lounged on her pillows, one arm behind his head and the other grazing against the ridges of her hand where the nectar stained. It was all too easy to get used to this—a lazy togetherness, content in his company.

"You should get some rest, Este dear." His voice sounded faraway, a tin-can telephone line.

Her pillow welcomed her as she slumped onto her mattress. They were so in over their heads. Too many dead ends, not enough clues to connect them. Este's eyelids fluttered closed. It would feel so nice to take a nap. Fifteen, twenty minutes tops.

She wasn't sure how long she lay there, somewhere stuck between consciousness and a silver daydream, but when she peeled her eyes open, daylight poured through the windows. All she saw was Mateo. The bridge of his nose, the dimple on his chin, the rim of dark blue around his irises. Beams of dazzling yellow illuminated her room, making him fade in and out of opacity as thin clouds wafted across the sun.

It wouldn't be so bad, an eternity like this with him: crisp October breezes tapping at the windowpanes, wool-socked toes padding across polished floors, dawns and twilights running together like watercolors.

"Good morning, sunshine," he said when her eyes finally reopened.

"What's good about it?" Este groaned, stretching her arms over her head and a reluctant smile over her lips. She woke up her phone screen to see the time: 8:37 a.m.

8:37 a.m.?

"Oh no," she said, flinging herself off the mattress. Black dotted her vision, and she caught herself on the bedside table, steadying only a moment before surging toward her closet.

Mateo pried himself from the blankets. "What, oh no?"

With her dad's sweatshirt half-pulled over the tee she fell asleep in, Este mumbled, "Meeting with Ives. She moved it to Thursday this week, and I totally forgot." Hair tangled over her face when her head popped through the neckhole. "I can't be late."

He propped up on his elbows, head tilted. "What's the meeting about?"

"Well," Este said, wiggling into a pair of denim jeans behind the closet door. "This week's meeting is probably going to be about how I also slept through *last week's* meeting."

She hadn't meant to, of course. But between the Fades' attack and the late-night shifts, her body needed a break. Plus, she hadn't exactly been eager to return to the library if that was the only place the Fades could reach her. And, besides, everyone deserved sick days, right? Ives hadn't said anything to her about it, but the thought of the head librarian sitting in her office, tapping her nails against her desk two weeks in a row, sent shivers over Este's skin.

In a frenzy, Este shoved her English textbook and the almanac they'd spent the last night staring at into her backpack. Mateo kept hold of *The Book of Fades.*

Standing in her doorway with her backpack slung over her shoulder, it felt humanly impossible to leave Mateo like this. All she wanted to do was waste the day away lying beside him, memorizing the dark ribbons of his hair and the slant of his smirk.

"I'll be back before lunch," she said.

"I'm not going anywhere." Mateo's mouth hung open, something lingering there, but whatever it was washed away with a shake of his head.

Brisk winds whipped Este's hair across her face with cold lashes when she plunged out onto the worn paths. She swiped a finger underneath her eyes, smearing off yesterday's mascara. On her trek toward the Lilith, she passed a few others, cramming for their exams or chugging coffees as they sprinted toward the science labs. Long nights and early mornings were prying up the school's photo-perfect veneer.

When she climbed up the Lilith's polished stairs, the head

librarian's office was closed. Este gave the handle another tug, but it didn't budge. Locked tight. No light filtered beneath the doorway. Had Ives even bothered to show up this morning to give Este the benefit of the doubt? What kind of high schooler didn't *occasionally* screw up and lead a conniving yet adorable ghost to a cursed ancient text, get optioned for sacrifice, and forget her morning meetings?

Behind her, the door to the spire creaked open, and Este spun on her heels with her arms up to block her face. Instinct. Where she'd expected the Fades' molding hands despite the glow of morning light drenching the fifth floor, she found Ives with a red handkerchief tied around her head like Rosie the Riveter.

The head librarian dropped a cardboard box at the foot of the door to prop it open. The stairwell's yawning cavern didn't look any more welcoming in the daylight, still thick with stale darkness and clammy stone walls. Ives brushed off her hands and wiped a bead of sweat from her forehead.

"Miss Logano," she said, out of breath. "I'd begun to think you were avoiding me."

Este yanked her sleeves over her palms, balling the extra fabric up in her fists. She raised her shoulders and plastered on her best *please don't kick me out* face, which she hoped shared uncanny resemblance to Posy's *sorry I ate your last ramen* expression. Big eyes, pouting bottom lip—knowing but apologetic. "Sorry I'm late. Do you need help with anything?"

Ives wiped a hand across her face and left a dirt smudge. She peeked back over her shoulder before nodding with a smile. "I figured it was time to do a few repairs upstairs, and a couple extra hands from a future librarian couldn't hurt."

Future librarian. The words rang like a dinner bell, calling Este home. She still had a future. But how many chances— second, third, fourth—could Ives give her before she ran out?

Ives nudged the cardboard box toward her, and Este scooped it into her arms. Her side groaned with the effort, but she tried not to grimace.

"Carry that while I grab the pruning scissors."

"The what?" Este asked, but Ives was already unlocking her office door. She returned with a pair of hedge trimmers the size of Este's torso. The box she gave Este held a half-dozen cheese-cloth pouches, a couple spray bottles, and a jar of dirt wriggling with worms. These weren't any repairs Este was familiar with.

Ives trudged up the stairs, and Este echoed her footfalls. The heavy spire door clanged shut behind them, dousing them in a stiff black darkness. Este knew to expect windows halfway up, but it didn't stop the prickly chill from creeping up her spine.

Without looking back, Ives said, "I trust you'll ensure all books stay on the shelves this time, Miss Logano. This is a privilege, not a right."

Este gulped. "Of course."

When they pushed through the door at the top of the stairwell, the spire basked in dewy morning light. Este wondered if the awe would ever wear off. All these relics, the jewels and the gemstones, the art and the arcane, all preserved through the years as if time itself could not breach the restricted collection.

"I found the spire key in the archives a few days ago," Ives said. Her blades sliced through a thick band of greenery, and all the color seeped from the stem. The cut section faded to black and dried like a snakeskin. "You wouldn't happen to know anything about that, would you?"

Este tugged her hair into a ponytail to get it off the nape of her neck, now flushed red with guilt. Through her foggy memory, she recalled the chime as the key slid across the splintered floors, but between the poison in her veins and the Fades at her back, she hadn't picked it back up.

"N-no," Este said.

"Sometimes it's better to prune things back before they get unruly," Ives said to the ivy as she trimmed. Another snip. Another vine blackening and curling. "Have you seen anyone hanging around the archives during your shifts?"

Este rattled her head with her lips shrunken into a sour stripe. Meanwhile, Ives wore the same practiced smile, but it didn't reach her eyes. Dark hollows had begun to form under her eyes, and the concealer she'd used to cover them caked into seams where the crow's-feet spread. Midterm stress must have been getting to her, too.

"I see." Ives pointed to the cardboard box with the sharp edge of her trimmers. "We'll clean up the floors and plant new seeds for the bookcases."

Este nudged a creeping vine with the toe of her sneaker. She could almost see the place where she'd walked with the ghosts, footsteps carving through the layer of dust on the stone floors. "Is this safe for the books? The plants."

"Oh, yes. Rivean ivy has unique protective qualities." The blooms were closed in the daylight, but the fragrance seeped from the pores of each stem like an uncontainable magic. Ives drew a long breath through her nose, relishing. In contrast, the scent sparked trippy flashbacks that made Este's empty stomach clench in defense. She tried not to look too green. "Good for keeping out all kinds of pests. Ladybugs, beetles, roaches."

Ives instructed Este how to plant the ivy seeds, and her hands followed like they were pulled by puppet strings. Her fingernails scraped half-inch divots into soil tucked in clay pots. She poured a teaspoon of seeds into each, covered, and spritzed. Este lost track of how many she planted.

As she went, Este skimmed the bookshelves like she might see the imprint of her father's fingers on the bindings. He'd either stashed the stolen chapter somewhere in the Lilith or shredded the paper, sent it to recycling, and let the invisible ink wash away to be remade into stationery or grocery sacks. This whole search could be useless.

"I should be thanking you," Ives said.

Este gaped. "You should?"

Ives propped one of her pots on top of a bookcase. Her long, black curls wore white streaks of dust that instantly aged her.

It reminded Este of Mateo, trying to trick eternity to show him what might have been. "You returned the spire key to me in the first place. These magnificent heirlooms could have been lost forever."

There was no vocabulary for saying sorry and you're welcome at the same time.

Clapping the dirt off her hands, Ives said, "I want to show you something."

Este followed the head librarian around the last corner to the center of the spire. The ceiling's coned point loomed overhead, glittering with gossamer cobwebs. Oil paintings, charcoal sketches, and ribbon-tied scrolls dotted this final concentric ring of shelves, and in the middle sat a high-backed chair dressed in embroidered black and Robin Radcliffe's desk.

"They say that when Lilith and Mateo were kids, they loved to read in the spire with their father. A quiet place where anything was possible between the pages of a book." Ives ran her hand along the chair's chiseled armrest. "This library has been that for many people, myself included. Do you have a place like that?"

Este's mouth formed a small circle, tongue pressed behind her teeth, ready to say *No, I don't*, but she stopped herself. Even in the inconstancy after her mom uprooted their lives on the west coast for a pledge of nomadic isolation, libraries had been her one sliver of comfort.

They were all different but somehow all the same. She loved

the smell of yellowed pages, the way each wrinkled sheet held inked stories and a piece of every person who had read them—sand from high schoolers' spring-break vacations, smudges from dirty fingers, perfume trails of illicit affairs.

Whether her mom was working in Tacoma or Tampa, Este could wander the stacks without getting lost, following the familiar trail of decimal points to any destination. Recipes for no-bake cookies? Turn right at 641.81. Techniques of rococo painting? Straight ahead to 709.4. Eliot's unmetered poetry? 821.9.

Libraries were the rope tying her to the fading memory of her father. Her soft landing, her solace.

Ives didn't wait for her to answer. "I've noticed the company you keep," she pressed as if searching for the weak spot, the tender bruise that would make Este squeal.

Este's mind flared with images of the ghosts, laughing as they sailed through the stacks on the ladders. Was having fun cause for expulsion? "You have?"

"You don't want to get too close to the Fades," Ives said, sharp and cold as an ice pick. "Not while *The Book of Fades* is still missing."

It felt like Este's body had been dunked into one of those carnival booths. Like a scrawny ten-year-old with the arm of a fastball pitcher hit the bull's-eye and flushed Este beneath a tide at a county fair. "You know about the Fades? I didn't think you'd believe in ghosts."

She'd assumed Ives would discount the school's ghost stories as child's play the same way Este had written off Posy's paranormal antics at the beginning of the school year. A stroke of severity washed across Ives's face, one that revealed she definitely didn't think this was a game.

"Certainly, I do. I know everything that goes on at the Lilith. I've been tasked with protecting *The Book of Fades* like every head librarian has since the Radcliffes were alive. The Fades have wreaked havoc on this school for the last century. It's my duty to safeguard the book and control them. And I have for my thirty years as head librarian." Her nails rapped against the glass inlay on the empty case where *The Book of Fades* should've been. "Without this book in my care, the Fades can be quite unpredictable."

Well, Este couldn't argue with that. She had the scars to prove it. But Ives knowing about the Fades kind of made her feel like she'd just donated blood on an empty stomach. "Have you ever seen them?"

Ives shrugged. "I imagine they're as ancient as these walls. You know, Este, some things are inevitable. There is life, and there is death. Within the walls of the Lilith, all of eternity resides on these shelves. The Heir of Fades is also inevitable and will stop at nothing to stay as immortal as these books."

Este nodded, but Ives's soliloquy barely sank in through the blood pounding in her ears. Her body ran hot, a sheen of sweat gathering at her hairline. Even the things Este thought she'd figured out suddenly felt misshapen, the edges no longer lining up.

A metallic taste flooded Este's mouth, one she couldn't wash away. She grasped for every fragment of truth she had, trying to form the full picture.

Mateo was obsessed with resurrection, guilting her into helping him have a second chance at life. And the Fades. Este had only seen the Fades when she was with him. He could have been leading them to her, little more than a lab rat in a labyrinth. He said he needed *The Book of Fades* to come back to life. Maybe Shepherd had a point—if he were truly immortal, he'd still be alive, right?

Unless he'd only become a ghost thirty years ago after her dad escaped, immortality slipping through his fingers, tricking the other ghosts with his promises of new life. She assumed he'd been a sacrifice like the others, an unwilling participant in an immortal scheme. *But what if,* Este couldn't believe she was thinking it, but *what if he'd raised the Fades for himself?*

He'd insisted that he required the help of a student, and Este was the perfect candidate. Her father was to blame for breaking the Fades' vicious cycle, and her mother was a one-woman traveling show. There was no one waiting for her. No one to notice if she never came home.

Plus, her name was already written in blood.

On in the card he had just reunited with the book.

With her help.

The pot slid from Este's fingers and crashed to the floor in a terracotta explosion. Soil stained her shoes, the floor, the grout between stones. It was as if all the air in the spire evaporated. She darted to the windows on the perimeter of the room and pried one open, pushing twice as hard when it snagged halfway up. She sucked down a long gulp of autumn air, begging her heart rate to slow with every inhale.

"I've spent my entire life studying this collection," Ives said, cutting through Este's spiraling thoughts. "There are things too valuable to lose here. If you know where *The Book of Fades* is, you need to return it. Imminently, Miss Logano." Something dark passed over Ives's face. It twisted her lips in an ugly sneer, like she hated the thought of what might happen without the book in her hands, the damage that might be done. And then her face relaxed. Maybe she had realized how much she had scared Este. "I'll grab us a broom."

As soon as Ives disappeared around the corner, Este slipped her phone out of her pocket and pulled up Posy's contact. The motion was second nature—they were supposed to be friends, even with whatever that was at The Ivy last night. Their last text was a discussion of which animals they could successfully fight in hand-to-hand combat (Este: *a quokka*, Posy: *what's a quokka?*) and Este typed something new.

emergency PI meeting before english

And then another, just to be sure:

!!!!!!!!!!!!!

Posy would know where to start, what to believe. She could help her sift through the accusations against Mateo, panning for truth like gold on a Colorado riverbank. Her roommate was the lifeline Este needed to feel tethered to the shore of the living rather than swept away into the strong currents of the Lethe, pulling her toward the realm of the dead.

Este reached down to the part of herself she'd bottled up when her dad died and uncorked it to pour a little more heartache in. She knew Mateo—she liked him, and she'd wanted him to kiss her in the senior lounge. He'd been growing more and more real to her with every day, and she hadn't exactly been sad about it. This had to be one big misunderstanding.

Ives reappeared with broom in hand as Este nudged her phone back where it belonged. She brushed everything into a small pile and swept it into a dustpan. Este's phone dinged, loud and obnoxious.

"Sorry," Este said. "Probably my roommate. Actually, I need to go. Don't want to be late for class."

Ives sank into the seat, crossing one leg over the other. It was a sight to see—Ives in her gardening gear perched on Lilith Radcliffe's chair, one hand cocked beneath her chin, red lipstick slanted into a smile. "Is it already time for next period? I always wish we had more time together. And with every hour that I don't have *The Book of Fades* in my hands, it is more dangerous for everyone."

Este stammered, unable to form a response. How could she

think straight through everything? The Fades wanted her dead, and there was a nonzero chance that Mateo had been behind it all along. She'd trusted him, and he'd betrayed her—the realization was a silver dagger between the soft of her ribs, straight to her bleeding heart.

"Go on," Ives said, batting her hand toward the door beyond the stacks. "But don't be late for your shift tonight. This library needs you, Este."

TWENTY-ONE

The notification that had interrupted her meeting with Ives flashed on her phone screen. It wasn't a text from Posy like she expected but a Pizza Town coupon. *This Side of Pizza-dise! A deal so good you've Gatsby kidding!* The bubbly cartoon letters advertising extra cheese were antithetical to everything Este felt right now. Not even BOGO 50 percent off pizzas could fix this.

Este tabbed open Instagram. Her feed was embarrassingly bare. Spending nearly every waking hour in the library didn't make for many photo ops. She scrolled through photos of her classmates—a girl from her poetry class posted an aesthetically pleasing Emily Dickinson–themed flat lay, a senior on the rowing team documented his practice regimen, and a few of the theater kids promoted their next program. She typed Posy's handle into the search bar and clicked her chipped nails against her case as it loaded.

Posy had captured the entire quarter in still frames. Her photos were carefully curated, all with matching colors and thoughtful editing. Some boasted doodles and handwritten captions more like a collection of Polaroids than social-media posts.

First, a selfie of Posy and the Paranormal Investigators this afternoon, crowded around a picnic table on the greens with heaps of textbooks piled next to coffees the size of their heads. Then, a photo of Shepherd kissing Posy at the Hesper Fountain, rivulets of sparkling water streaming behind them, one of her legs bent at the knee and a bouquet clutched in her hand. Este kept scrolling. Posy and Bryony grinning in their History Buffs outfits, an overhead shot of their séance setup, and a photo of the Paranormal Investigators' club flyer.

At the top of the page, a green dot flashed next to Posy's name. *Active now.*

Este pressed her fingers beneath her eyes to catch a few stray tears. Posy had shown up for her, relentlessly so, but not now. Not when Este needed her most. She'd pushed her away so many times that she almost couldn't blame Posy for not texting back.

Around her, the rest of the student body filtered into their classrooms, and Este should have been one of them. How was she supposed to focus on Mr. Donohue proselytizing about the genius of Virginia Woolf when everything she thought she knew was turning to dust in her hands?

Instead, her feet carried her to the library and upstairs to the senior-lounge door. She hesitated with her hand halfway to the knob. Weeks ago, when she first stepped through that door, she'd barely believed in ghosts, but somewhere along the way, she'd done more than just believe. She'd begun to trust them. All of them. She wasn't sure what would be worse—the ghosts knowing Mateo was the Heir this whole time and not telling her or them not knowing at all?

If they were his accomplices, walking into the lounge was a death sentence. But if they didn't know, if they were kept in the dark like she was, then she owed it to them to discover the truth. It was what a friend would do. And maybe, just maybe, she was wrong about Mateo. They had stockpiled bits and pieces of the past—surely something in them could clear his name.

The study was quiet when she walked in. Aoife had traded her typical hardback nonfiction books for a paperback romance, and now she and Luca giggled over the saucy bits. Daveed dragged an ink pen over the pages of a notebook, dangling upside down on the sofa cushions.

"Hey, Este," Daveed said. "How's it hanging?"

She marched to the trick floorboard and stomped down on it so that the other side leveraged up and she could reach in for the stack of clues. "It's been better."

"What's eating away at you?" Luca asked, peeking over the cover of the bodice ripper she and Aoife each held one side of.

On the table in front of her, Este spread out the evidence

they'd gathered—*The Book of Fades*'s borrowing card in its plastic bag, the almanac, books on poetry and herbal remedies from her dad's circulation history, and the scroll of parchment from the Hesper Fountain—like maybe she could summon the solution. But she'd looked at these clues so many times that they'd burned into her retinas, she could map out every spill of ink with her eyes closed, and she still didn't know what her dad was trying to lead her to.

"What was it like for you?" Este asked the phantoms, her chin in her hand. "When it happened."

"I'm actually still a virgin," Daveed said.

"Not *that*," Este chided. "I meant when the Fades separated your body from your soul. Do you remember it?"

"Plain as day," Luca piped up. "Or, as night, I suppose. It was late on October 25, and I was taking books back to the archives when the Fades sank their claws into me. I never saw them coming."

"Because it was so dark in the archives?" Este asked.

Luca frowned, a distant thing. "I know how it sounds, but it was almost as if they were the dark. There was nowhere for me to run."

Este scooted the borrowing card closer. Next to Luca's name, her death date had been penned in blood red. She found Aoife's name next. Someone else's name had been scribbled out, with Aoife Godrich crammed on the line below. "Aoife, did you die on October 3?"

Aoife eyed Este like she was annoyed to have her reading interrupted. "I did. I was supposed to work that morning, but I'd traded shifts. One minute I was shelving books, and when I woke up, I was here with the others."

"And Daveed," Este said, "October 22?"

Daveed flipped off the couch and landed wobbly on his feet. "Yeah, I was working that night and a couple friends stopped by. One of them asked me to grab a book for her. Next thing I knew, everything went black."

Este tried to imagine it—the suffocating snare of the Fades' grasp, the light blotting out into nothingness, and the waking up dead. "Did you know? That you'd died?"

"Not at first. But I remember Mateo bringing me here, sitting me down by the fire." Daveed shook out his shoulders like he could still feel the cold.

"Could he touch you?" Este asked.

But Daveed rattled his head. "I don't remember."

If Mateo *were* the Heir, and he had been immortal, he wouldn't have been able to physically interact with any of the ghosts until . . .

"Why are you asking?" Aoife scrutinized Este with a precision that cut straight to the quick.

Este tapped the card marred with their names. "The Fades didn't kill me. There's no date next to my last name. But the days you died, they're on here."

Aoife looked at Luca who looked at Daveed who scrubbed

the back of his neck. "Maybe they weren't hungry yet?"

Somehow, Este was pretty sure loss of appetite wasn't a huge concern for the Fades.

"But that doesn't explain Mateo," she thought out loud, dread welling at the base of her sternum. The date next to his name was smudged, mostly unreadable. October something, 1917. "He told me that it happened to him in the spire, but . . . that doesn't make any sense."

She'd never seen the Fades venture beyond the third floor, the darkest corners of the library. When she escaped them, their tendrils recoiled from the light as if singed like the edges of paper curling up into ash. They were clearly most powerful in the darkness, and there were more windows in the spire than she could count—she couldn't imagine the Fades lasting more than a minute in the moonlit landing.

And that made Este think of Robin Radcliffe writing about his late wife by the light of the stars, which she quite frankly did not want to think about right now or ever again, because a love that persistent, that loyal, that defiant of death made her chest feel too tight for reasons she didn't care to examine. Robin must have known something she didn't. He'd sat in that spire, charting the stars and penning love letters to the dead. He knew the skies better than anyone.

Este touched the curled edge of the newspaper clipping. October 15, 1917: the night that the fire started in the spire, when a spark erased some of the most precious Radcliffe memories, including Robin's letters. Any sage wisdom he might have left in those pages had cindered.

That was why her dad checked out the farmer's almanac—not for a quick-start guide to growing his own vegetables, but to see the moon and stars in memoriam.

"Luca," she said suddenly, "I need you to grab almanacs for each of your death dates. This year, too."

While Luca collected those, Este traced her fingers down the pages of the 1997 almanac's chart of historic moon phases. The new moon came and went on October 1, only to return on October 31. But someone—her dad?—had only circled the first date with the broad stroke of a blue pen. Luca splayed the rest of the almanacs out over the coffee table, and the ghosts gathered around the table, vultures hungry for answers.

"Look up the moon phase for the night you were sacrificed," Este instructed, tabbing through the pages of the current year herself.

Daveed found his first. "New moon."

Aoife said, "Me, too."

"Me three," said Luca.

"That's why the Fades couldn't fully sacrifice me before. It can only be done during the new moon. That's when the night is darkest, and that's when they're strongest."

Este flipped through the pages until she reached the moon phases for 1917. Her dad's blue ink circle outlined October 15. For a long, shocked moment all she could do was stare at it, heart thundering and head dizzy with shards of black. Her stomach clenched like she was on the precipice of a free fall, the tipping point between being on top of the world and bottoming out.

The night of the new moon was the same night of the fire in the spire.

Embers flickered in the fireplace, casting streaks of light and long shadows as they breathed. Este recalled the words from *The Book of Fades*, the way Mateo's voice sounded as he read *You cannot know darkness without first knowing light*. With Mateo's blood on the pages, a match in his hands, and a moonless sky, the Fades must have been summoned that night, drawn out of the shadows created in that blaze.

The Heir was Mateo. It had been Mateo this whole time.

And she'd fallen for his lies the whole time she'd been falling for him.

"Este, are you okay?" Luca asked as Este lurched out of her seat.

The ghosts watched her, waiting. Every drop of self-assurance left her bones at the sight of them. If she told them the truth about Mateo, what good would it do? They must have already known. He told her that he didn't want to let them down—what bargain had they already struck?

She fanned ahead to the current month in the current year for an answer some part of her already knew. A pit opened up in her stomach so deep Este thought it might swallow her whole.

The new moon this October was tomorrow night, and she was the soul du jour.

"Um, yeah," she said, flustered. "I . . . I can't stay."

She shoved the catalog card into her bag, heart racing.

Apparently, she was like her dad, after all.

Following his footsteps, that was why she'd come here. She always imagined that meant drinking coffee by the carafe in between classes and losing track of time at the library. The truth was that his footprints led past the iron gates, back down the mile-long driveway, and as far across the country as he could get. The Fades could only hurt her here, and she needed to be as far from the Lilith as possible when her time came.

She needed to get out. Out of the Lilith, out of Sheridan Oaks, out of the state. She might get all the way to California and sink her knees into the desert dirt before she stopped looking for shadows over her shoulder.

TWENTY-TWO

October's breeze turned bitter as Este followed the sugar maples and their bloodred leaves back to her dormitory. Vespertine Hall was a flurry of motion as evening crept in early over the horizon. Term papers scattered through the air. The coffee maker in the first-floor kitchen gurgled, a caffeine buzz in the making. A boy in a Hawaiian shirt brushed his teeth in one of the doorways, dodging an airborne pair of Doc Martens. Este ducked a few seconds later as the rubber soles hit the shiplap wall next to her.

When she finally reached her floor near the top of the building, her teeth ached from the clench of her jaw. She angled her head high, mouth drawn straight as she stomped into her dorm, slamming the door behind her.

Her bedroom door creaked open, and Mateo's head popped around the hinges, shoulders swaddled in her duvet. "You're back!"

She hated how his face illuminated and then how his eyes dimmed, eyebrows cinched, when she didn't say anything back. Her footfalls were heavy, too loud as she barged into her room, purposefully leaving a generous radius between them. She scooped heaps of laundry off the floor and onto her bed. Sweaters and socks, plaid skirts and ripped jeans.

She growled, "I didn't ask you to stay."

That was always how it happened, wasn't it? One moment, Mateo was a stranger, and the next, she knew all his favorite songs (then, "Somewhere a Voice is Calling" by John McCormack, and now, "Levitating" by Dua Lipa), the sound of his laugh across a crowded room (low and lingering, like thunder on the horizon that sent electricity under her skin), and the way he looked first thing in the morning (curls frayed around the edges and sticking up in odd directions). She hadn't asked him to come in, to make a space for himself in her heart.

"Technically true, I suppose," he hummed, still feigning a smile. "What are you doing?"

"Packing." Another heap of clothes tugged from the hangers in her closet. All of it needed to go.

He inched forward. "Why?"

Este didn't answer. The taste of copper seeped onto her tongue from where she bit into her cheek. She yanked her suitcase out of her closet and shoveled her clothes inside.

Another flash of confusion washed over Mateo's features. She loathed how easy this was for him—pretending he didn't know exactly what he was. Seriously, he deserved an Academy Award for this performance.

He asked, "Este, dear, is everything okay?"

"Don't call me that anymore," she snarled. "Don't call me anything anymore."

His lips thinned into a fine line. "What happened at your meeting?"

Este stalked to the window and twisted the blinds. The last dregs of amber sunlight splashed through her room, and Mateo was caught in the tide. He striped transparent in the angle of the blinds. "You know my dad used to talk about this place all the time," she said with a hoarse laugh. "Called it the best time of his life. I guess he left out a few key details."

When her dad spoke of his school days, he'd always worn a far-off look—the same kind Este later recognized glazing her mom's eyes whenever she spoke of him. The look of something lost. Maybe sepia-toned nostalgia was its own type of haunting. The ache of missing something you could never have again.

"Will you please just tell—" Mateo started, but Este grabbed the drawstring for the blinds and pulled them wide. Beneath the harsh beam, his head vanished. Mateo's hands found his hips. Even without seeing the frustrated slope of his mouth, she could hear it when he said, "You're acting incredibly immature right now."

"I'm acting immature? You've been lying to me. This whole time."

He sidestepped out of the sunshine, coming back into his full form. It didn't matter how far Vespertine was from the Lilith—somehow he always managed to look fully corporeal in her bedroom. "Este, you know me."

"I know you're the Heir." A callous laugh tore up her throat. "No, it's worse, actually. Because you told me to my face weeks ago, and I was too naive to see it. That borrowing card—the Fades can't choose who to sacrifice, only the Heir. And you chose me, didn't you?"

He'd set his sights on her during orientation, and she hadn't even realized it. All she'd seen was a ghost, dreaming of a second chance and grieving for the first one he never had. Now the Fade's touch would scar her skin for the rest of her life, and if she didn't leave soon, she wouldn't have much life left at all.

He held his palms upright, a subtle surrender. One Este didn't believe for a second. "I don't think you fully understand."

She cocked her head back, stifling a sob she couldn't let him see. Her side throbbed in time with her pulse. It was like her wound worsened being around him. Like her side knew he'd caused the pain and rioted in response.

"You think I don't understand how you framed me so that I'd end up on the night shift? And my first night in the archives when things kept going missing—that was you, wasn't it? You've always known I was the only sacrifice the Fades could take, so you led me right to them." Everything was hot—her face, her hands, the burning coals of her heart. "Or that I don't know why you always carry matches in your pocket?"

"I told you. I have those for reading—"

"You started the fire to summon the Fades." She slipped the sliver of newsprint from her pocket. *Radcliffe Legacy Goes up in Flames.* "1917, the prodigal son and daughter vanish less than a year after their parents died. No bodies found. Family records destroyed. And all you remember is smoke."

The comforter fell from Mateo's shoulders as he stepped forward, but Este dodged right and stepped onto and over her mattress. She wouldn't let him get close to her—not again. It was all a ruse with him. A foxhunt, and she was the prized kill.

"I've waited lifetimes for you, Este Logano." His voice cracked and so did his porcelain facade, a sliver of something like sadness slipping through. "I promise that it's not what it seems like."

A strangled sound snagged in her windpipe. She never thought the Heir would be so spineless. "My dad knew the truth about you."

A seam split between his eyebrows. He finally took a step away from her, and a relieved breath found Este's lungs. "I never lied to him, just like I never lied to you. I do need you. We all need your help."

"Then, tell me you're not the Heir of Fades."

"Este—"

"Tell me."

His shoulders sank, wilting flowers at the end of their

259

season. His time was up. Nothing could stay hidden forever. Mateo's eyes dipped toward her waist, the damage already done. Este wondered if he could tell the scabs kept chipping off, leaving the skin angry and vulnerable. Not unlike herself. She thought it would've healed by now, but the cuts carved into her side were gorges growing deeper every day.

"You aren't safe here," he said instead.

She made herself look at him—at the heavy set of his brows, the dimple on his chin, the divot in his sternum beneath a row of buttons where she used to wish she could rest her head. The place where his heart had once beaten.

He grabbed handfuls of his hair in both palms, leaving his curls sticking in mismatched directions. Frustration rippled off him in storm tides, powerful enough to knock Este off balance. She half expected the Fades to appear out of the shadows at his command.

Hollow, she said, "Well, that's fine because I'm leaving."

Mateo shoved both hands into his trouser pockets. He stood too rigid. "Good. It's the only way you'll be safe."

"As if you ever cared about that," she spat.

"You think I care more about this? Take it with you and never come back," he said as he dragged *The Book of Fades* off the side table. He dropped the familiar tome with its painted edges on top of her dresser next to a stack of textbooks. "Without you, Este, none of this matters."

His image faded, retreating into his sanctuary of nothingness, but the door opened as if moved by the wind and closed behind him. Este waited until her dorm had gone completely silent to let herself cry, let the floodwaters wash her away.

It was dark when her tears ran dry and darker when Este tucked her arms into the sleeves of her heaviest coat to trek across campus. The Lilith was a beacon through the night fog. Este clutched *The Book of Fades* with tight fingers, shaking hands. She'd tucked the bloodstained borrowing card back into its pocket, the book back as close to one piece as she could get it.

The head librarian's office door was closed when she approached on leaden legs and knocked.

"Este. Nice to see you early for a change," Ives said as her door swung open. She'd braided her black hair over one shoulder. Her mouth slipped open when she spotted the tome in Este's hands, eyes dragged to the book's magnetic pull. "You found it."

"I wanted to make sure it was returned," Este said, throat raw. "That it was kept safe."

Away from Mateo and locked in the spire beneath the ivy's roots where none of the ghosts could reach it, like it had been for the last thirty years. No more names on the catalog card. No more sacrifices. No more bloodshed.

Ives snatched the book away from her, the rough texture grating against her skin. Her nails rapped against the backing, the *tap, tap, tap* like rain against shingles. Her blue eyes squinted as she scrutinized Este's features. Could she still see the paths carved by tears against her cheeks?

"Consider me impressed," Ives said with a breezy smile. "I look forward to your future here at Radcliffe."

Este forced a grin that didn't last. This was everything she'd thought she wanted.

And it was everything she would have to leave behind.

TWENTY-THREE

Applewood bacon and a short stack of pancakes could abso-lutely wake the dead. Este didn't remember falling asleep. All she knew was one moment she was bleary-eyed, trying to make sense of an escape plan after returning from the Lilith, and the next moment the sun was up and the whole dorm smelled like a twenty-four-hour diner.

She hauled herself out of bed, rubbing a palm against her crusted eyelids, but paused in the doorway. "I guess you guys should change your name to the breakfast club."

The whole PI club crowded around the cramped kitchen— Bryony leaned over her plate of sticky pancakes at the island, Arthur perched on the counter with his swinging feet tapping against the cabinets, Shepherd shoveled food into his mouth at superhuman speeds, and Posy stood next to him, stealing bites off his plate.

"She lives," Bryony cooed around a syrupy bite.

Posy peeked around Shepherd's shoulder. There was no hint of a smile, no excited recognition of Este's continued existence, the straight face of someone with enough siblings to perfect the silent treatment. Bryony turned back to her plate, Shepherd focused on his flapjacks, and Arthur offered her a flat smile but nothing else.

Seeing them like this, padding around her dorm in their flannel pajamas and wrinkled sleep shirts, sheared through a heartstring Este didn't know she was holding on to. They were planets revolving around each other, just like the ghosts in the senior lounge—a solar system anchored by each other's gravitational pull. They'd found their place and fit into it perfectly. Este was an asteroid, blazing through their quiet harmony.

These, she realized in the stiff stillness, were Posy's friends. Not hers.

For a moment, they stood like that in a speechless stalemate. Neither Este nor Posy was willing to dive into the trenches. Then, Este's stomach grumbled.

"You want some grub, Logano?" Shepherd asked with his dorky lax-bro grin, breaking the tension with a sledgehammer. "Dr. Kirk's downstairs dishing up, and I grabbed double."

Shepherd slid a plate across the counter to Este. Two strips of bacon and two pancakes topped with a slice of butter and a drizzle of maple syrup. It smelled divine. Este's diet had consisted mostly of bowls of frosted shredded wheat and almond milk at odd hours of the day for the last few weeks, supplemented with the occasional black coffee that her brain refused to believe didn't count as a meal. She stifled a moan when the syrup hit her taste buds.

"These are so good," she said around a bite too big. "Why is Dr. Kirk making breakfast?"

"Fall break starts today," Bryony said. The *duh* was silent.

Sticky pancakes lodged in Este's throat, and she swallowed hard to get them to slip down. She glanced at the all-pink calendar pinned to the fridge with cactus magnets—Posy's doing. Sure enough, in glittering ink, Posy had drawn stars around the day. A long week of freedom before midterms kicked into high gear.

Este's eyes focused on the tiny circle in the corner of the dated box where tonight's new-moon symbol had been stamped. "Big day."

Arthur and Shepherd gathered at the island, but Posy cradled a plate in her hands, propping herself up against the back counter instead. She made a big show of clanging her silverware around her plate like she wanted to make sure no one forgot she wasn't speaking. So, she was *mad* mad.

Bryony zipped her bacon through pools of syrup before dripping it on her tongue. "I can't wait until we're in Paris drinking wine for breakfast, lunch, and dinner."

Arthur clicked his tongue. "No one will be doing that."

"*Au contraire, monsieur,*" Bryony said through the crunch of bacon. "You might not, but who's going to stop me?"

"The legal drinking age?" Este asked, earning a steely glare in response. "Is that what you're doing for fall break? Paris?"

"Hell yeah," Shepherd said. "I'm gonna carb-load so hard. Bry's parents own this, um, what's it called?"

"*Pied-à-terre.*" The word rolled off Bryony's lips like ivy nectar, sweet and sickening in equal measure.

Shepherd funneled breakfast into his mouth in heaping fork-fuls, but that didn't stop him from talking. "Yeah, that, and it's in the fourth, uh—"

"*Arrondissement,*" Bryony supplied.

Another bite. "Which means there's all this cool old shit like the church from that movie."

"Notre-Dame?" Este offered, and Shepherd shrugged.

"Yeah, the one with the hunchback or whatever," Shepherd said, waving his fork.

Arthur's eyes narrowed. "You know there's not really a hunchback there, right?"

Este's shoulders sagged. She could almost imagine Daveed and Luca bickering and found herself missing the pauses where Aoife would have snarked and smiled, the human embodiment of a Sour Patch Kid.

And if she wasn't careful, she could all too easily imagine a different reality where they were the ones jet-setting to Paris for fall break instead. Aoife would buy too many books at Shake-speare and Company to fit in her carry-on, Luca would make them all eat crepes at Champ-de-Mars, and Daveed would drag them to a club where Este and Mateo could sneak outside beneath an awning as the rain poured, one of his hands in her back pocket and the other tracing the line of her jaw, and—

"You were right," Este blurted. A ripped Band-Aid. It would only hurt for a moment. "About Mateo. You were right."

Mateo would never make it to Paris, and Este would never see him again. Leaving before she got left was her mantra, and she had let him get much too close without pulling away, so the radiating ache in her chest was what she deserved in return. All she had left to do was finish packing.

"Don't act so surprised," Posy said with an exaggerated roll of her eyes. Patches of red painted themselves across her roommate's cheeks as if she'd been lounging in Cannes all week, sunburned, and not huddled indoors to escape Vermont's October gloom. Posy's plate rattled against the counter. "I've been trying to tell you there was something seriously spooky going on with him, and you weren't listening!"

"You could've kept trying!" The room felt too big and too small all at once, like Este was both suspended in air and suffocating. She timed her breathing, in through her nose and out through her mouth, blowing waves in her plate's syrupy sea to try to calm the storm inside her.

The Paranormal Investigators excused themselves with some flimsy excuse about Bryony needing to buy a beret and insisting Shepherd wear pants that weren't shorts, and then it was the two of them. Posy had nowhere to look except right at

Este with her jaw clenched and her arms crossed.

Este's throat was hoarse from the well of emotions bubbling up when she asked, "When do you leave?"

Posy lifted her nose. "After the last class this afternoon."

By the time they got back to campus after fall break, Este would be long gone. In a cabin deep in the Smoky Mountains or applying for part-time work at cafés in Chicago or, by some miracle, at another library like all the other libraries: worn in and familiar like a paperback with curled corners she knew well. It would be as if she had never existed here at all.

Este walked her dishes to their tiny sink and nudged the faucet on. She needed something to do with her hands. "That'll be fun. Escargot, champagne, the whole nine yards."

It took Posy a moment to respond, and even though Este had her back turned to her, she could imagine the way Posy gathered her short hair into a ponytail at the nape of her neck, considering how much snarl to put in each syllable when she said, "I would've invited you, but you've been *so* busy keeping secrets from me that I figured you didn't have the time."

Chiseled words with sharp edges Este hadn't truly intended slipped out. "I know I've had a lot of weird stuff going on lately, but I wanted to tell you about Mateo sooner. I did."

"As if." Posy rolled her eyes so far back she probably saw her frontal lobe.

In another timeline, one where Este hadn't said yes to the boy with the keys, where her scholarship and family legacy hadn't demanded she sell her soul to the Lilith to make amends, she could have been toasting lattes over exam notes and cramming onto their couch to watch black-and-white horror movies the way the rest of the Paranormal Investigators did. Instead, she'd pushed Posy away in all the ways that mattered. Alone was a canyon, and Este had carved it out herself.

"I'm going to ask for a new roommate in the spring," Posy said, words clipped.

Despite the way it felt like the very cobblestones that held this school together vanished beneath Este's feet, sending her into a spiraling free fall as her one new constant left the way Este should have known to expect by now, she said, "Good because I won't be back after fall break."

Something softened in Posy's timbre. "Why not? Where are you going?"

Este watched the soap bubbles pop. "Anywhere else. I can't stay here."

"After everything you've done?" Posy asked, hushed. "Did Ives kick you out?"

Because even mad at her, her roommate knew that Este had slumped into bed in the middle of the night for weeks, bones weary and brain fogged after late-night shifts. She knew that Este had been willing to sacrifice everything else for a chance to stay in this prestigious program—skipping every party, cramming for quizzes during breakfast, and slowly but surely fading into the background of her own life.

"Oh, Este. I'm so sorry." Posy rounded the island and wrapped her arms around Este to reel her into a hug.

Or, at least, she tried to.

Instead, her fingers dragged through Este's skin like she was a Disney theme park hologram, like she was Leia Organa begging Obi-Wan Kenobi for help, like she was a ghost.

Este jolted backward, away from her roommate. She flattened her palms against the countertop to prove she could. Her shoulders felt *weird*. Tingly, alive with electricity. Heat striped the place where Posy's arms should have touched.

"No, it's fine," Este said in answer to the absolutely dumbstruck look on Posy's face—her eyebrows arched into her hairline and her jaw had gone slack. "I was in the spire yesterday, and there's this ivy up there that makes me temporarily impermanent, or caught between life and death, or something." Each word was rushed, panicked. "I can hear dead things when I taste it and touch dead things if it's on my skin. I must've brushed up against a vine or something, I don't know. This is a side effect, I guess."

She was fully aware of how incredibly delusional it sounded, even to Posy, the P.T. Barnum of paranormal. But her roommate's hands had gone straight through Este's body, and without delusion all she was going to have was a full-blown meltdown.

The spark reignited in Posy's eyes, and where Este expected to see a journalistic curiosity, there was only concern. It must have outweighed every ounce of pent-up bitterness and frustration Posy harbored toward Este because she scrambled to grab her notebook from the coffee table. She flipped frantically through the pages in a way that made Este feel a little too much like a science experiment. She touched the tip of her ink pen to her tongue. "What are your symptoms?"

"I'm fine," Este huffed. She needed to believe it herself. The brief lapse in her corporeal existence was nothing more than a blip in the matrix.

"Denial," Posy said as she wrote. "What else?"

"Mild irritation."

Posy nodded. "Like, skin, or what?"

"Something like that," Este muttered. She darted through the apartment. Everything in her room was either fake or dried—a faux succulent, a fiddle-leaf fig formed from plastic, the fading remnants of the ivy blossoms in a Tibetan singing bowl she bought at a hippie town in Arkansas. She needed something living. She had to try again.

Posy was hot on her heels, pen scribbling. "Okay, and?"

Este sprang toward the door, favoring her left side that whined beneath its bandages, and Posy stumbled out of her path. She whipped a coat around her shoulders, swiped her cell phone from the counter, and slid her feet into slippers—all incredibly real to her—on her way out.

Posy snuck out behind her with her socked feet, one of Shepherd's shirts skimming the skin of her thighs, and her pen pressed to the page. Este swallowed a groan. She didn't need

271

an audience, but there was no way Posy was going to miss this.

They tore through the Vespertine Hall doors and out onto campus. A layer of mist cloaked everything in swirling white. Este's feet crunched leaves into pulp as she ran into the fog, but that didn't slow the frenzied pace of her heart. Which, at least, was still beating.

The trees. The leaves were dead, but the trunks were alive, dormant as they waited for their time to bloom again.

Inhale. Eyes closed.

"Where are you—" Posy started but cut off abruptly.

Este reached her palm out, waiting for the moment where her skin scraped against the sycamore. It never came.

She opened her eyes and tried again. Her hand slipped inside the trunk, which was warm, humming, alive, but not solid. Back and forth, back and forth. Nothing. She was a shimmering mirage, a fool's prayer for water, there and not all at once.

It's a fluke, she reminded herself. This was fine. A side effect of the ivy. Tomorrow, or the day after, or after that, everything was going to be absolutely, 10,000 percent fine.

Her esophagus was going to earn the MVP award for somehow holding down her heaping breakfast. She held her head in her hands, counting the things she knew without a doubt— what she could and couldn't touch, the stinging in her side, the spire dirt still under her nails, and the ivy sap that might still be coating her skin.

A glimpse of midmorning sun fought through the overcast

shroud, tearing seams in the clouds. It filtered to the earth in a diaphanous sheet like soft tulle. Este leaned into its rays and measured her breaths, *in and out, in and out,* until she'd warmed all the way through. This, this was real. She was still real.

Posy's footsteps tapped against the cobbled path as she surged through the fog to catch up with her. "Este?"

"I'm right here," she said, but Posy's head still swiveled in search of her. "Posy, I'm *right* here."

"Where'd you go?" her roommate asked, stepping hesitantly forward. She pushed through the haze toward the wash of sunlight, toward the sound of Este's voice, but her eyes were focused somewhere in the distance behind Este.

Through her.

Holy shit, *through her.*

The clouds stitched themselves back together, and the sun's warming light got trapped in the stratosphere. Posy jumped when she saw Este, inches away from her own face. She must have had no idea how close she was. She was disappearing in direct light, just like Mateo did. But Mateo was a ghost. And, as far as Este knew, she didn't have the prerequisites for that.

"Are you sure this is just from the ivy?" Posy asked. Her fingers twitched at her side like it was killing her to refrain from trying to touch Este again. "I can do some research on—"

Este forced her voice level when she said, "I don't want your help anymore, Posy."

The words were harsh. They needed to be. Flint strike and

kerosene, enough to burn a bridge to ashes. She was protecting Posy. It never would've lasted anyway. If their friendship didn't end now, it would once they graduated, disappearing beneath the shadow of their thrown commencement mortarboards once they traded Radcliffe for higher education. They had always been destined to be "friends from high school."

It took only seconds for Posy to morph the freckled planes of her face back into stoic indignance, her mouth set with the determination of a middle child. "Then what *do* you want?"

"I want you to go to Paris and eat as many French vanilla macarons as you're physically capable of." Este's voice caught on the jaded edge of a fragile, shattered thing inside her chest. Each ragged breath sent needles through her side. "Go and read Fitzgerald on the Left Bank of the Seine. Ride around on one of those little scooters and make a wish at Point Zero in front of Notre-Dame."

"So, that's it?" Posy asked, rubbing warmth along her goose-bumped arms. "You're going to shut me out like it's no big deal while you're, what, dying?"

"It's not a big deal," Este said as calmly as possible. Which was admittedly not very calmly. Black webbed at the edges of her vision like she might pass out if she didn't sit down soon, and some quiet part of herself wondered if that feeling would ever go away. "I can handle it on my own."

Posy, with her face flashing between stubborn iciness and genuine concern, settled somewhere in the middle, a mask of hardened resolve despite the way her bottom lip quivered like she was a dam on the brink of spilling over. "But you don't have to."

Este turned, welcoming the fog as it wrapped around her shoulders like a silk robe. Her slippers scuffed along the path, and shivers crawled over her skin. She wasn't sure if they came from the mist or from some ancient cold front swelling inside her. Posy didn't call after her as she faded into the mist, and Este didn't look back. Loganos never did.

TWENTY-FOUR

Este was almost positive she wasn't dead. The unfiltered adrenaline coursing through her limbs assured her that her heart was still beating, and her side seeped red where the Fade grazed her skin, aching something awful. At least, she could only hope death had the decency not to hurt this much.

As the sun lifted overhead, some buried part of Este was cognizant that she was missing her last class before fall break. A week ago, that would've sent her spiraling. With her bags half-packed, today her priority list was preoccupied with things like *regain corporeality if at all possible* and *try not to have an entire mental collapse in front of my classmates.*

Students flooded the pathways, shuffling from building to building on the clock tower's chime, and she brushed against them, hoping to feel something solid, but everyone slipped by untouched. Instead of the warmth of the living beneath her fingertips, a dull numbness spread through her tired limbs.

Este wandered beneath the barren trees, wondering if anyone saw her fading in and out of vision whenever the cloud cover split, and the sunlight spilled through. Not everyone would leave for fall break, some preferring the solace of campus and a quiet week of studying. Others carried suitcases and wrapped themselves in cashmere scarves, sprinting to catch their cars at the iron gates early for their fall break getaways, and they didn't spare a second glance for the girl almost gone.

Her feet paused at the front entrance, the wrought iron swirls of the gate looming ahead. Beyond that, evergreens and the stripped limbs of deciduous trees scraped the overcast sky as they lined the winding drive. Este held her hand through the bars, wiggling her fingers on the other side. The farther she reached, the more her skin shimmered as if made of glass.

Este jerked her hand back inside the gates. Her head felt cloudy, the way it did when she was nursing a head cold. Like her thoughts were too far apart and couldn't find their way to each other. She thrust her hand out again with the same result. Skin: see-through.

This could not be happening.

She pressed her back against the iron and slid down until her knees coiled to her chest. If she left, she knew she'd end up like the 1937 sacrifice Henry Bordeaux, like her dad, like everyone else who had ever lived and moved on—a figment of people's memories faded into the nothingness that came next.

The ghosts were chained here, prisoners to the Heir, and now so was she.

In a feeble attempt to stave off the asphyxiating panic that roped around her chest, Este fumbled for the cell phone tucked inside her coat pocket. It rang and rang and rang, screen pressed against her ear, until her mom's bright voice broke through the other line: "Hi, my North Star."

And despite the gnawing fear working its way through her body and bone, Este smiled. "Hi, Mom. How are—"

A gunshot blasted the other side.

"Wait, where are you? Are you okay?"

"Seeley Lake, Montana. Biathlon," her mom said. When Este's brain couldn't supply the difference between all the -athlons in order to figure out why it justified someone shooting near her mother, she added, "You know, the skiers with the guns at the Olympics."

Este let out a small *oh*. "You're not participating." She could all too easily imagine her mom, one hand on a ski pole, one holding her phone to her ear, and a rifle draped across her chest. "Are you?"

Her mom laughed, fair and fleeting. "No, no. Let me hike back up to the chalet where my service is better."

Este would've never put *watch a biathlon* on her bucket list, but her mom was always doing things that Este hadn't consciously considered important—kayaking the Louisiana bayou, singing at seedy Sunset Strip open mic nights, a brief stint walking Fifth Avenue pooches through Central Park to make enough money for them to eat lunch at The Plaza. But now, with Este's world quickly shrinking to the square footage of campus, she wished she had done more.

"How is everything going?" her mom asked. After her dad died, Este had been her shadow for so many years, and now she pictured her mom's brown hair flecked with gray, tied back in a braid beneath one of those knit caps with the huge pom-poms on top. They had the same bunny-slope nose, her mom's probably ruddy from the cold. "Your classes going okay?"

Este's throat constricted. "Yeah, things are alright. Fall break starts tomorrow, but I think I'll stay around here. Get some extra studying in."

"I bet there are some amazing ski slopes over your way," her mom said. "Don't work yourself to the bone, okay?"

"Yeah, okay." Este's voice trailed off.

There was the sound of her mom drinking something, maybe hot chocolate, before she asked, "You making friends?"

"Sort of." She rubbed her thumb over the crease between her brows. "A boy named Mateo was helping me look for one of Dad's old things, but we got in a fight this week."

"Mateo, Mateo, Mateo, Mateo . . ." her mom cycled over his name like an ASMR video trying to lull Este to sleep. "I wonder if he comes from a long line of Mateos? What are the chances he's the son of your dad's friend?"

"You know about Mateo?"

"Said he saved his life once." Her mom sighed, a wistful, longing sound.

"Saved him?" Este balked. *Tried to sacrifice him* was more likely.

"Your dad always said he was the one who told him to leave Radcliffe and never go back. And then he met me, and now I have you, so, really, I owe him all the best things in my life."

Este leaned her head back to stop the tears brimming in her eyes from falling. She pushed out a shaky breath. Give and take, that was life.

"Yeah, well, he didn't save him enough," she said. "We still lost Dad."

The phone line held an understanding quiet, letting it pass despite all the miles and unsaid things between them.

"You know I still feel like your dad's with me sometimes?" Her mom's voice sounded dreamy, distant. "He always wanted a new adventure, to try new things. When I met him, he said life was too short to spend it all in one place."

"He said that?" Este asked.

"Absolutely. Before he transferred high schools, he'd never been west of the Mississippi. When I met him, he said he wanted to go everywhere. He would've loved to see cross-country skiing in Montana. That's why I'm here." Her words lifted, and Este knew she wore a faint smile, lost in memories. She used to think her mom was sad when she looked like that, mourning for what she couldn't have. She never imagined she wasn't running away from something but toward.

"Mom, I—"

A stiff bout of static surged through the line, cutting Este's words off. Then, her mom's laugh sliced through. "Apparently Montanans don't need reliable cell coverage. Sorry, I keep losing you."

"That's okay. I have to go," Este said, shaking her head. She promised she'd call more often as she pried herself off the ground, knees shaking beneath her weight, frozen stiff. The words felt faraway, tucked into the corners of her mind, but Este dragged them out like a dusty encyclopedia. "I love you."

"Love you too, sweetie. Don't be a stranger." Her mom made a kissy *mwah*, and the call flatlined.

As Este drifted down the paths, the call replayed through her head. Could Mateo have saved her father? Vespertine Hall met her with a hearth-warmed swell of cinnamon. Mateo saved her father? Her dorm room welcomed her, quiet and still, and she trudged into her bedroom. She tossed balls of fuzzy socks into her suitcase, just to keep her hands busy. *Mateo?*

Physically, she grabbed a heap of sweaters and folded them into her suitcase, but mentally, Este was unraveling thirty years of knots tying her and Mateo together. Even as she packed up everything in her room, she could still see the traces of him here in negatives—the empty spot on her bed where he had lain next to her, the absence of his shadow in her periphery.

Her mom said Mateo warned her dad. Which meant he must've taught her dad about the Fades, told him he was being targeted, and maybe he even led him to *The Book of Fades* the same way he did Este.

But it was a trap, right? The same kind he used to snare Este in his scheme.

Except that if Mateo wanted her father dead, he would've done it quietly. He would've stripped soul from bone to use its power to stay immortal, remained in control of the Fades, and lived happily ever after—at least for the next ten years when he'd need another sacrifice. Her dad would've kicked a Hacky Sack with Daveed, debated modernist theories with Aoife, and danced a foxtrot around the senior lounge with Luca. He would've become part of the tapestry, and Este wouldn't have existed at all.

She zipped up her suitcase and rolled it toward the door. On her dresser, she rapped her nails against a stack of books she needed to return to the library, the yearbooks her dad had checked out. No need for those anymore. It was over—who cared if they never found the chapter missing from *The Book of Fades*? She'd slide the books into the first-floor drop box and pretend this quarter had never happened.

Even so, she flipped the 1967–68 yearbook open. Este fanned through the pages until she found a familiar face—Aoife in her natural habitat: tucked behind a book. She and another student craned their heads together over an atlas. Este couldn't make out the other girl's face, hidden behind a swath of black hair, but she had a ring on her finger with a blue gem the size of a pepperoni.

Something about it felt familiar, and Este yanked open the 1987–88 yearbook, fanning to the photo of Daveed in the stacks. There he stood, smiling. The girl next to him had her arm around his shoulder, and on her hand was the same sapphire ring

Este reached for the yearbook from 1977–78. She'd never met the ghost from this decade, but instead she looked for a streak of black hair, for the glint of a ring. She found them in the front row of a journalism club photo, hands folded in the lap of a girl who stared right at the camera. Someone had encircled the girl in blue ink, smudged with the heel of a left hand Este knew had to belong to her dad.

It couldn't be the same student, but it was definitely the same ring. Was that one of the sacrifices? Pressure built behind Este's eyes. Someone had to have the answers she needed.

Este reached for her laptop and loaded the Ghoul School forum Posy was obsessed with and did a quick search for the Radcliffe disappearances. The top thread had been started by someone called PocketfulOfPosy—the profile's smiling face was undeniably her roommate.

Doing a deep dive on the Radcliffe legacy, Posy wrote, *and look what I found in the archives! Original photos from before the fire of 1917, compiled by a former student. You guys have to see these.*

With each scroll, Este traveled back in time. In 1901, there was a ribbon across the gates announcing Radcliffe Preparatory Academy at its grand opening, and then mustachioed Robin Radcliffe dusting off a plaque naming Vespertine Hall, followed by Judith holding a toddler wearing a crowned nest of tangled curls who Este immediately recognized as Mateo.

The next photo was a vignette of school life in the early twentieth century—a snapshot of the architecture, students in their old-fashioned clothes, and toward the center of the photo a girl with long, black hair stared at the camera with a lopsided smile. Basked in sepia, it was a hazy fragment of what life must've looked like in full saturation a century ago, and the girl's features were grainy, softened by time. Slanted, smudged blue ink scrawled a handwritten caption that read: *1917—Lilith Radcliffe, age 15, shortly after her parents died.*

A noise escaped from Este's mouth, something small and involuntary between a gasp and a laugh. It was unmistakably his handwriting. Her dad had been here every step of the way.

In the photo, Lilith wore a smile like a harnessed stallion— wild and desperate to escape. She was trapped in time at the library, frozen in a moment otherwise forgotten. Clutched in her arms was a stack of textbooks, and Este touched her fingertip to the screen over one in the middle, a book with black binding and gold lettering that Este had returned to the library last night. On her finger, a familiar stone glistened.

The same dark hair. The same blue eyes. The same cocky smile. Every ten years.

Panic zipped through Este's chest, each breath short and burning. She stared and stared, waiting for something to convince her that she was being deceived, but the truth smiled back in the photograph, wide-eyed and determined. Lilith's hair had since lost its impossible luster, and taffeta wrinkles now webbed across her skin, but Este knew the deep wells of Lilith's blue eyes, the soft curl of jet hair, and her dignified, rod-straight posture, not only because they resembled Mateo's so starkly but also because she'd seen glimpses of them since September. She'd spotted her between the stacks, heard the echo of her steps against the library's floors, and helped her in the archives for weeks.

Which meant that Mateo wasn't the Heir of Fades. Lilith was.

And Ives was Lilith Radcliffe.

TWENTY-FIVE

Ives couldn't be Lilith Radcliffe because if Ives were Lilith Radcliffe, then Este had just handed *The Book of Fades* right back to the Heir, and if Este had done that, then they were all royally fucked.

She wrapped her arms around her knees as she bent them to her heart. Jagged, shredding sobs clawed out of her chest. She pressed her palms to her eyes as she wept for herself, for her father, for the ghosts they shared.

Este stared at the photo of Lilith in 1917, a bright-eyed fifteen-year-old with the gleam of amusement in her eye. She'd returned every ten years like clockwork and wormed her way into the lives of the sacrifices until they trusted her.

God, and *she'd* trusted her. Chosen her word over Mateo's.

Everything they'd worked for had been compromised, and it was all her fault. She'd offered *The Book of Fades* to the Heir on a silver platter, and she hadn't even known it. She hadn't found the missing pages, Mateo thought she hated him, and when he found out what she'd done, he'd have every right to despise her as well.

When Este saw Ives yesterday, she had looked significantly older than Lilith did in the photos, but she wasn't *The Walking Dead* either. Without her dad's sacrificial soul, Ives must have aged in accordance with time for the last thirty years, which put her squarely at forty-five. That was soccer-mom territory. How was Este supposed to realize she had been born in the early 1900s?

When her dad left Radcliffe Prep, he'd saved three decades' worth of students from being sacrificed, but that wouldn't save Este now. Death was painted in faded grays, not stark black or white. She was a contrapposto marble sculpture, one foot in the grave and the other on solid ground. A sigh cleaved Este's chest, deliberating which to bury, herself or the hatchet.

It was within her right, she felt, to be mad at Mateo for not telling her the truth about Ives. She'd spent weeks kissing up to a known murderer, and he hadn't said a word. He'd let her yell at him and encouraged her to leave. Why? To save her?

Then, breaking through the brume of her memory, she heard Posy's words through the coffee-drenched haze of The Ivy: *Maybe they're protecting something else. Everyone has something they can't stand to lose.*

When they said chivalry was dead, Este didn't know to take it literally.

He'd been trying to protect her. Was she any better than him? Este couldn't count on one hand the details she'd hidden from Posy in a feeble attempt to keep her safe. It worked, too. Shutting her out, letting her down. It meant that Posy was preparing to soar across the Atlantic for a relaxing fall break filled with profiteroles and pirouettes.

But it didn't feel *good* to keep secrets or lie to the people she cared about most. It was like chugging a strawberry milkshake only to have her nerve endings seize up, freezing her throat and chest and brain. She'd wanted it, but not like this. If she hadn't pushed everyone away, then maybe she wouldn't have had to face this alone.

Este pressed a gentle finger into the swollen skin on her side and gasped in staccato bursts at the knife-point sear that followed. She knew, and maybe deep in the folds of her consciousness she'd known all along, that a Fade's touch would always kill. It wasn't the rivean ivy sap on her fingers that let her feel the solid weight of Mateo's hand in hers. For weeks, she'd been slowly dying. Life, too, wasn't the harsh beam of a fluorescent bulb, on or off. It was a dimmer switch, a candle-wick burning down to the quick. Fading and fading away.

Dread and disassociation sparked inside, burning a hole through her chest. She was here in the bathroom, body failing before her eyes, but she was also thirteen again and crying next to the stucco exterior of the funeral home. In the reflection of her toothpaste-flecked mirror, she saw the ghost of someone she once was.

A shuddering breath escaped from her lips. She closed her eyes tightly and opened them again, trying to ground herself back in this reality. Before she lost her dad, it was impossible for her to know she needed to learn the sound of his voice and the way he laughed across the dinner table before it was gone forever. Watching her grieving mom caravan aimlessly around the country, Este had buried her heart, letting the weeds grow wild. She'd assumed that if no one could be hers forever, they didn't need to be hers at all.

But her dad had also been the first person to show her how to search for books at the library. She'd found security among the stacks in those lonely days, and the stories Este read stayed with her long after the two-week borrowing period. Mateo was right—the words on the page were always there waiting for her. And Este missed the comfort of something that understood the quiet parts of her, the curls like inkwell spills and the blue-eyed windows, the lilting whispers and the laughter.

She couldn't let it end like this.

Right now, every other Radcliffe Prep student was probably either tucked behind a desk studying for a midterm exam or on their way to some extravagant fall-break excursion. Since Ives had *The Book of Fades* and the Borrowing Card of Death, what would stop her from pricking her finger to write someone else's name? No one was safe.

Este put a call on speakerphone as she clipped fresh bandages into place and shimmied into a knit sweater. The phone's trill was cut off when the Safety and Security receptionist answered with two annoyed syllables: "Yeah, what?"

"Hi, Tammy," she said sweetly. "Long time, no talk. I'm calling to report an incident at the Lilith."

"All incidents at the Lilith need to be reported to the head librarian. Let me transfer—"

"No, no!" *Dammit*, Este thought as she slid into her sneakers. The wounds around her waist protested as she bent her knees to her chest to tie her shoelaces in double knots. She'd need something bigger to convince Safety and Security to evacuate the library—and she needed to get everyone out before the head librarian grew horns and a red tail, or whatever it was the Heir of Fades would do. On her way out the door, she dropped her keys. Bending over, she muttered, "Rats."

"Rats?" A spark of interest ignited in Tammy's ordinarily monotone drawl. "Been trying to get those nasty suckers out of the walls for months."

"What?" she asked, locking her door. "Oh, yes! Rats! And, um, a water pipe burst? Yeah, there's water everywhere. I guess the rats chewed through it. Is there any way you could send maintenance to help clean it up?"

More clicking. "Yes."

"How soon?"

Tammy's acrylic nails clacked against the keyboard. Her voice eased back into her usual drone. "How much water?"

Este clicked her phone back to normal audio and tucked it between her chin and her shoulder as she took the Vespertine

Hall stairs in leaps, nearly face-planting when she fumbled the landing and scrambled outside, ignoring every dagger pang twisting through her waist. "It's leaking . . . sludge. Thick, brown sludge. Smells like pennies and sulfur. I really don't think it's safe for students."

Tammy smacked her gum. There was a stream of steady air and then a quick *pop*, like she'd dug her nail into a bubble. "You think it's toxic?"

"Pennies and sulfur, Tammy. I'm in the restroom, and it's like someone tried to summon a demon here."

"Gonna have to close it down until we can get it cleaned up. And you've gotta report this to Ives. Transferring you now."

But her words peeled apart, sound waves unraveling as static rustled the line.

Sandpaper against wood grain. Polyester track pants swishing with every step. The crackle of a bonfire, flames licking the summer air and embers drifting into the thicket, or a pyre preparing to burn her at the stake. That was the sound of the static that replaced Tammy's pinched soprano. The last sound Este heard before the Fades sang.

"The dying light with shadowed hands will spin you in eternal dance. What blooms tonight—"

Este halted on the cobbled sidewalks, the boughs of evergreen trees reaching toward her like greedy hands. A veil of darkness washed over campus, blotting out the afternoon light. Black creeped at the corners of her vision. Night had come early.

"—a secret sworn, and you are ours until the morn. The dying light—"

The song of the Fades wove through Este's rib cage, squeezing until she'd run out of room to breathe. Somehow, she managed to have the wherewithal to end the phone call. Their voices extinguished, but their haunting melody dragged Este closer to the Lilith. On the one night she knew she shouldn't, she had to go back.

The library was a formidable beast of Bodleian proportions built from carved arches, pedimented windows, and balustraded parapets. Low-hanging, full-bellied clouds parted for the spire. A storm was brewing, and Este was about to walk right into it.

A Safety and Security officer with a walkie-talkie pinned to his chest held the door open for everyone leaving, and Tammy's deadpan seeped through the tiny speaker: "Go ahead and evacuate."

A rush of students flowed out the front doors and down the shallow steps, but Este swam upstream. She pushed through the current into the atrium. Shadows wept beneath the sconces, flooded the floorboards, and wedged into every nook and cranny of the first floor. The central staircase rose before her. She needed to get to the senior lounge, even if her side bled with every groaning step.

She made it to the fifth floor before she saw Ives, weaving through the collection. Este lunged behind the stacks, keeping the head librarian within view between the tops of books. Despite her silk blouse and tailored pants, the knowledge that she was looking at a century-old Lilith Radcliffe shot chills across her frame.

She squinted to keep her sights set on Ives. The head librarian pivoted, and for a moment, Este was certain she targeted her between the shelves. Desperation flashed across her features—the hunger of a starved hunter. Este refused to even breathe with Ives's jungle-predator gaze searching through the stacks. Maybe she deserved to die for walking straight into the devil's lair on the darkest night of October.

Overhead, a streak of piercing white flared, and thunder crashed—a jarring boom, close enough that books rattled against their shelves. Every light in the library zapped out at once. The wall sconces sizzled, electricity fried. As the storm opened up, sheets of rain hammering against the glass ceiling, Este was enveloped in an instantaneous darkness.

Three visions in hot pink seeped out of the shadows beside the head librarian. She lifted a hand, little more than an outline as Este's eyes adjusted, but the Fades were unruly. They tugged a sheet of black across the fifth floor, a hum on their chapped lips as they stalked along the balcony's ledge. Looking for dinner, no doubt.

"I said stay," Ives grumbled to her ghouls. "Why won't you listen to me?"

Este tiptoed down the aisle without taking her sight off the back of the Fades' tracksuits. To get to the senior lounge, she could skirt the perimeter, taking the scenic route through jade relics and antique atlases. It would take longer than cutting through the bookcases, but she might make it in one piece without being skewered by a rhinestone manicure. She had until moonrise to make it out alive, but only if she didn't get caught.

Beneath her, a floorboard creaked.

So much for that.

The Fades' frontwoman with her straw-blond ponytail whipped around at the sound, and a frigid wind blew with it, rustling book pages. Este dipped toward the floor, burrowing into a ball. *Please don't see me, please don't see me.* Her spine trembled as the Fades leered toward her hiding place.

Another jagged stroke of lightning painted the sky, blinding and then black again.

"This way," Ives boomed. "I said *this way.*"

Este didn't dare breathe until the warmth returned to her fingers, the only sure sign that the Fades had moved on.

She'd cried more in the last two days than she had in years, and salt water edged her lash line. Este rested her head against the top of her knees, lungs aching. She didn't see the frayed hem of bell bottoms until they lined up with her toes. Aoife's voice was a flat can of soda when she whispered, "On a scale of one to ten, how dead are you?"

TWENTY-SIX

"Uh, eight?"

It must have been the wrong answer because Aoife huffed. "You don't look like an eight. Are you positive?"

"I-I don't know," Este muttered, gliding a hand beneath her running nose and drying her cheeks with the pads of her fingertips. She peered over the book tops, but Ives had vanished beyond the trove of Old English stories. "I need to see the rubric, I think."

Aoife was flanked by Daveed. Este couldn't help but try to peek over their shoulders for a familiar lock of black hair, for a mischievous glint in sapphire eyes.

"Can you feel the temperature of the air?" Aoife asked as they walked. "Have you lost your sense of taste? Can you do a cartwheel?"

"What does that have to do with being dead?" Este asked as they nudged through the senior lounge's green threshold. She sighed as she landed on the soft curves of the velvet chaise, her waist throbbing and legs aching.

"Your center of gravity shifts, and centrifugal force doesn't work the same," Daveed said, lighting a few candles so they could actually see. "I found out the hard way."

Este rubbed soothing circles into the skin above her eyebrow. "Duly noted."

The door slipped open, and Este lurched upright, but it wasn't Mateo. Luca slipped inside with a debutante smile on her red lips. "You look worse than the Fades."

Este didn't have time to be offended—frankly, she couldn't even argue—before a weighted blanket landed firmly on her belly, knocking the air out of her, and then another. Aoife dove into the lower cabinets for spare comforters and knitted throws, piling each of them onto Este in a colossal heap.

Luca perched on the cushion next to her. "We used to have all-night study sessions up here. That should keep you warm."

"I'm sure I can find something to dull the pain." Aoife turned another page in her book, skimming her fingertips over the lettering as Este succumbed to the gravitational pull of the chaise and all nine thousand of its new blankets.

And on top, the ghosts splayed across her chair like a patchwork quilt of bygone eras. Their presence warmed some long-dormant creature inside Este that now raised its head for the first time after a cold winter.

She cleared her throat, suddenly choked up. "I made a mistake, and I need to apologize to Mateo. Where is he?"

"He went out looking for you," Luca said. "He said you were leaving, but he also said he'd never met someone as magnificently stubborn as you."

Este's voice snagged on the way out. "He lied to me. And I . . ."

Technically, Mateo had said he couldn't tell her that he wasn't the Heir of Fades. She'd misread it as self-preservation, used his diversion to convince herself of his guilt, but the truth was that he'd only been trying to save her like he saved her dad. If she'd left earlier, if she'd run and not looked back, she might have been safe. He'd only been trying to do what was right.

Weeks ago, Mateo had said he didn't want to get the ghosts' hopes up when he believed there was a way to bring them back to life in case he let them down *again*. Without Mateo's death first feeding the Fades, Ives never could have wreaked havoc on Radcliffe's students, wielding immortality like a blade. He must have blamed himself for their deaths. The burden fit him like well-worn denim.

Except he wasn't the one who was going to disappoint them—Este had willingly handed *The Book of Fades* over to Ives. He'd given it to her, trusted her with it, told her to take the book with her when she left. And she'd betrayed him, all of them. They deserved to know the truth.

"I turned *The Book of Fades* in. I didn't know it was her." With each word, some part of her cracked open. She didn't know when she started crying, only that tears dribbled off her chin. "I thought I was helping, I thought I—"

"Ives?" Aoife asked. "Ives is the Heir?"

Este nodded. "Ives is *Lilith.*"

Luca tucked a blanket tighter around Este. "Este, Este, Este. It's going to be alright."

It was the kind of white lie you told little kids when they messed up—everything was decidedly not alright, and the jury was still out on all future alright-ness.

Somewhere downstairs, there was a crash and a subsequent scream. The shrill note shot through the floorboards, jerking Este to attention. The sudden movement made her side stitch.

Daveed jumped to his feet, but he smoothed a cool mask over his face when he looked at Este. Apparently, she looked fragile enough that he needed to tiptoe. "Luca and I can go take a look."

Luca mimed a fake yawn as if shrieking was common practice within the Lilith. "Me? Haven't I done enough today?"

Daveed hauled her up by the hand. "Bro, I am not going alone. Are you serious?"

"*Bro.* I hate when you call me that. So unseemly," Luca whined but followed Daveed through the doorway.

Which left Este under Aoife's care. She shuddered beneath the iron gaze of the gray-eyed ghost. Stretching for levity, for anything to break the silence, she asked, "So, how bad is it, doc?"

"Honestly, I thought you'd already be dead," Aoife said,

gesturing vaguely at Este's body, the way it shimmered in the candlelight.

Este couldn't wash away the bitter tang of rising panic. She would become as dead as them. "Will it hurt? When the Fades finally . . ."

Aoife shook her head. "At first. Then, it's like floating or falling. A weightless plunge. It's not a bad way to go."

A laugh forced its way between Este's lips. She spread her hands as if painting a headline. *"An Eternity of Purgatory Earns Rave Reviews from the Critics."*

The light dimmed behind Aoife's eyes. "I suppose it could've been better. Not having to watch everyone you love leave, knowing they'd grow old without you, would've been nice, I imagine."

Este muttered quiet condolences, the same kind she hated receiving after her dad passed. Looking at Aoife like this, snug in the shape of a sixteen-year-old hippie, it was all too easy to forget she should have been nearing eighty, drinking lukewarm bourbon and watching golf championships at max volume in a retirement home somewhere sunny. Instead, she was still here, still smooth-skinned after all those years.

"You know how I said I'd traded shifts that night?" Aoife said. "I had a friend who had been assigned the late shift originally, but he was exhausted that night. He'd been running himself dry for weeks, doing too much for too long, and I . . . well, I would have done anything for him."

Este couldn't close her mouth, stuck in an open cavern. "Did you know what would happen to you?"

"No, but I saw what was happening to him. I never told him, but I loved him, and he was miserable—always tired, failing classes. It was him or me, and if one of us had to suffer, I was going to choose me every time."

"So, Ives crossed his name out, and the Fades took you instead?" Este asked. Even speaking their name in the library felt like a death sentence. She could practically feel their Charonic hands tightening around her throat.

"Yes," Aoife said. Her voice didn't waver, and her shoulders didn't bow, but something shifted in her posture, and for the first time, Este knew its name.

Love was the dreamy, offset look Aoife wore and the heartbreak written on her face without a hint of regret. It was the same way Posy edged into Shepherd's body in the corner of the booth when there was plenty of room to stretch out. It was her mom on the road to anywhere, every eighty-miles-per-hour twist down a turnpike, every cold-salami deli sandwich, every middle-of-nowhere pit stop in a desperate hope to find a sliver of the man she couldn't keep. And it was Este, searching for Mateo in the stacks, whispering to him in the back of class, closing her eyes as his lips brushed the soft skin of her hand like it might last.

It was love, and it always had been.

The moment passed when, outside, a gale screeched. The

sound struck the Lilith and pierced Este's chest, between rib and tendon. The longer the storm raged, the wilder the winds.

Este stood too suddenly and black rushed to her head. Her pile of blankets streamed lazily onto the floor. "I have to find a way to fix this."

"There's no glory in trying to do everything on your own." Aoife reached for the pendant at her neck, a smooth onyx oval encircled with silver. Maybe it was a gift from her lost love. Her face fell back into its comfortable steel trap—cold and indifferent, protective—but her words were spoken in a delicate timbre that made Este think she still had one hand dipped in her well of memories, that maybe she wasn't speaking only to Este but also to herself.

Aoife's gray eyes zipped toward Este, who was suddenly more interested in her cuticles and the rough edges of her fingernails. The ghost said, "If you feel the way I felt, don't wait to tell Mateo. You don't want to lose something you never had the chance to have. Trust me."

Este considered pretending she didn't understand what she meant, gaping at Aoife wide-mouthed and confused. That option flashed for a millisecond in her mind—an easy scapegoat, an excuse for the emotion bubbling inside her like water in the kettle on the stove, slow and then sudden.

Then, she thought about denying it. She could write everything off as a misunderstanding, an incorrect assumption. Obviously, Aoife had meant she should tell Mateo about Ives's knuckles tightening around *The Book of Fades*, dooming them all to failure, and not the way she wanted him, all of him, for all eternity.

But instead, Este matched Aoife's challenge. She nodded once, curt and final. That was that. She would face love—its canyon cliff side, this suspension bridge between here and the point of no return—head on or not at all, and not at all wasn't an option anymore. Her body was quickly decaying. Ives had *The Book of Fades*. She would either find a way to save them all, or she'd join the ghosts, and then there would be nowhere to hide from how she felt.

Este swiveled, favoring her good side as she marched toward the exit.

Okay. *Okay.* No turning back, not even when the storm let loose another sharp exhale and rattled the latched windowpanes. Not even when the marks beneath her bloodstained bandages begged her to stop fighting. Not even when she pried open the lounge's door and Mateo stood on the other side.

"Sorry I'm late," he said. "There's a woman downstairs who thinks the drainpipes are possessed."

TWENTY-SEVEN

❦

He looked like a Greek sculpture.

Mateo was soaked from head to toe, water contouring the white planes of his collared shirt to every line and dimple of his torso. Phidias himself would have envied the immaculate wet drapery, carving marble features beneath the flimsy fabric. Mateo's hand had frozen in midair, poised to knock, and now he brushed it over the back of his head as a coy smile dawned. Droplets sprayed from his hair as he shook it dry.

Then, as if remembering their latest argument, his eyes rounded, cheeks drew downward, and he bobbed a step back.

Este wiped a stray bead of water off her lip. It tasted like copper. The clunk they heard must have been Safety and Security searching for a fabricated leak and causing a real one. Mateo appeared to have been caught in the deluge. What had he said? Something about ghosts and plumbing?

"Oldest excuse in the book," she said, not fighting the

matching grin that creeped up. They stood like that for a moment, all the unspoken things taking up space between them, until Aoife coughed conspicuously behind Este.

"Oh, were you two leaving?" Mateo threw a thumb over his shoulder, stepping aside in case they wanted to get around him.

Este shook her head no, but Aoife said, "I am." Two stark syllables as she slipped back into the buttoned-up version of herself Este knew well. She vanished from sight, nothing left of her but a sliver of shadow, and one of the candles shivered as she passed them and headed out into the hallway.

Este backed into the lounge, and Mateo followed. The door clicked shut behind them. Alone together at last. She said, "I was actually coming to find you."

Mateo moseyed around the edge of the room, hand skimming the spines of books lining the shelved walls. Este ran over her list of confessions in her head. Standing in the center of the lounge, she picked at the loose threads of her shirt.

"I'm sorry that I—"

"Este, dear, I thought you'd be—" A slow, hesitant smile bloomed across Mateo's face. "You go first this time."

He met her in the middle. Her heart thumped, thankfully still beating but a gentle reminder of everything at stake. Her only option was to say everything and get it out in the open. There was no other way around it. The truth was the very least she could offer him.

Este sucked down a deep breath that reached every corner

of her lungs. "I'm sorry, Mateo. I know you're not the enemy. I was scared and foolish and wrong, so wrong, to believe you could be. You asked me to believe you, and I should have." She cleared her throat. "I know you're not the Heir of Fades."

His voice dipped low, rasped like a deckle edge. "You don't have to be sorry for anything. It was my fault for not telling you the whole truth, but I couldn't let anything happen to you. It was my fault you were in the spire. I never meant for you, for anyone, to get hurt."

"It's not you," Este said, words cracking down the middle. "You're not to blame for any of this. Ives is." She reached for his hand and found it heavy in hers. Their fingers threaded together. Este memorized the groove of his knuckles and the callus between his index and middle fingers where a pencil would sit. She squeezed his hand like if she held on hard enough, she might be able to pull them both back to the world of the living.

He stared at their clasped hands, mouth open. "How—why?"

"It's been an interesting few days." She untangled their fingers to hold his hand face up and traced patterns along the flat expanse of his palm.

Her shoulders felt lighter with one difficult truth out of the way. The next one, unfortunately, was going to be much harder to speak around the lump in her throat.

Este closed her eyes. Some things were easier to admit in

the dark. "I was scared and hurt, and when you gave me *The Book of Fades*, I returned it to Ives. I thought it would be safe that way."

When she opened her eyes, a fold had formed between Mateo's brows. "That's not exactly what I meant when I told you to take it with you."

Este hated how her voice cracked. The walls of the lounge shrunk around her. "I'm so sorry. It's over. Where the Fade touched me, it . . . it's not getting better. I'm dying, Mateo."

Mateo cupped her face in his hands. A look she'd never seen before fixed itself on his face—something between agony and apology. He wrapped his arms around her, and her cheek pressed against his chest despite the wet wrinkles of his shirt. There was no heartbeat, no rise and fall of bated breath.

She would've given anything to stay like that forever with him, but he deserved more. Whatever it took, she would give him another chance at life.

"The Fades only came back when I showed up. They need my soul, but there's still time." She was grateful that she couldn't look him in the eyes as the words tumbled out. The thought had been formulating at the back of her mind for a while, but it wasn't so much of a plan as it was frantic desperation. "Maybe they'll leave again if I leave, too."

His hands gripped her shoulders, holding her at elbow's length so that she had no choice but to watch as a spark flared behind his eyes, determination refusing to become a smothered ember. "You're not going anywhere."

"I think it could work." She tilted her head back, pinching her eyes closed, and composed herself for a split second. "You'd have to wait until Ives died of old age, of course. Steal back the card and make sure no other Loganos ever ended up in the library. It could take another thirty years, maybe forty, fifty, I don't know, but eventually it will happen. And maybe, with her gone, your souls would be free. You'd come back to life."

Mateo's fingers found her chin, tilting her head so that she'd face him. "But you never would. If you walk out of those gates like this, you'll be gone forever. I won't lose you like I've lost everyone else. We'll figure something else out."

"But you've waited so long for this—"

"I don't want to know another life without you in it."

His thumb ran figure eights across her cheekbone. He must have felt the frantic pace of her heart, clinging to what little life it had left, as it thrummed inside its ivory cage.

Don't wait to tell him.

Aoife's words echoed through Este's head. She knew she should tell Mateo that, in another version of reality, she wanted them to spend fall break in France with her classmates, sipping cappuccinos and debating which Gilded Age writer was superior. She should tell him that she wanted them to have gray hair and laugh lines and all the quiet moments that came between. She should tell him that even though she was never supposed to know him, knowing him made her a better version of herself.

307

An Este who wasn't afraid of the dark crevices of her heart. An Este who learned it was possible to hurt and hope at the same time.

No matter how hard she tried, the words didn't come. He blinked in anticipation, eyes flicking toward her open mouth. She didn't know how to say all those things at one time. She didn't have that kind of language in her vocabulary anymore.

Instead, she lifted onto her toes and kissed him once, like a long pull from a bottom-shelf whiskey bottle—something she wasn't supposed to have but wanted anyway. She let it speak for her.

Mateo made a soft, surprised noise and leaned in. He was solid beneath her fingers. She splayed her hand across his cheek, holding him steady. The pressure of his lips against hers made her head spin, stars circling behind her closed lids.

She was kissing Mateo Radcliffe, and Mateo Radcliffe was kissing her.

His hands skimmed down the length of her waist, and when she tore herself away, she could feel the heat of her blood humming beneath her skin: on her cheeks, on the slim of her neck, on the ridges of her spine where he traced his fingertips. He was careful at first—slow and patient—but Este was a storm that swept him up. She closed the space between them as his palms slid down the bell of her hips, gentle over her split side, until his hands were underneath her, pulling her closer.

Mateo dropped onto the chaise, shoving aside the mountain

of throw blankets and quilts. He tugged her onto his lap, and the soaked fabric of his shirt was cold against her skin as she pressed into him. His mouth found the hollow beneath her ear, the smooth stretch of her neck, the curve of her collarbone.

With his lips against her skin, his hands shimmied beneath her sweater, gingerly over the soft of her bandaged skin. He pushed the fabric up and over her head, tossing it to the floorboards. Goose bumps spread like wildfire down her skin. The sports bra she had on was hardly impressive lingerie, but Mateo didn't seem to care. When he looked at her like that, with the crooked smirk she'd come to love, every one of her senses shifted into high alert.

With a finger latched to her belt loop, he reeled her closer as he reclined on the velvet. He propped a hand behind his head as one of her legs slotted between his. His other hand brushed through her hair, weaving between the strands, as she worked the buttons of his shirt and kissed down his chest as she went. One button, two buttons, three. The drenched cotton brushed aside, leaving cool patches on his skin.

She paused against his breastbone. Resting her head against his chest, she imagined the thrum of his heart, the way it used to beat. Este ran her fingers tenderly over the length of his sternum as if she could stir it awake. With peppered kisses back up to his lips, she lost herself in him.

The door creaked open as Daveed said, "Yo, Este, have you seen—whoa, sorry!"

Este jolted upright, throwing her hands across her chest, and rolling off the chaise. She landed on the heap of blankets, but they barely softened the sharp jab to her side.

"Daveed!" Mateo lurched forward, fumbling for his buttons as Este dove back inside her sweater. He stood, frazzled. There was no way to hide the crooked way his shirt fell over his shoulders, the rumpled tousle of his curls.

"Next time put a sock on the door, dude." Daveed retreated into the hallway as quickly as he'd opened it.

Mateo offered a hand to Este, helping her up. "I should've known we were on borrowed time."

Maybe it was the way he looked at her, blithe and bashful, bottom lip sucked between his teeth like he could still taste her there, that stoked the flame of defiance. Or maybe it was the infectious heat radiating from the Fade's mark on her waist that reminded her what fate was waiting for her on the other side of the door. But mostly, it was the adjective he chose.

"Borrowed," Este repeated. She said the word over and over, two syllables dripping off her tongue, before gripping both his shoulders with white knuckles. *"Consider it a loan*. I knew it had to mean something."

Brilliant as he was, Mateo blinked like the cogs of his brain had seized.

"The souls are *loans*, Mateo. Like library books." Her head was spinning with possibilities. Her weary body demanded she'd need to sit back down soon, but she was on the brink of a breakthrough. "Ives doesn't own them. We can get your souls back."

"Ives must have already put the book back in the spire, and I don't think saving our souls from an eternity under her control is going to be as simple as stamping a borrowing card." Something gleamed in his gaze, affectionate and amused. "Although, I have to admit, I've never tried it."

This wasn't over yet. It couldn't be.

Este dropped Mateo's hand, and she was pretty sure she saw him form a pout before she paced away. She drifted back and forth, fingers pressed to her temples. She needed to work through her tangled thoughts out loud. "Could you repeat everything I just said back to me?"

"Okay, um," he stammered, sinking back onto the chaise. "Dean wrote, *Consider it a loan*. Stolen souls are like library books. Dean also left the book's epigraph in the Hesper Fountain. Ives has the book but not the missing pages."

Her feet stopped moving. "What did you say?"

Mateo rested his elbows on his knees and his chin in his hands, and he looked up to echo, "Ives has the book but not the missing pages?"

"No, the poem in the Hesper Fountain," Este said. She scrolled back the panel to reveal the chalkboard with their harried thoughts from a few weeks ago. With a piece of chalk, she added the word love next to Mateo's curved penmanship, the words life and death leftover from their last brainstorming sesh.

"Life, death, and love. You're a genius."

"Thank you?" Mateo said, more question than statement.

She grabbed his face and planted a kiss firmly on his lips. "Gather the rest of the ghosts in here. I'll be back before you know it."

"Este, where are you going?" he asked, but she was already halfway out the door.

Her dad's voice filtered through her memories. *Everything you need to know, you can find in your library*, he'd said. They'd searched the Lilith from ceiling to floor, peeked inside every hidden passageway, and pried open every locked door. Este only had one place left to look.

TWENTY-EIGHT

Este was eight the first time her dad took her to the library.

Her birthday was firmly situated in July, at the peak of summer's heat, and she remembered the way the library's air conditioner swept stale breezes through the stacks, winding around her legs like snakes that made her shiver. The bespectacled woman at the circulation desk waved to them as they walked in. They filled out sheet after sheet of paperwork, and in turn, the clerk slid a thin, green library card across the counter. Este had been barely tall enough to reach.

That afternoon, they left with a pile of paperback chapter books tucked neatly into the back of a blue wagon. Este knew how libraries worked: the books weren't hers forever, only for two weeks, and that was enough. She would read them over and over until she had nearly memorized the pattern of ink on the pages, so that even when they were back on the shelves where they belonged, she could carry a piece of their stories with her.

Her dad was the one who introduced her to that world, and she could still see the day in a grainy, sun-bleached film photo.

Este trudged toward her dorm room as a tempest roared with bough-breaking gusts and downpours like down comforters, thick and enveloping. Biting rain soaked her straight to the bone marrow. Her teeth clattered, waist drummed with pain, and shoulders sagged in relief as she thrust into her Vespertine suite.

Thankfully, there was no trace of Posy and the others. Their uncomfortable brunch felt like a lifetime ago. The day, now dark, had slipped away from her, but at least her roommate and the rest of the PI club were probably heading to the Burlington International Airport by now, trading Vermont for Versailles.

The pile of yearbooks still sat faceup on her unmade bed, but Este lunged for her suitcase. Inside, she found three photos. In one, her dad grinned outside the suite to his junior-year dorm room, Vespertine Hall 503A. In the next, he shook hands with Robin Radcliffe's statue in the middle of the Hesper Fountain. And lastly, in a cracked frame, he stood outside the Paso Robles City Library with an eight-year-old Este by his side. She gripped her brand-new library card in one hand and wrapped the other around her dad.

Digging deeper, Este peeled out wool socks and consignment-shop sweaters and at the bottom, next to a few stray lip balms and wrinkled syllabi she hadn't looked at since the start of the school year, sat a small, green book.

As far as books were concerned, this one was nondescript.

There was no title, no dust jacket, no gilded lining. When she and her dad returned home from the city library on Spring Street that day in July, there had been a small stack of wrapped presents waiting for her on the kitchen table. The best day of her young life had just kept getting better. She'd peeled off glittering wrapping paper in long streams. Her dad sat next to her, tapping his fingers against the tabletop in anxious anticipation, and her mom buzzed around the kitchen, lighting cake candles and dimming the lights.

Este ran her hands along the book's smooth cover now the same way she did after she unwrapped it, heart swelling with appreciation as she memorized the texture of the backing. She pried open the front cover, loose from years of reading and rereading. Underlined on the first page, her dad had written, *From the library of Este Logano.*

Her dad had taught himself to bind books, a holdover from his days at the library, and he'd woven together all her favorite stories. She recalled the scent of his cramped office—like repair glue and old books with fresh ink—so thick that for a second, she could've sworn she was there again.

Este's fingertips pressed against his penmanship like it might make him feel closer. He had walked this path before. He knew the way. She didn't have to do it alone.

A breath shuddered out of her as she flipped the page. She knew what came next. The first time she read these words, she hugged him in the kitchen. He was still alive, breathing and laughing and there when she needed him. Then, after he passed away, she had to skip past the dedication page every time she cracked open the storybook. It hurt too much.

She'd been avoiding that hurt for so long. But now, on the floor of her Radcliffe Prep dorm, with her back pressed against the stiff side of her mattress and her legs sprawled out in front of her, she read his inscription through a new lens. One she hadn't dared look through since arriving at Radcliffe for fear of what she would find.

"There is life, there is death, and there is love—the greatest of these is love." Her finger drifted over the smudged blue ink. He'd written it quickly, like he was running out of time. And he had been. Still, each crooked letter was his promise to her that even when he was gone, he would never truly leave her.

Este sucked down a steadying breath. She fanned past the fairytales and fables she'd committed to memory, straight to the last chapter where a signature block of blank pages had been bound past the last story.

She'd always assumed they were meant for her to write her own story someday, the way that some school texts had workbook pages at the back for assignments. All this time, she'd been too afraid to press pen to paper, too concerned with following his path that she never considered forging her own.

Now, as the pages unfolded in front of her, they weren't blank at all. As promised, the answer she needed was found inside her library—the library of Este Logano.

TWENTY-NINE

The missing chapter from The Book of Fades *was bound in the* back of Este's storybook.

She recognized the text immediately, ancient and meticulous. Her stomach clenched as she fanned through the pages, and Este could read them without translating them from Latin, without squinting through the ivy blossom nectar, without even trying. The language of the dead was more legible to her than it had been all semester. The words ran together, spindly sentences next to sketched diagrams, all of it in thick, black ink.

For weeks, these words had been within reach. The reason Mateo had felt so *real* any time he was in her dorm was because of these pages, the tether to his soul stronger in their proximity—it had never been the ivy at all.

This chapter didn't look particularly special at first glance—What had she expected? A resurrection checklist?—but there had to be something here worth protecting. Fingers crossed,

Mateo would know what to make of it.

She didn't have any other choice but to go back to the Lilith. She'd be that much more likely to end up skewered by the Fades' fake nails, but Mateo was waiting for her. And since Ives had the book, who knew what she could do to him if Este was even a minute too late. Este would save him, even if it was the last thing she ever did.

Este closed her eyes and sent a silent plea to the patron saint of books to forgive her as she ripped the pages out and folded them into a tight square, shoving them deep in her pocket. When she stood, blood rushed to her head, and she held on to the post of her bedframe until it passed. Her body was running on fumes and scraps of bacon from breakfast.

First: defeat the evil, immortal librarian ruining her life.

Then: consume an egregious amount of frozen Tater Tots because that was basically the only thing left in her freezer.

Este halted by the front door. She'd left her coat discarded on the floor of the senior lounge, but a thundercrack snapped the sky in half and reminded her that she wouldn't make it back to the Lilith like this without the pages getting drenched. Posy's coat had disappeared from the hanging rack by the door, prepared for a brisk week of sidewalk cafés and window-shopping. Este needed something that would protect all of her. A poncho or a tarp or a—

She'd emptied the contents of her closet, shoving it into duffel bags and suitcases, and left behind splotches of peeled wallpaper, a few rusted racks, and a burgundy stain in the woodgrains that Este hadn't questioned for the sake of her own sanity. In Posy's room, she checked the usual places—the back of her desk chair, the hook on the closet door—but Posy must have already packed her rain slicker and her peacoat.

Instead, Este found a pile of paisley. The printed sheet wasn't a poncho, but it would work in a pinch.

Posy's ghost costume dragged across the floorboards as Este raced down the Vespertine Hall staircase and out into the frigid gales. Her sneakers splashed in wading puddles, soaking her up to her ankles and leaving a muddy rim along the hem of the sheet.

Hazy through the gray storm, the Lilith's spire was a dark streak along the darker skies. Every light inside the library had been extinguished. Each window was a black eye, watching her with every step toward the doors. Plastered to the carved panels, a sign read: Closed for Maintenance. When she tugged on the handle, it didn't budge.

"Dammit, Tammy," Este said to the storm and the wind and anything else that would listen. She jiggled the handle again. Nothing. Then, there was the scratching sound of a window sliding open.

"Este, is that you?" Posy's stage whisper was unmistakable. Her head jutted out one of the classroom windows above.

Este shouted, "You were supposed to be eating a baguette right now!"

"And you're supposed to be opaque in the sunlight." Posy clamped a hand down on the brim of her Paranormal Investigators hat so that it didn't fly off. "I don't think you're really in a position to judge."

"You can't get in." Another head popped into view. Arthur. "They evacuated the whole library."

Este's squinted expression was questioning enough for Posy to add, "We hid in the storage closet."

"We?" Este asked.

Two more faces appeared, Bryony next and then Shepherd. The sight was enough to make Este's chest cavity feel like a butterfly sanctuary, fluttering and filled with light. She never thought she'd be so glad to see the two of them in her life.

Este held a hand up to shield her eyes. Droplets clinging to her lashes made their faces all swirl together, one stacked overtop another, and they all wore their PI hats over their brows. "Can you come unlock the door, or are you just going to leave me stranded out here?"

"We can't," Bryony said, and Este tried not to roll her eyes at her signature sass. At the back of her brain, she wondered how Posy convinced her to ditch their trip to Paris at the last minute, but maybe Bryony and Posy were more alike than she realized. Neither of them could turn down a good ghost story.

Shepherd clarified, "That library lady is guarding the front."

On cue, the front door's lock unlatched, and Este dove for the shrubs to hide herself as the hinges yawned open. If her side could speak, it would have been screaming a string of curses, each one ruder and louder than the last. Brambles shredded through the paisley costume, pricking her skin as Ives stepped out.

Her falcon eyes scanned the perimeter but never once looked down. The rest of campus was mausoleum quiet as icy rain splattered against the cobblestones. Ives had no reason to believe there was a junior hiding in the bushes. Este held her breath, staying perfectly still, until the door closed behind the head librarian.

Posy jutted her head back outside. "You'll have to come in another way."

Este's arms felt like overcooked spaghetti noodles and reaching the second story window looked like a Herculean task for which she was ill-prepared, but she couldn't think of a better option, and the pages in her pocket were dangerously close to disintegrating to a fine-print pulp.

The only way out was through, and the only way through was . . . up.

Her fingers searched for grooves in the Lilith's facade, fitting into the mortar. Fragile flesh ripped around her waist as she twisted to grab Posy's outstretched hand. Her side was not happy with her, but if she could make it a *little* farther.

Her hand should've gripped her roommate's, but instead her skin slid through Posy's. Este plummeted back to the muddied ground. Every ounce of air in her lungs was knocked out with a *whoosh*. The costume tangled around her body a little too like mummification linens.

"Are you okay?" Posy called.

"Do you have anything that isn't alive that I can reach for?" she asked from her pitiful place on the ground. "I forgot that I'm halfway haunted."

Everything hurt. Everything was wet. And if she didn't find a way inside soon, everything would be over. She lay there, unmoving, as Posy ducked back inside the classroom. Este nearly submitted to the swallowing soil, resigning her bones to become worm food, when a lacrosse stick poked out the window.

"Grab on!" Shepherd yelled.

With a moan, Este hopped to her feet and reached, reached, reached, but her hand missed every time. "Can you lower it?"

Posy turned back, saying something to the others that Este couldn't make out over the howling wind and the pounding rain, and then Posy hooked her legs around Shepherd's waist, extending down and down again until the lacrosse stick bobbed within grasp.

Posy lurched downward as Este caught the stick, eyes wide, but they didn't fall. The handle was solid in her hands, but slippery. Coated with rain, Este's white-knuckle grasp nearly skidded right off the pole, but she laced her fingers through the netting and kicked her feet against the Lilith's wall. Shepherd reeled Posy back inside the window until Este clamped onto the windowsill and hiked herself up and over.

She lay flat on the floor, sufficiently soaked and her body throbbing. Between labored breaths, she huffed, "Thank you."

A wad of fabric dropped on her stomach. "Get changed," Posy said. "I don't know if the living dead can get pneumonia, but I don't want to find out."

Este pulled herself up until she was sitting straight, and for the first time, she took a good look at the Paranormal Investigators. Not only did each of them wear the caps sporting the familiar flashlight logo, but they'd tucked themselves inside a matching set of purple coveralls. Their names were stitched in gold over the breast pocket.

"Plumber chic," Este said.

Posy smiled. "I was going more for *Ghostbusters*."

Este spread out the coveralls on her lap, brushing over the back panel. Paranormal Investigators had been embroidered around the beaming flashlight. When she flipped it over, she found her name. A bubbling joy spilled into every part of her.

"I thought you'd have kicked me out by now," Este said as she traded her ghost costume and drenched clothes for soft, dry cotton. Modesty was the least of her concerns right now.

Posy rattled her head left and right. "Once a PI, always a PI."

After she buttoned up, Este fished the soggy pages out of her pants pocket and carefully spread them flat across the nearest desk. They were damp around the edges, fragile and flecked with rain, but the ancient ink didn't run—Este wasn't even sure if it could—and the pages didn't tear. It was more than she could have hoped for.

"I have to get these to the fifth floor," she said.

Arthur laughed. "You really do have a death wish."

Este turned to Posy for reassurance. If her roommate was still mad at her for pushing her away, it didn't show. Posy had a tape recorder strapped to her belt, an electromagnetic field reader clutched in one hand, and a headlamp looped over the brim of her hat. This was her Super Bowl.

"Arthur's right. I don't know how we'll get up there without being seen," Posy said, "but we'll help any way we can."

A lightning strike like a street race gunshot jolted them into action. Este gently refolded the stolen chapter and tucked it safely inside the deep pockets of her coveralls. Posy doled out ghost-hunting gear like a hot dog vendor at a baseball game until everyone was fully loaded.

"Ready?" Este asked. This was it. When everyone nodded, she didn't walk toward the classroom door. Instead, she skirted around the edges of the room, pushing on each wall panel until one gave. The pocket door slid back into its catch, opening to a dark hall. "After you."

As they stalked through the service hallways, Posy lighting the way with her headlamp, Este caught everyone up to speed—the red herrings and the riddle, the true Heir and the mark of the Fades on her skin, the missing pages in her dad's

324

book. Saying it out loud made her feel like she really had a chance.

The corridor led them right to the fifth floor like Este knew it would. She'd learned the ins and outs of the Lilith, every winding passageway, every labyrinthian floor, every alcove and atrium balcony. Este peeled open the hatch just enough to peek into the staunch darkness. So far, so good.

Este said, "The senior lounge is on the other end, back behind the dictionaries. That's where we'll meet up with the ghosts."

"We get to meet them? Real ghosts? Live ghosts? No, wait. That's an oxymoron." Posy froze, nothing but her mouth moving. Este wasn't even sure if she was breathing or if that part of her brain had malfunctioned.

"I always knew there was something weird going on over there," Arthur said.

Posy's lips were blabbing a mile a minute. "I need to document this. I could set up a tripod to record heat-sensing video. Arthur, you brought the high-sensitivity microphone, right?"

Bryony reached into the fanny pack she'd strapped around her hips and handed Posy a pair of geothermal goggles. "Here, so you can see them."

"You won't need those. Trust me." Este intercepted the goggles. "Pose. Pull it together. You look like you're going to burst a blood vessel or seven."

Swatches of bright, burning red splotched Posy's porcelain

skin. "Sorry, it's just that this is the biggest moment of my entire life."

"Well, it might be the last moment of mine, if we can't—"

Her sentence was cut off by the distant wailing of the Fades. They sounded hungry, harshness marring their words. Bryony perked an ear upward, listening. With a sinking stomach, Este recognized the glazed look in her eye.

Thwacking Bryony on the shoulder with the goggles to break the seal the Fades had on her, Este asked, "What are the chances that Mary Poppins fanny pack has earplugs in it?"

"One hundred percent," Bryony said with a thick swallow. She pulled out a new pack of earplugs and dished them out to everyone. "Always thought we'd use them for banshees."

"If you hear singing, put them in. If the Fades come near, our thermometer readings will nosedive," Este said, quieter now. "Shepherd, you keep an eye on average temps. Bryony and Arthur, you two keep an eye out for Ives. Posy, your EMF reader has never been wrong. If we get separated, use that to find the ghosts."

Este took the first step onto the fifth floor. The storm outside had only grown darker. Heavy winds lashed against the atrium ceiling as they slinked through the stacks.

"Sixty-eight-point-eight, sixty-seven-point-two," Shepherd whispered as they tiptoed.

Every dropping degree made Este pick up her pace. By the time they turned the last corner, the green door to the lounge coming into view, she was sprinting. She blazed into the room, skidding to a stop in front of the ghosts.

Luca, Aoife, Daveed, and Mateo huddled around the chalkboard, turning at the commotion. Behind her, the Paranormal Investigators were hot on her heels, each of them wide-mouthed and stunned silent. Este wedged in the middle, the bridge between them.

"Posy, Arthur, Shepherd, Bryony," Este said, "meet the Radcliffe disappearances."

For a long moment, the ghosts watched the Paranormal Investigators, and the Paranormal Investigators stared back at the ghosts, blinking like they weren't sure if they were hallucinating. Este must have looked the same way a few weeks ago.

Posy's voice shook when she finally said, "Big fan of your work."

Mateo stepped forward. "What'd you find, Este dear?"

Reaching into her pocket for the pages, Este smiled. "Who's ready for resurrection?"

THIRTY

Everyone huddled around Este's shoulders, craning for a better view of the pages. Daveed's eyes shifted from the paper to Este's face one, twice, before he finally said, "But what do we do with them?"

"That's what I can't figure out." Este sagged against the shelves. Her waist rioted beneath the weight of her own body, begging for relief. "This chapter is about *summoning* the Fades—the ceremony, the smoke, the whole shebang. It'd make more sense for my dad to steal it if he were trying to rule the Fades, not escape them."

"Perhaps that's exactly why he didn't want my sister to have them." Mateo hummed, thumbing through the chapter again and again until handing it back to Este. She stuffed the pages back into her pocket for safekeeping. "Maybe we missed something in an earlier chapter that will tell us how to release the souls? It's all connected."

"We need the rest of the book," Este said, the realization hitting her with the weight of an encyclopedia. "You're right. Ives told me the book needed to be returned in one piece. It didn't matter which chapter he took. They need to be bound together again."

A deep-bellied groan cut off her thought and scattered the ghosts, each drifting out of sight. The Fades' cold front swept down the hallway, and the Paranormal Investigators pressed themselves into the shadows of the bookcases. The figures haunted toward the senior lounge, knuckles clicking and a putrid breeze preceding them.

Este pressed a firm finger to her lips, begging Shepherd not to say something stupid and get them all killed. She didn't come this far for a *your mom* joke to ruin them. Only after the Fades swiveled right, following the scientific journals toward forgotten histories, did Este fill her lungs again.

"Since I gave the book back to Ives, I'm sure it's already back in the spire," Este said, focusing on the scuff marks her shoes left on the floor rather than the inevitable way that everyone's faces fell.

"Can we sneak up there somehow?" Arthur asked.

"The door's locked, isn't it? That's, like, its whole thing," Posy said, picking at the hem of her sleeve. Nervous, maybe, finally facing the spirits she'd been so keen to hunt at the beginning of the semester.

"There's another way up," Este said as Mateo's shape

re-formed next to her. He had told her the truth the first day she met him, whining as they hiked the spiraling stairs to the archived collection. "There really is an elevator in Ives's office, isn't there?"

Mateo's hand fit into hers, skin against ancient skin. He pressed a kiss to her knuckles, the sensation swirling fizz through her entire body. "Este Logano, you're a beautiful mastermind."

But Bryony made a hideous noise of disbelief. "Breaking into the head librarian's office is *Mission: Impossible*."

"We could take the long way," Daveed offered. "Go through the service hallways. They connect to her office, don't they?"

Mateo released Este's fingers so that he could grip his hands behind his back and stretch the lengths of his neck. "Via brick wall. We'd have to deconstruct century-old masonry to even enter."

"Not to mention," Luca said, "what would we do if she goes back *inside* her office?"

"We split up," Este said. All eyes on her. She straightened her shoulders. They were relying on her. Yes, it meant she might let them down. But it also meant that she had backup. "One group will distract the Fades and preoccupy Ives, while the other goes to the spire, finds the book, and finishes this before she realizes we're there."

"How are we going to keep her busy?" Posy asked.

Este swiveled to face Arthur, her mouth scrunched up in a

devious grin. She raised her eyebrows, and his furrowed.

"Oh, no," he said, elongating each vowel.

"You're the best actor I know," she said, laying the charm on, heavy as honey on a biscuit. It didn't matter that he was, in fact, the *only* actor she knew.

Arthur nodded once and fastened a serious expression on his face. He shook out his neck, circling his shoulders. His lips flapped together as he warmed up his vocals. "Peaches and princes, peaches and prunes."

Shepherd squinted. "That sounds like the worst fruit salad in existence."

"Do you need medical attention?" Aoife asked.

Arthur held out a flat palm to shut them up. "Let me warm up. If I'm doing this, I need to get into character."

"While you do . . . whatever that is," Luca said, "Daveed, Aoife, and I can distract the Fades."

Aoife's flat expression didn't shift when she added, "It's not like they can kill us any more than they already have."

Mateo wrapped his arm around Este's shoulder. "Then, we'll take the elevator."

All nine of them nodded, each with their own mission. This wasn't a job for one person. Too much was at stake for that. They could do this if they did it together.

The ghosts vanished, trailing the scent of molding bouquets through the stacks, which left Este and Mateo with a loose-lipped Arthur, Posy and her headlamp, and Shepherd, who clutched his lacrosse stick with both hands.

When they reached Ives's office, the door was closed, and a thin strip of yellow poured out from the seams in the threshold. She was inside. A cold chill on the back of Este's neck told her that the Fades weren't far, but she could only hope the others were masters of distraction.

As Arthur approached Ives's door, the rest of them crouched behind the nearest bookshelf. Posy flipped off her headlamp as the office's light flooded the dark floor.

"What are you doing here?" Ives barked.

Arthur launched straight into a fabricated sob story about failing his acting midterm because he was in the middle of memorizing his monologue when the power went out. He wept believable tears, gripping onto Ives's shoulder and dragging her by the sleeve of her silk blouse toward the stairwell.

Arthur flung his hands around in wild gestures, but his words were muffled with dramatic sobs. It wasn't enough. Ives's smile turned sinister. "Tell me where Este Logano is, and I'll make sure you get the leading role. How does that sound?"

Este's life flashed before her eyes, and it had a Tony Award–winning soundtrack.

"She left already," Arthur said instead of ratting her out so that he could be a shoo-in for Erik in *The Phantom of the Opera*. Este sucked a breath in through her teeth, relieved. "I heard she was going skiing at Sugarbush for fall break."

Ives rolled her eyes and angled back toward her office.

"You're not half the actor you think you are. Tell Este that I'm waiting for her. All other students must leave the Lilith immediately."

"It isn't working," Posy whispered over Este's shoulder. "What do we do?"

Bryony pushed out a stiff breath. She straightened the shoulders of her coveralls, smoothed down her hair. "I'm going in."

Este's mouth fell open. "Bryony, what are you—"

But she was gone, steering across the open floor with her head high.

"Head Librarian Ives," she said too loudly. Her tone kicked into the snotty, entitled cadence Este and Posy had first heard at the Safety and Security office. "I believe my parents donate good money to this school so that the lights stay on. Wait until my mother hears about this."

"Dolores Pritcher is the least of my worries," Ives snarked.

Just as Ives was about to close the door, Bryony said, "I know where Este is."

Ives inched the door open wider. "Is that so?"

With their efforts combined, Arthur and Bryony lured Ives away from her open doorway. The door inched closed behind her, and Este clutched Mateo's hand as they sprinted toward the office. Shepherd jammed the end of his lacrosse stick into the doorway at the last second, saving it from latching shut.

The office dripped in golden light from a menagerie of candles. The only lights left on in the entire library. Lopsided stacks of books, wrinkled papers, dried droplets of spilled ink covered every inch of her desk. The desperate searching of a desperate woman. She hadn't known the pages were missing until Este handed her the book back.

"No offense," Posy said as she wandered through the amber alcove, "but I don't see an elevator."

"Look again." Mateo paced toward the wooden hatch on the wall and tapped his knuckles against it. A low-end echo responded. The sound of an empty elevator shaft.

Este had seen it during every meeting, but it wasn't anything special. The Lilith was filled with hidden doors and secret passageways, so she hadn't given it much thought. In the corner, a small brass latch clamped it shut. The key was surely dangling from Ives's wrist right now.

"Letter opener?" Mateo asked.

She lifted the gold tool from Ives's desk and slotted it into the hole. She was practically a professional locksmith by now. The mechanism inside clicked as pins moved into place, and the door loosened enough for Este to scrape her fingernails beneath the ledge and pry it open.

"You call that an elevator?" Shepherd asked.

Inside, a book trolley sat on rusted wheels. The dumbwaiter was only wide enough to fit a single cart, a box with an old-fashioned pulley system installed as an easy way to transport books in and out of the spire. The rope was frayed, which was not the most reassuring.

"Our chariot has arrived," Este said to Mateo.

They dragged the cart out of the elevator, trying and failing to keep its clanging wheels quiet. Este folded herself into the plywood box first, her back against the flimsy board, and Mateo followed. There was nothing to hold on to, and they had to hope the old joists didn't decide to give out.

The machine groaned as Shepherd and Posy wound the rope around their wrists and pulled. The cart lurched along the guide rails with each tug, and the light from the office was lost behind the stone walls of the chute. The weight of everything waiting for her, whether salvation or certain death, flattened against Este's ribs until each breath burned.

"You okay, Logano?" Mateo asked, nudging his shoulder against hers. In the lightless chute, she couldn't follow the lines of his mouth, but the lift of his smile was self-evident.

For a moment, there was only the sound of aching metal not up to current building codes. The rope creaked but didn't split. Blood rushed through Este's head, pumped by her weary heart.

She raked her teeth across her bottom lip. "What will happen when we get upstairs? To you? To us?"

When the pages pressed back against the book's spine, would the ghosts earn a second chance at life? Would she get lodged in the in-between, stuck in the same collegiate purgatory? Or would their souls go on once and forever toward the same peace her dad had found?

"I'm not sure." His hand found the soft bend in her neck,

thumb tracing the line of her jaw as he nudged her to face him. "But whatever it is, I'm by your side."

Don't wait to tell him. But she couldn't form the three simple syllables.

Not because they weren't true but because the dumbwaiter thudded against the machinery at the top of the elevator shaft, and the words died on her lips.

THIRTY-ONE

The first time Este saw the spire, it had been a sparkling won-
derland, shimmering in moonlight and fragrant with a million
night-sweet blooms. Now, the magic had vanished. The spire
was a carcass—book spines, limbs of rivean ivy, stone-cold
flesh gone stiff with rigor mortis.

Shelf after shelf, Este and Mateo breezed past the antiques
and artifacts toward the bookcase near the heart of the spire.
Her frantic thoughts were drowned out by the din of rain
against the windows. As they rounded the last corner, a pit
formed in her stomach.

She splayed her hand against the glass, no concern for the
fingerprint smudges she'd leave behind. The shelf where *The
Book of Fades* should've been proudly situated was completely
and totally empty. Este's hand twinged toward the pages in her
pocket, their one chance at redemption rendered useless.

"I believe I have what you're looking for," Ives said behind
them.

The head librarian leaned against one of the shelves, a hand slipped in her pocket and hips cocked in a stance so much like Mateo's that Este couldn't believe she hadn't seen the resemblance sooner. In her other arm, Ives cradled the gilded tome that should've rested on the empty shelf.

"The matching outfits were a bit of a dead giveaway, don't you think?" Ives asked, words toxic behind a saccharine smile. "And Este, there are debts to be paid. You of all people ought to know why."

Their plan hadn't worked. Somehow, Ives had managed to shake off Arthur and Bryony and hightail it up the spire staircase to cut them off. Este felt a twist in her chest, hoping they weren't hurt.

"That's why I'm here, isn't it?" Este clenched the papers in her pocket to remind herself they were real. That she'd made it this far, and she'd do whatever it took to make this right without anyone else getting hurt. "That's why you offered me a full-ride scholarship to Radcliffe Prep. So that I'd come back, and you could skin me alive like you did all the others."

"Like I've always said, you have a legacy to fulfill." Ives tossed a look over her shoulder, eyes glinting. She strutted through the stacks, heading toward the center of the spire, and Este and Mateo followed. They skidded to a stop at the carpet dais leading to the high-backed chair.

"Enough, Lilith," Mateo said. His voice had gone deep, serious. In different circumstances, it would admittedly be kind of hot. "You have to end this. You can't live like this forever."

Ives sank into the black tufted chair at the middle of it all. Her rightful place as Heir. As she flipped through the pages of *The Book of Fades*, shadows congregated in the corners of the ceiling and sank to the floors. She ran a painted nail along the vellum page, tapping the ink. With a smile as sharp as a silver dagger, Ives said, "Certainly I can, and certainly I will."

The temperature plummeted, raising the hair on Este's arms. The Fades' song broke through the shadows first. Este pinched her palm to keep her grounded as their hypnotic lullaby swirled through the spire. All three of their grotesque bodies shifted into view behind a layer of black clouds.

The Fades were supposed to be downstairs, preoccupied with the ghosts, but their forms reappeared in the shadows at the edges of the room. Este thought they would lunge for her, wrap their bony hands around her throat and finish the job once and for all. Instead, they flitted through the bookcases, reprising their tired tune.

"This isn't a game. Lives are at stake." Mateo's jaw clenched, mouth set firm.

"Believe me, I know." Ives swirled Lilith's sapphire ring around her finger. *Her* sapphire ring. "You think I don't remember watching Mother and Father grow ill while you promenaded around campus? I had to care for them, and you only cared for yourself."

Mateo's throat bobbed. "I know I didn't show it, but losing them was difficult for me, too."

Ives feigned a yawn. "I'm sure you think so. I watched the light fade from their eyes, and I swore I would *never* let what happened to them happen to me." She kicked her legs over the arm of her chair, eyes locked on Este's. "Let's make this easy. I'm doing you a favor. You wanted to work in the library so badly, and now you'll have the next millennium to study the archives. Isn't this fantastic news?"

"You know they invented Botox, right? Maybe give that a try instead of sacrificing people," Este snapped.

"Simmer down. You've done well. You returned *The Book of Fades* before midterms like I asked. The only problem is that it's missing a few important pages. You wouldn't happen to know anything about that, would you?"

"Why would I tell you?" Este sneered.

Ives tapped her nails impatiently against her chin, groaning. "I really didn't want to have to do this."

Waves of black swelled as the Fades inched closer. The air evaporated from Este's lungs. Plumes of ink spun through the spire, as smothering as smoke in a wildfire, but a frozen bodice tightened around Este's chest.

There was more to the fire of October 1917 than Este had realized, more that her dad had pieced together, that his clues were trying to tell her. He'd been pointing her to it the way the statue of Robin Radcliffe pointed to the evening star. When her dad had discovered the truth about Ives, he'd vanished from campus before she could add him to the library's collection of souls. But before he'd left, he scribbled a passage from *The Book of Fades* on the back of a newspaper headline describing the blaze. It wasn't a coincidence.

What burned, come dawn, will not be lost. What buried roots will grow,
and when the ink fades, we will see what only love returns.

"Of course," Este whispered, punctuated with a breathy laugh. And then, louder, she said, "Ives, wait. You're right. I do know something about the missing pages."

In her periphery, Mateo's mouth was fixed in a fine line. Almost imperceptibly, he shook his head. A warning she couldn't afford to heed.

Ives spared a petty laugh. "Convenient timing. Do share."

"After three decades, the Fades returned this fall. But it didn't have anything to do with me." She forced her chin high, her words steady, no matter how much her hands shook as she pulled the timeworn pages from her pocket. Shadows crawled up her legs, a layer of darkness along the floorboards emanating from the Fades. Reaching for the pages. "My dad stole a chapter from *The Book of Fades*, and I brought it back. That's why the Fades are here. You said you needed the book in one piece. Without these, they're nothing, and so are you."

Fury lit behind Ives's eyes. She pointed a single, stiff finger toward Este's chest, and the Fades roared, piercing notes like banshee screams rising to the rafters. She snarled, "Hand those over immediately."

The Fades' vicious snarls didn't give Este a moment to hesitate. She crumpled the pages into a ball and tossed them toward the stacks. Ives launched out of her chair and dove to the floorboards, spreading the damp paper out, smoothing them flat with her palms.

"You once told me to destroy *The Book of Fades* with hellfire and brimstone," Este said to Mateo, loud enough that Ives, even as she rushed to puzzle-piece the final pages back into *The Book of Fades*, was certainly listening. "I wish I'd listened to you then."

Unlacing their fingers, she dipped into the silk inlay of his pocket until she found a small rectangle, five smooth sides and one sandpaper. Matches. Exactly where he always carried them.

Este pressed her lips to his ear. "Do you trust me?"

She pulled away enough to see the cut of his eyes, diamond sharp and just as dazzling. Rimmed with heavy lashes, his irises webbed with navy. She smelled cedar smoke and fresh ink and felt the touch of his fingers on the pulse point of her wrist when he whispered, "Explicitly."

God, she hoped this worked.

"It's all connected. The book, the pages, the ghosts you've

created," Este said to Ives. "Tell me, what good is a story without a last page?"

She struck the match, a seed of light blooming. With her other hand, Este dragged one final folded page from her pocket. She lifted her sights to Ives—she wanted to see the look on Lilith Radcliffe's face when she realized her tutelage had come to an end.

"Este Logano, I assure you that you will not live to see tomorrow." Ives stood now, flanked by the Fades.

Este raised a brow, a smirk ghosting over her lips. She was as good as dead anyway. "I'm afraid your loan is long overdue, Lilith, and it's time you pay the fines."

All she needed was one ember.

Fire licked along the bottom edge, smoking against the damp parchment. Este floated the flame beneath the page, praying for it to light. Her heart buried itself behind her navel, sinking, sinking with every passing second it didn't catch.

The paper was soaked from the thunderstorm. No matter where she held the spitting flame, it sputtered. The match burned out before the last page could spark. The page slipped out of Este's fingertips.

There were more—more matches to strike, more chances to burn—but there wasn't more time to spare. Ives plucked the page from the ground, wearing a grin like a scythe. The Fades gravitated around Ives's makeshift throne like worker bees to their queen. *The Book of Fades* was whole again. Ives's power restored.

With a flick of her hand, Ives once again had the Fades obeying her every command. She pointed a manicured finger straight toward Este's beating heart and said, "Do your worst, ladies."

Este fumbled for another light but she slid the box open too quickly and spilled matchsticks over the floor. They disappeared behind the Fades' veil of darkness and skittered across the stones. She dove after them, hands pressed blindly to the cobbles, each breath coming more ragged than the last.

"Este, dear." Mateo crouched to the floor next to her, but she didn't look up. This couldn't be how it ended—a fade-to-black credits roll overlaid with the Fades' sweeping melody, calling her into an eternal rest.

"Este, Este. Stop." Mateo's hands wrapped around hers, cutting her search short. He folded them together, an anchor in the writhing sea of shade.

She saw it in his eyes, the same quiet concession Aoife must have worn when she chose to take the night shift. Mateo looked at her, calm and composed amidst a maelstrom, like they were the only two people in the world, or at least the only two who mattered.

"They're too damp, but I-I'll make it work." Frantic, hurried breaths heaved her chest, but Mateo was steady.

"I'm so glad I got to meet you," he said, smoothing a strand of hair behind her ear. "More than you know, and more than I deserve."

The Fades in their Juicy Couture tracksuits and their sweet pea body spray and their a cappella theme song closed in, one 4/4 measure at a time. Mateo's thumb swiped a gentle path along her jawline, and his lips brushed against the crease between her brows. "You're the most exquisite girl I've ever met."

"Mateo, I—" Her lips parted, primed to say the one thing that mattered most, but it was cut off with a shriek as a scarred hand wrapped around the collar of her coveralls, dragging her off the floor.

Este kicked against the Fade's exposed midriff and her eternal belly button ring. It did nothing to deter the spirit who raised Este to eye level, forcing her to peer into the black caverns of empty sockets, an infinite, swirling darkness like cemetery soil on a closed casket.

The Fade dragged a skeletal finger down her cheek. The touch seared through her skin, white-hot pain flashing behind her eyes as a scream wretched from her lungs. As if the Fade wrapped her hand around Este's throat, her airway blocked. Panic bubbled inside her chest, but there was no oxygen left.

The Fade was going to siphon her soul like she'd done all the others.

Then, something sparked in Este's periphery.

Across the spire, Mateo pinched a match between his fingers, a lit orb of orange. In the other, he dangled the corner of *The Book of Fades*'s borrowing card over the flame. He must have stripped it from the back of the book while Ives was preoccupied with the missing chapter. It was dry. It would burn. But if he torched the tie that bound him to the Fades, what would it mean for his soul?

"Mateo!" Este screamed. It didn't stop him.

First, there was smoke. Gunmetal rivulets that rose to the rafters. Then, the fire caught. Cinders dripped from Mateo's fingers as the page disintegrated.

Mateo's figure blurred in her vision as the Fade tugged and tugged at the very threads of her. But him, she wouldn't let him out of her sight. Wouldn't lose him. He smiled at her, a coy thing on his lips that sent her heart rate soaring. *The Book of Fades* would never be complete again.

"What have you done?" Ives shrilled.

But she wasn't looking at Mateo. The pages underneath her hands curled at the edges as flames skittered over the parchment. She couldn't stamp them out, trying and failing to smother them with her feet. The fire burned wild, wicked. The match in Mateo's hand had fizzled out, but the pages acted like he'd taken the spark straight to them.

The Fade holding Este hostage hissed. Her grip loosened enough that Este wriggled out, dropping to the stone floors in an aching pile, gasping for air. Everything tasted like smoke. The Fades' familiar haunting song faded into minor scale runs, and they retreated toward Ives.

Flickering red coals clawed up the hem of their velour pants as the same flames eating away at the pages burned right through them. Fire lapped at their waistbands, their sleeves, their collars, soot swirling around them, until all that remained of the Fades was a pile of crematory ash.

Este and Ives dove toward *The Book of Fades* at the same time. Before they reached it, a beveled flame appeared at the center of the book. Its tendrils spread. The pages smoldered, the binding incinerating. It went up in a blaze, sputtering vile ink-black smoke.

Ives fell to her knees and cupped the ashes in her palms like a prayer. When she looked at Este, her eyes were blades, sharpened and merciless. "I should've never let another Logano walk these halls."

"You should've never lived this long in the first place." Este squared her shoulders, a boxer in a ring. Ives was powerless without the Fades by her side.

Mateo sidled up next to Este, and his hand fit inside hers. He squeezed. "It's over, Lilith."

"If I'm dead, so are you." Ives's mouth twisted into a cruel smirk. She stalked toward one of the glass cases. From within, she unsheathed a stripe of silver, a pointed dagger.

Of all the ways Este thought she'd die this quarter, she hadn't truly considered the possibility of getting shanked by the head librarian.

"You should've been mine," Ives said, a manic laugh lifting the edges of her words. She clutched the dagger in her fist. It was all a little too *Psycho* (1960) if you asked Este. "The Fades had you in their grasp and you escaped, just like your worthless father."

Ives couldn't touch Este while she was stuck between life and death, but the dagger could. Ives aimed the silver edge at the soft of Este's throat.

Then, a wrinkle daubed Ives's forehead. A fine line between her brows. Crow's-feet webs crawled from the corners of her eyes. Her hair paled, deep black dissolving into cool gray. The flesh at her chin sagged, and then her cheeks. Worry lines etched into valleys, deepening like tectonic plates shifted across her skin. Every breath aged her.

The dagger fell, her grasp weak. Hoarse, Ives asked, "What is happening to me?"

"It was only ever a loan," Este said.

Ives's paper-thin skin heeded to rot and ruin. Two slits where her nose was. Lips and gums sank away, leaving only teeth behind. She shriveled, burned. Este held her breath as an inky wisp of smoke, all that was left of Lilith Radcliffe, dissipated.

Este smiled so widely it ached. "Mateo! We did it!"

But when she turned to Mateo, the ghost staggered backward. He slid down the length of the shelf, head lolling weightless on his shoulders.

"No! What's happening?" Este asked, a half-choked plea. "What do we do?"

His eyes glazed over, losing focus with every passing second.

The edges of his body feathered into nothingness. Where he'd been whole to her minutes before, now he flickered in and out. A light bulb with a loose connection. As if it took all his effort, he raised a slow hand to the back of her neck. The soft pad of his thumb smoothed away a stray tear.

"Este Logano," he said, eyes dimming. Her name, both a promise and a threat. The last thing he said before his eyes closed.

Este made an ugly, splintered noise like a nail in a coffin. She fell to the stones next to him, pressing her palms against his face, his hands, his chest. He was still dead, and she was still dying. She barely registered the heat flaring at her side as rapid breaths inflated her lungs. It didn't feel like she was getting any air.

"You were supposed to stay," she sobbed, cradling his head. "*What only love returns*. It was right there in the book. Come back to me. Please, come back."

Her side seared, heat lashing the broken skin. Pain throbbed, too blinding to ignore. As if the flames that consumed the book were tearing through her skin, the mark of the Fades burned and burned, a brushfire blaze. She grasped at her bandages, splaying her palms flat to smother any stray flames, but it did nothing. The fire burned from within.

Each inhale was sharp, stinging. Her lungs couldn't expand as the skin on her side tightened.

"Wake up," she whispered. "Please, please."

With a gentle hand, she brushed a curl away from Mateo's forehead.

"I don't care if I have to love you in this life or the next," she said, planting her hands firmly against his chest to hide the way they shook. "I need you to know that I love you."

Este wrapped her arms around Mateo, sinking into the shape of him.

"I love you," she said, as she laid her head against the empty cavern of his chest. "I love you." As if the words would echo inside his rib cage atrium like a hallelujah chorus in a cathedral nave. "I love you." Even if it always had to end like this.

The spire quieted as the rain pelting the window retreated and rivean ivy halted its trek across the cobbled floor, searching for light in the darkness. Everything stilled, everything silenced.

And then, Mateo's heart beat.

THIRTY-TWO

Este definitely flunked her midterms.

"No, you *didn't*," Posy said, finally sick of her incessant complaints. It had been two weeks since she chewed through the bottom end of her pencil, scribbled down any archived factoid about the invention of cataloging conventions she could scrape off the recesses of her mind, and turned in every exam half-blank.

Now, Este wrapped her arm through Posy's as they drifted through a fresh coat of powdery snow on their way toward the Lilith Radcliffe Memorial Library—new name pending. She wrinkled her nose, undoubtedly red from the cold. "I got a D-plus on my history test."

"Exactly," Posy said. "The plus makes all the difference."

Frost glistened on the arched tree limbs bowing together overhead, a silver lining that led them straight to the heart of campus. November's sun wasn't strong enough to melt the icicles but it was just enough to make the snow sparkle.

A small crowd had already gathered on the steps of the Lilith, but Este could've spotted that head of ink-spill curls from a mile away. Mateo waved one mittened hand when he found her in the distance. Beneath her scarf and sweater, her heart hammered—she'd never get tired of seeing him in the sunlight.

"Has it started?" Este asked as she stepped into place next to him.

"No, not yet. Here," he said, nudging a coffee into her hand. "Got this for good luck."

The first sip spread heat down to her toes and quieted her chattering teeth. When she leaned into Mateo, he slid a hand into the back pocket of her jeans. That warmed her up, too.

"It's like we don't even exist," Daveed said, and Luca's birdsong laughter brought Este back to reality.

The ghosts—well, they weren't really ghosts anymore—flocked around the Paranormal Investigators. Aoife's nose was tucked deep inside a wrinkled paperback, as she tried to ignore Arthur's stream of questions, letting Daveed answer. Luca's hands were folded inside the new-to-her mink muff she'd found at the vintage store on Main Street during her first off-campus excursion in decades, and her eyes dragged toward Bryony any chance she had. Posy had slipped into the warmth of Shepherd's arms.

When Mateo's dormant heart thrummed back to life inside

the spire, Este thought at first that she'd imagined it. A desperate hallucination. But then, it happened again and again, and a dusty breath shuddered out of his lungs.

Once the book was destroyed and Lilith fell from power, the trapped souls had been set free. What Este hadn't anticipated was the tremendous effort it took for a soul to find its way home, but maybe she understood that best of all.

First Mateo, then Luca, Aoife, and Daveed all powered back on, souls reunited with their bodies as if they had never left. The Fade's touch left silver scars along the dip of Este's waist and a jagged line across her cheek, but otherwise, the five of them were perfectly whole.

The massive library doors swung open, and the crowd quieted at once. Dr. Kirk smiled as she addressed the crowd: "As the newly appointed head librarian at Radcliffe Prep, it is my honor to welcome you to the Dean Logano Heritage Library to announce the dean's list for academic honors in our first quarter."

A grin touched Este's lips at the sound of her dad's name, and Mateo moved his hand to her waist, hugging her closer. If her name was on that list, she could keep her job as an archival assistant and actually do what she'd come here for—and this time, she wouldn't have to worry about the shadows breathing down her back.

Dr. Kirk's sight landed on Este. "Radcliffe Prep is a place of prestige and powerful history, and while the school has spent the last century upholding its tradition of excellence, I want to encourage all of you to pave your own paths in this world. After all, it's not about the legacies we are left with—it's about what we do with them."

From the pocket of her plaid coat, Dr. Kirk retrieved a tightly wound scroll. She peeled off a thin, red ribbon, and the parchment unfurled. Este couldn't tell if her hands were shaking from the cold or the adrenaline. Archiving had always been her dad's dream. She'd come this far—she didn't want to let her dad down now.

"That being said, I'm pleased to announce Radcliffe Prep's top performers." Dr. Kirk taped the list onto the door and disappeared back into the amber warmth of the library.

The crowd didn't wait.

A tidal surge of rare-books hopefuls flooded the stairs. The thin scratches of ink didn't register at first, a blur between bobbing heads. Este elbowed to the front of the line and skimmed the list for a familiar four letters, down, down, down.

But when she reached the bottom of the page, she hadn't found her name.

"Read it again," Mateo said behind her. He was Velcroed to her back, sturdy in the sea of eager students, a hand firm against her side where her waist had stitched itself back together.

A few cheers went up, excited gasps as her classmates read their names. But it was a short list, and when Este raked through from top to bottom one last time, she wasn't one of them.

The way she deflated could only be described as a leftover happy-birthday balloon trapped in a ceiling fan: slow, wheezing, and stuck. Life had moved on around it. She pushed out a long, swirling breath and turned back to Mateo, letting the floodgates break around her as others found their place in the program.

"I didn't make it."

At the beginning of the semester, that revelation would have sent her into a downward spiral, but she had found her own footing somewhere along the way. She'd waded past the quicksand, and there was solid ground for her to stand on.

"I'm so sorry," Mateo said, brushing a strand of hair off her shoulder.

"It's okay, I think," she said, shaking her head, and she meant it. "I've seen enough of the archives for a while."

"What will you do instead?"

Este chewed on the inside of her cheek. Honestly, she hadn't considered the possibility of not being able to continue as an archival assistant. For starters: she already knew the job. But Ives had made her the exception, allowing her into the restricted area early—her intentions anything but altruistic in hindsight—and Dr. Kirk had inherited the head librarian position with no obligation to keep Ives's promises after she vanished.

Reports had circulated about Ives's sudden disappearance, like so many at Radcliffe before her, but Posy's first big byline at *Sheridan Oaks Daily* as a student contributor broke the news on the head librarian's departure from Radcliffe, claiming she left to reunite with her family.

"Maybe I'll take an elective on library acquisitions instead. Get some new books on these shelves." Dr. Kirk was right. It was time to start looking forward instead of back. She slipped her hand into his. On her tiptoes, she whispered, "Come with me."

"Anywhere," he said, and for once, it was true.

They darted down the stairs, ignoring the inquisitive looks on her friends' faces—they'd find out soon enough that she hadn't made the cut—and crossed the quiet copse of frostbitten trees until they stood outside the Hesper Theater and its fountain. Robin, with his hand outstretched, smiled down on them. The mosaic basin had been drained for winter, and its sculpted, stone tiers were dry, but the base glimmered with copper promises, and Este had one of her own to make.

"You know most people make wishes when the fountain's turned on," Mateo said with a laugh. "Did you bring any coins?"

She circled her arms around his waist, reeling him closer. They didn't need pennies for the kind of wish she wanted. Este nudged her ear against his chest, listening to the steady drum like she had every morning for the last two weeks. He was there, he was whole, and, somehow, he was hers.

"Did you know a kiss at the Hesper Fountain is supposed to

mean your love will last forever?" she asked, tilting her head back to meet his gaze.

He hummed. "And do you believe that?"

Este smiled when she said yes. She kissed him, warm and sweet and soft, and she'd keep kissing him until their hair grayed, until their skin wrinkled, until dust gathered on the bookshelves. Eventually, they'd become nothing more than sun-faded ink, a final line in her favorite story, one she was no longer afraid to write.

ACKNOWLEDGMENTS

When I was a kid, I'd ask my mom to drop me off at the library so that I could spend all afternoon getting lost in the stacks, carrying around a pile of books half my size and daydreaming about seeing my name on those shelves. This is the book that makes that possible. So, thank you, Este and Mateo, for meeting me in the library.

Thank you to my agent, Claire Friedman, for not only enduring but encouraging even the wildest of my ideas. You make it feel like the sky's the limit, and you've got the ladder. To everyone at InkWell Management who made this possible, thank you, thank you, thank you.

To my editor, Sara Schonfeld, you are a dream to work alongside. I'm fully convinced you have editorial superpowers like X-ray vision that lets you see straight to the bones of a story. And to the entire team at HarperTeen, I couldn't have imagined I'd ever get so lucky. Thank you for every second spent transforming this book from something that lived inside my Word document into something I can hold with two hands.

To my writing soulmate and pseudo-sister, Kara Kennedy, thank you for always knowing exactly what I'm thinking because you have court-ordered custody of the other half of my brain. This is one hell of a sparkle. Mackenzie Reed, thank you for championing this story from the very first draft. You're the best alpha pal a girl could have. Phoebe Rowen, you're the softest place to land and the firmest stronghold in a storm. I can't believe it's time to break out those Sharpies. Taylor Gates, thank you for being one of the first people to explore Radcliffe with me. (RIP Ulrich's gingerbread lattes.) Skyla Arndt and Maria Pawlak, thank you for introducing me to everything I didn't know that I didn't know when we started a writing group together in 2020. Without you and Hex Quills, I wouldn't have known where to begin. To Abby, Alex, Brit, Cassie, Crystal, Darcy, Helena, Holly, Juju, Kahlan, Kalla, Kat, Lindsey, Marina, Olivia, Sam, Shay, and Wajudah: long live Starscream, the prophetic pigeon.

I'm so wordlessly grateful to have been selected for Author Mentor Match and for everything I learned and everyone I met because of it. Jo Fenning and Serena Kaylor, thank you for selecting me as your mentee and helping me peel back the layers so that I could get right to the heart of this story, à la artichoke. This book only exists as a rom-com (a *real* rom-com) because of you. Meredith Tate, thank you for cheering for this story every step of the way. Barb, Brittany, Brooke, Cat, Hannah, Kate, Kennedy, Kila, Libby, Lindsay, and Morgan, there is no one else I'd rather have in my corner—cheers, DGIAB!

To Kaleigh, who has unflinchingly supported every overly enthusiastic pursuit of my heart since the fifth grade, thank you for bribing me to write with celebratory milkshakes, for sharing in every win and loss like they were your own, and for a lifetime of laughter. And to Taylor, thank you for being my bookstore buddy, my favorite QDOBA date, and my loudest hype-man for the last twenty-three years.

Thank you to my parents, Trey and Linda, for believing in everything I've ever written—from picture books and poems to school papers to these pages of my debut novel. Mom, you've always been the Crystal to my China, the Connie to my Becca. I'd be lost without you. Dad, your faith in me means more than I can ever say. I promised I'd give it a Trey ending because I know I'll never live down the *Tristan & Isolde* fiasco. To the brothers I look up to both figuratively and literally, thank you for being my built-in best friends. Tyler, thank you for letting me use your copy of *The Legend of Zelda: Ocarina of Time* when we were little so that I could play make-believe in Kokiri Forest. Alex, thank you for all the times you knew I was being ridiculous and didn't stop me. I love you all more than I could ever describe (and that's saying a lot, since writing's kind of my whole schtick).

Of course, to Christopher, I owe a million thank-yous and

I-love-yous. You've shown me the kind of joyful, selfless, unconditional love I used to think might only be fictional. Without your support and encouragement, it would have been all too easy to give up. If you've read this far, you'll know what I mean when I say I'd kiss you at the Hesper Fountain, and if you skipped to the back to find your name, I'd kiss you anyway.

To everyone who's no longer with us: yes, you are. I wrote this book on the heels of my grandmother's passing, and every word is for her.